— UNRAVELLED —

ZOE FANNING

This book is non-fiction. It reflects the author's present recollections of experiences over time. Some names and characteristics have been changed, some events have been compressed, and some dialogue has been recreated.

First Published by Bermingham Books January 2023
Printed by Clark & Mackay, Brisbane, Australia

ISBN: 978-1-922784-54-4

Author: Zoe Fanning
ABN: 955 068 404 98
Facebook: Zoe Fanning
Instagram: zoe_z_fanning

CONTENTS

PROLOGUE

The tarot cards were turned one by one. The alternative, intuitive, and almost angelic gypsy sighs.

"Well, my darling, I'm sorry to inform you that your husband is having an affair."

My body twitched; my heart raced and seemed to inflate at such a speed I thought it would burst through my chest at any given second. Every heartbeat seemed to be magnified, it felt like my entire body was pulsating as if I'd just run the race of my life. I knew at that moment, my race had only just begun. Somehow, deflatingly, I knew how it would end.

My body knew and was prepared for this, I however hadn't been consciously aware of what was to come. My mind caught up to my body in what felt like long, slow minutes, but in reality it was more like a nanosecond when it dawned upon me the horrible secret my soul had kept safe under lock and key to steer me away from storm looming.

Through now blurred vision, I watched the tarot reader of the past, present, and future matter-of-factly continue to spill the beans on what this man I had devoted my entire life to was doing. As each card was turned over to reveal itself, the readers' words accompanying them were simple yet terrifying. It was all put into what seemed like one long, sickening sentence of torture.

"He is with a brunette woman who he works with. Not the same office but in the same company. She isn't originally from Victoria but from Sydney. It's been going on for five years. She loves him and I'm afraid to say he loves her too. I'm so sorry to tell you this."

Her words began to be overshadowed by the thumping of my blood pulsating through my ears as rage welled up inside of me. I wanted to scratch her eyes out, push her off her crystal ball chair, and maybe even for good measure stomp on her, like all evil witches bearing bad news! My anger seared, but a voice within my soul reached up to me gently persuading my thoughts to stop, breathe and wake. It appeared I had slumbered too long. Fragments of the past few years quickly flickered into my mind, like a silent movie, showing me what I had missed, and what I hadn't but just didn't want to see. There were more signs of deceit than I cared to admit. Love is blind, and I had headed blindly for heartache.

She then asked if I was worried about my marriage before seeing her. Then followed by asking about any strange behaviour I may have experienced in the past. Sitting for a moment still grappling with my head, heart, and anger, I finally thought to myself, "How far back does she want to venture, and is it all relevant?"

I began picking furiously through the memories in my head—the colourful, peculiar, terrifying, funny, and most definitely memorable journal of what was my life. And what sort of strange things did she mean? Did she mean the headless woman who wandered my house growing up? Or maybe the piano playing songs by itself, or the decapitated bird and the lifeless cat that sent me into early labour? Or was she talking about the strange things I had done like my stint of pony thievery or the experiment I took on myself with LSD? The list of possibilities swirled wildly in my head.

I cleared my thoughts and thought of something else she may have meant before asking for confirmation.

"Do you mean from Jim and our marriage?"

"Yes", she replied, eager for me to confirm her very talented theories. It was like I was frozen to my chair in her tiny incensed, spiritual room for what felt like a long while. The stories of Jim and his strange behaviour purged out of me like they had been exorcised. So many, it surprised me and left me thinking how I could have ever missed putting them all together and seeing them sooner.

The tears welled up and a river of sadness, disappointment, and betrayal deep inside me threatened to burst its bank. Every story I told her, I heard myself justifying him or his actions. Speaking it aloud, it became clear, I wasn't seeing the woods for the trees. I felt like a twit, a loser for not seeing it how it was.

Three secret credit cards were discovered, no sex life, and excessive nights out for work were only the beginning. A heavier and heavier training regime away from his family, and the suspicion of giving me free rein to spend all the money I wanted on anything that took my fancy. Then of course his obsession with what was now his very locked, and very private, Blackberry phone.

I didn't want to believe the clairvoyant, but hearing her, hearing myself, I had to. I left her rooms sad, angry and confused all in the one, trying to figure out my next move. I talked to a few friends, chatted to Mum and went on a bit of a fact-finding mission.

Later, I was to find out the enormous lengths people go to hide their secrets and how smart or conniving you need to be to coordinate them and keep them running for great lengths of time.

You know what they say, don't underestimate a woman scorned. Scorned, huh! That didn't even come close to how I felt. Dusty and bruised from having the wind knocked out of me, I may have been brought to my knees, I may have cried an ocean, but what I wasn't about to do was be beaten. Not to be underestimated, I was determined to get right back up again with strength, dignity, love, and success! This is what the situation needed I told myself, and this is just what I did!

Whatever the dream we're chasing, no matter how rocky the climb, we are certain to get there by trying our best, and taking one day at a time.

I'd done it! I had come out the other side, and you know what? I'm ok. Thank God! Well sort of anyway. A few small scars, more of the emotional sort, and some good old-fashioned growth of character that people talk about getting after a whole lot of crazy "full on" experiences. That sounds like my life to date, full of excitement to say the least. What doesn't kill you makes you stronger. I'd say so. I am still alive I guess, and stronger, well, maybe. I can cope with more without falling to pieces if that's what you call strength.

I adopted Monty Python's "always look on the bright side of life" and it became my mantra, regardless of the sometimes-unbearable moments I endured. I knew positive experiences only resulted from positive thoughts, and God knows I needed as much positivity as I could get!

I didn't take myself too seriously. I smiled, laughed, and remembered the good things life has to offer. I was determined to make a good life for myself and my kids with the passion and zest for life I had before it all happened. I had lots of love to give!

I may not have done everything right, but hey who does? I've made some real WHOPPING mistakes believe me, but none of us are perfect, nor do we have to be. The adventures and life experiences I've had have made me into the woman I am today.

CHAPTER 1

STRIP TEASE

There was a knock at the door. I wondered if it was to be a special delivery as it was my birthday. I opened it hesitantly, hoping I didn't have to show my face for long as I had picked up a bug a day before and was feeling wearily awful. Two men in police uniforms stood there. Strippers? I wondered. My girlfriends were as crazy as I was, could be plausible. I quickly glanced at my watch and thought it was eleven o'clock in the morning, I was only thirty-eight, no great milestone and it wasn't my big 4-O yet, nothing was adding up. Then I heard a sound from behind me and saw my kids in tow, "Really?!" Surely these guys had come to the wrong house.

"Zoe?", they asked calmly but firmly. Uh Oh.

"Yes," I replied confused and a little anxious all at the same time.

"Were you at your husband's residence last night?" One of the two officers asked. They barely looked a day out of school, young and fit-looking, to be honest, I was still half thinking it was some kind of stripper gram and expecting the music and seduction to begin. I wanted to play along and not seem like I was falling for their serious and heavy-handed act, pinch one on the butt perhaps, and put my hands out for the other to cuff. To fall to pieces or look too worried was just what I imagined the prankster behind this little birthday wish would have loved. But just in case, Zoe, the well-behaved, good citizen took over, and just to be on the safe side I complied.

"Yes," I answered calmly. They appeared sterner with their eyes burning into mine, and in that second, I knew they weren't strippers, and this was no joke. One of them quick to respond piped up loudly words that will be etched in my memory forever, "Zoe Fanning, you are under arrest for the assault of Jim Brown."

My birthday had previously brought happiness and lots of Leo love my way. A typical day often consisted of breakfast in bed, possibly with flowers and pressies, and always being right. We had a tradition in our family—no one is allowed to argue with you on your birthday, and certainly, no arrests are supposed to take place! It's just not in the rules, but in all, a day that flows perfectly and wonderfully your way. This was how it was supposed to go anyhow. I should have known it wasn't to be my typical celebratory day, beginning with the virus that had taken hold of me and made me suffer all through the night. Note to self, if the universe sits you on your arse for your birthday or the lead up for that matter, don't fight it. It is often for a reason. God works in mysterious ways they say. Or in my case, he was yelling it straight at me, but I just wasn't listening.

I felt like death warmed up in general, as did the kids (they had the bug too), so it was weird after I had gotten over the fact that two strippers were now not standing at my door for sheer entertainment value but officers of the law, my mind swiftly reverted to the more serious matter of why I was being arrested. So please jump into my nightmare, the water is warm. Let me fill you in on my life's little challenges.

Rewind, twenty-four hours. I was rushing around getting my nails done and booking hair appointments as I was due to meet friends for dinner to celebrate my birthday. Now although my husband and I had been separated a good year by this point, we were still speaking, but only just. Not to say there weren't volatile moments at times, but leading up to my birthday, we had made an amicable arrangement. He would have the kids on the night of my birthday so I could go out, and I would do the same for him when his birthday came around. I'd had a bit of a rough week. The moon and stars were clearly not aligning for me. But hang on a wee bit, let me slow this story down. I'll get to all that a little later. I really in fact should start at the beginning...the very beginning!

My adventures began during my entry into this world. Birth, Portland Victoria, Australia, July 1973.

Birthing, in my opinion, is an important and almost sacred event. Most of the women of this world take it in their stride and just get on with it, often with a wee bit of pain; tongue in cheek ladies! But in the end, the baby comes out and you hope for a healthy one with no complications. It's a scary but powerful event for both women and children. One you don't forget in a hurry.

I think Mum had all those thoughts. I was her first child, and she was ready. Apparently, I wasn't though!

The smooth birthing process we were experiencing suddenly went wrong. My mum heard something on the monitor, it was my heartbeat. Well, the lack of it. She asked if there was a problem.

"Stay calm Tilly and David, your baby has just decided to turn sideways and get the umbilical cord wrapped tightly around its neck."

"I'm just going to use the forceps around the head and get it out."

Hmmm not great I'd say. Nerves were high at this time. Mum prepared herself as Dad stood back praying for a positive outcome. The next minute the doctor placed his foot at the end of the bed for leverage and with all his might pulled. Imagine the trouble my mum and I were having hanging on for dear life as the doctor, with one foot up, was yanking and pulling at the forceps (attached to my head!) like he was in some kind of tug-of-war competition! Yep, didn't sound like I was quite ready. Maybe I had an inkling of just what life lessons were ahead of me and I wasn't too keen to learn them! Whatever the reasons, I was happy in my current location... Mum's tummy. Well to Mum's and Dad's delight all the pushing and pulling finally resulted in me popping out. I took a big breath and lived to tell the tale.

And tell the tale I did. I can be rather vocal. Lots of talking, singing, and negotiating, I put that down to my Leo the lion traits. I wasn't always like this though. In the beginning, I was a bit of a shy little petal according to my mum, and it took a few years for me to come out of my shell.

I had Mum and Dad to myself for a while. I was spoilt. I'm sure part of me would have been happy to be an only child, but alas two sisters were on the way. It's kind of a funny thing. Poor Mum and Dad think the cord around my neck damaged me in some way, often blaming unruly behaviour on it, so I've used this to my advantage and whenever I was in trouble all I needed to say is something about my traumatic birth and I'm home free! Instant "get out of trouble" card. Works like magic.

I spent my childhood days in a very unusual round house on a hill that my parents built in Cape Bridgewater, Victoria, Australia. It was a beautiful place to grow up. Trees surrounded us, it was full of wildlife, and we overlooked the valley and ocean. Although we were in a gorgeous spot, we had lots of very strange occurrences happen in our house on the hill. The paranormal type! I think being exposed to such peculiar experiences at such a young age helped me develop skills and an awareness I wouldn't otherwise have had. The lush bush and adventures I had on our property instilled an open mind and a "never say never" attitude to life.

I know everyone has such different views on that sort of thing and I don't push my views on anyone, not everyone is a believer. It seems however, almost everyone you meet has at least one story of their own, in my case, my own would fill a book!

Before my sisters were born funny things started happening. I was around eighteen months old on the first known occasion. We had a room in the back part of our house that was my room as a baby. Apparently, my parents awoke one night to hear me yelling "Man man" and pointing to the corner of the room, absolutely hysterical. My dad David, a true sceptic, and an avid atheist always found a logical answer for anything weird and wonderful. He was closed-minded to several things, one of those being the supernatural. Dad was an extremely determined, almost brutal straight shooter—you never had to wonder what was on his mind, he'd tell you and make it clear, crystal clear. There wasn't a lot that gave him pause to change that. It was his weakness and his strength. Mum on the other hand was not a sceptic by any means. Far from it. She grew up with the paranormal. She has the incredible ability to remember as far back as her own christening at eleven weeks old—insane! She can't remember every moment but certainly enough to warrant it to be considered strange. At the age of nine, she also began to be able to predict if people were about to die. She would also start dreaming of future events that would almost all come true. Even shocking her mum one day as they saw her eighteen-year-old fit young neighbour pass by the house, Mum then turned to my Grandma (her mother) and said he is going to die. Unfortunately, the following day he was killed in a rugby accident. Needless to say my Grandma always took notice of any other predictions she made moving forward. Mum, like Dad, was strong. Strong on many different levels. She had a fabulous sense of humour, and although in some ways conservative and straight-laced at times, she was also a free spirit. Mum recalls one night when we were all young and tucked into bed, the adults heard heavy footsteps running down our wooden stairwell in the middle of the night with nothing, not a sound at the bottom, just silence. My grandparents were staying downstairs at the time. Everyone from upstairs and downstairs met at the top and bottom as soon as the noise was heard. There was nowhere to escape from what everyone involved thought was an intruder, but again no answers to show either way.

Next, our piano (with the lid firmly closed) starts playing a few bars in the dark of night. All spread out on different days. These spirits like to entertain! Oh, it's great to scare a whole family to death for years! And more was to come.

My little sis arrived in perfect form and with no major hiccups when I was three years old. Surprisingly, she was Mum's birthday present. Good work Mum! Always a nice present to have. Although, as I was to find out later on, it's no fun sharing your birthday. Her name was Caprice. I loved her. She was my baby to take care of. I was gladly Mum's little helper. Caprice was a thoughtful soul. Different from me, she wasn't particularly adventurous, she was cautious and sweet-natured. As she grew up, I would say she almost always considered others. She showed a keen interest in cooking, which she later developed.

And once again at approximately the same age I was when I was in the back room of the house Mum and Dad were woken with the same screaming, "Man, man". And when they arrived in the room Caprice was pointing to the very same corner, but of course, nothing was there. Mum was not too shocked and Dad, well who knows? Even if he saw something, would he admit to it and ruin his reputation for logic? Regardless, life in our home went on, and questions about such events went unresolved.

Caprice and I grew close and had many great days together. I liked being the big sister and tried to fill my job enthusiastically.

I once rescued her from a whole nest of bull ants devouring her tiny little body as she stood helplessly in their feisty home. Caprice unable to understand to move, screaming blue murder. Big sister to the rescue! I walloped those tiny critters until most of them dropped off before mum stepped in. The screaming took a while to die down, as did the dozens of bites on her legs. I felt proud I had been the capable sister to spot trouble, act, and get everyone away unharmed.

I helped Mum and a school repairman by keeping Caprices' head still while he used metal cutters to cut away two metal bars she had somehow wedged her head between. That was my first day of school. Always something exciting happening! The future Zoe would be so proud.

I continued with the big sister thing for the next little while and then my other little sister arrived, all of us three years apart, and… on my birthday! You have to be joking. Genius! How did mum plan this? Astral Twins, they call it. So Mum and Caprice on the same day and myself and Sky. Yep, that was my little sister's name, Sky. Now I believe being born on the same day made her similar to me in some ways personality-wise. Especially as a child, but still to this day, we can clash a little as we are so alike. Sky was much more sedentary as a youngster than both Caprice and I. Not keen on getting outside or socialising. She was happy just hanging out with our cats and Mum. Sky had a wonderful way about her. She was an interesting young girl and had a strong idea of who she was.

Our childhood was full of many wonderful and interesting experiences. I was a very curious child and pretty intense, traits that have stayed with me throughout my adult life. And I still have my curious character, quick to ask questions and learn as much about what's happening around me than most. I was a little accident prone too but always seemed to have the knack of coming out the other side all in one piece. Right from the get-go I've been a survivor. I almost always got the better of troublesome situations, and even if it was all wrapped in drama I made it out ok. A little unsure about my feet, I'm not certain if genetics or my rough birth had any bearing on the fact that I ended up with a slight clubfoot. It was tough spending many of my young years at night-time in bright red callipers I had to wear to bed to straighten my left leg out. I would scream the house down as a youngster when sleep time came, begging my parents not to put the metal bars on me. It was the worst thing ever when they were positioned, I couldn't move the bottom part of my body. It was like being in a metal straight jacket. Mum had to leave the room each night, tears in her eyes, it tore them up having to do it. Well, I assume it was all worth it because now as an adult no one would know, and it hasn't stopped me from doing anything. I think as time went on, I forgot all about it, only to be reminded occasionally as I found myself slipping over my own feet or bumping into things that I shouldn't have.

I was usually the one that stuff would happen to. From little things to big things. I was like a magnet! Constantly I would be the child who would step in the dog poo, if there was a hair or a slug or pretty much anything that wasn't supposed to be on the food, I would find it. Or it would find me!

A tad accident prone, and attractor of strange events, I have been caught in the middle of fires, hold-ups, and even had a possum hunt me down in the middle of a busy street to use me as a bridge to cross the road! Weird! In saying that I usually had luck on my side too, winning raffles, and getting picked from crowds for the coveted lucky door prize.

I think deep in my soul, I energetically send out vibes to the world. Good and bad. Law of attraction at its finest! I believe in the Law of attraction—how could I not with all I've had happen? I trust in the philosophy that like attracts like. Positive thoughts bring positive outcomes, and negative thoughts attract negative outcomes. I guess all that energy could have been channelled in the right direction a whole lot earlier and achieved my dream of being a child star! But I don't think I was wired to think like that then. So, I continued to be the only person I knew how to be... Zoe, love it, take it, or leave it. And so, with a string of crazy events under my belt, I started accumulating all my most amusing and not-so-amusing stories. I didn't mind telling a story. I never even had to make them up as my life just seemed to roll them out one after the other! It never occurred to me they were that far from the norm until later in life when I retold them to others, they'd all laugh. I was a constant source of entertainment for my family and friends, and happy enough to laugh at my own expense.

My parents were very caring towards us and just in general by nature. Mum was a stay-at-home mum in our early years, taking incredible care of us in all situations. Dad worked tirelessly to make sure we were taken care of as well. We all could afford some real luxuries in life. Unfortunately, my dad's job had him travelling the world as a chemical trader, and he would be gone for months at a time. I missed him even if he was stern and strict, he was my dad, and I wanted him around more. Luckily, Mum was, and I think my sisters would agree, "Super Mum". When Dad was there he was great too, but when he wasn't Mum was all over it. I'm sure Dad felt it being away from us too because he put his maximum effort in and tried to make up for the times he was gone when home. He was always a considerate and capable dad to us, involving us in his weekends, teaching us life lessons be it in manners, using a fishing rod, gardening, and even astronomy. I wouldn't say they were a quiet couple when together. Although there were peaceful moments, my parents both had strong characters and strong opinions, which led to a noisy household full of banter. My dad was very assertive and somewhat regimented, while my mum was confidant but more reserved with an occasional temper that reared up at certain times. No wilting lily, my Mum. Discipline was not lacking, and their strict parental guidance was always a challenge for me being the unruly character I was. Together, we all made great memories and had pretty much everything we needed, and most of what we wanted. I would like to think I took a bit of both my parents' personalities and focused more on their positive traits, although you never can tell what traits you end up taking with you.

I remember one day Mum and Dad battling with a dysfunctional fax machine and a paper roll. It was not behaving so Dad gave up to go the post office. Mum, however, decided she wouldn't let it get away with its defectiveness. After a wrestling match along with several frustrating moans, groans, and swear words, she threw it clean out the window and over the balcony. Good on you Mum, that taught it! Anyway, she soon realised her temper tantrum may not be looked upon favourably, so she quickly ran to the shops to buy another less faulty model before Dad arrived home.

My dad had a fishing boat and would love nothing more than to venture out to sea and fish. It turned out to be very handy for me as a child, there were no limits on the number and size of the catch you could bring home. Dad would take enough for dinner, and instead of wasting the rest, I was allowed to take the fish around to the neighbours and sell them. Keeping the profits of course. Great pocket money to be had. The neighbours didn't mind, it worked well for everyone. Unfortunately for the little minds out there (usually teenage boys), I was nicknamed "Fishmonger Fanning". Oh yes, that was our family name, Fanning. Oh, spare me all the Fanning jokes! Fanning has become quite popular now with a few well-known singers, actors, athletes, and TV presenters proudly sporting the surname. Wished they were in the public eye back when I was growing up, it would have been cool to carry the name!

My parents loved nothing more than to take us away on short getaways, locally and overseas too. Even something as simple as going to the nearby public tennis courts with other families for a BBQ, and running around with our friends while the adults played. We had our hit while they had a break.

The spirits in the house still hadn't given up and were doing their ghostly best to make themselves seen. Sky hadn't had the same "man man" experience as Caprice and me, but they weren't going to let her get away that easily. Mum said she was about four when she had her first occurrence, so a lot older than we were when we had our encounters. I can only assume that would be scarier as you are more aware of things that go bump in the night. One evening while sleeping in that same back room, she awoke. Unable to get back to sleep, she lay there restlessly looking out the window. To her absolute horror her attention was brought to the corner of the room where a lady in a 16th century gown floated above the floor, gently moving in a small area, and with no head on her at all. With one swift movement, Sky was out that bedroom door and was running hysterically down the hall. She was not yet safe from what I imagine wasn't ever going to hurt her, but try telling a small child that. I think it only wanted to show its presence, and of course, scare her to death. As she arrived at the top of our lounge room steps her eyes were led to three beautiful balls of light bouncing across the room heading for the stairwell that was in question earlier with the footsteps. Dodging them as quickly as she could she ran sobbing as fast as her legs would carry her to Mum and Dad's room, repeating the story in a jumbled and rushed fashion. My parents took a look, but again no remains to be seen. A rattling moment for everyone in the house.

I was safe for a little longer, but Caprice was next. We were all going out one day and headed down the stairwell and out the back door when my sis said she forgot something and raced back in the door to collect it. And collect it she certainly did. Her dose of scares me stupid! Standing in the bottom room was a man dressed in what seemed to be old-fashioned clothing standing in a pondering pose, finger to the chin, viewing a map in pressed copper we had on the wall from the 16th century. He was completely unaware of Caprice and stared intently at the world map.

Probably would have scared me more if I was there and he had glanced my way, so thank God he didn't, for Caprice's sake.

My grandma was next. She was staying over in one of the other rooms on the top level of the house and was peacefully sleeping. She slowly started to wake up only to feel what she described as a soft kiss on her cheek. When she rolled over, she saw what sounded very similar to the headless lady leaving the room.

We owned two cats, Levern and Smocker, and later adopted a third, Lucy. They were the most beautiful Himalayan felines with long, lush, and silky coats and piercing blue eyes. We also had a black ghost cat and it used to prowl the house (to the disgust of our feline part of the family) who would be caught hissing at invisible enemies in our rooms. We knew, or thought, that it was black because we would often see a very dark figure, like a cat, flash across in front of us. It would jump onto our beds during the night on and off over many years, and when we used to switch on the lights nothing would be there.

My turn! I woke up one night and happened to look out toward the dining room where I saw a girl standing there. She seemed a little younger than me and was wearing clothes that didn't match our fashions of the day, but I couldn't quite pick what they were. I stared for a while and eventually she faded away to my delight. Not long after I had a friend stay who reported the same thing, and poor Mum and Dad had to drive her home in the middle of the night because she was so freaked out. I couldn't blame her, I wanted to get the hell out of there too, but it was my house, haunted and all! I had to stay, although they say a captain (Mum and Dad) doesn't desert his ship, I can't remember anything about the crew. We all had to get used to it, I guess. Mum was very supportive of all these happenings, but Dad still never really believed. I think deep down he questioned his thoughts on the matter, but dads are supposed to stay strong and not fall apart at the paranormal, aren't they? Better to hold the fort and stay an atheist! That's ok Dad. There has to be one relatively sane person amongst us, right?!

CHAPTER 2

EQUINE FEVER

As a young girl, I was horse mad. Unfortunately for me, my parents and sisters were not! Although I had a kindred spirit in a friend I had since I was three, Aria. We developed our friendship over our early years, and into high school and beyond. With Aria being just as overwhelmed by these glorious steeds as I was, she would accompany me on many crazy horse expeditions. "I smell a horse Aria." "Me too, Zoe. It's got to be close by." So off we would venture on our push bikes and into the neighbouring streets pony searching.

Wherever we went, we were always on the lookout for them. We were lucky in that we had many riding schools in our area that we frequented. Those were the days with mucking out stables for a ride, taking out people on horse trails for free, and generally helping out just to be close to the animals we adored. Our parents did pay for us sometimes, but not enough for our liking, back then there was no insurance and no stress, it was basically a free for all in the sense that there were no restrictions, nobody telling you what to do, just pure fun with the true horsey people of this world. Not the insurance issues that we have now either with people suing each other left right and centre. Just good memories and innocent fun!

One day we were so determined to find some, we stopped at a local paddock where there were two lonely-looking geldings standing, begging for a ride! Or so we convinced ourselves. After a little brush and a pat, and of course some hay, we pounced on them. No saddle, bridle, or anything! Go, boys, run like the wind we said as we flew aimlessly around their large pasture, clinging legs wrapped tight around their bellies. Aria's horse was not impressed and decided to stop dead as we raced side by side up the hill flinging her through the air. All I could hear was her screaming with delight as she was flung into the air tumbling into the long grass. She looked up at me with happy tears rolling down her cheeks, pain and pleasure a fine line. Not much control was to be had but a lot of fun. It didn't take long and the owners arrived. Two cranky girls running towards us. Can't blame them, I guess, having two twelve-year-old's stealing their pride and joys. I know if someone touched mine, I would be on the attack.

"Get off our f…ing horses," they screamed.

Oh no! "Oh, we are sorry," we said apologetically. "We… we… we… were just…um… patting and grooming and um…riding your horses." They were a few years older, and I think in the end felt a little sorry for us and after calming down told us we could visit again but next time make it with them. Fair call we thought.

Time went on, and there was more pressure from Aria and me for our parents to buy a horse of our own. I was alone in my mission. Me versus Mum and Dad and not a sibling in sight wanting to back or support me in my plight. Aria was a little luckier than me. One of her two sisters was also horse-crazy, so she had a tad more strength in her arguments to purchase a fabulous beast to call her own. I on the other hand lived through her and other more fortunate girls who had become owners. My parents didn't deprive me completely of the horse experience though, they let me find horses that were offered on lease, which was just as good in my book.

I leased a few ponies before coming across Moyse. Super sweet with a high arched neck and an apple bum, Moyse was a flea-bitten grey—and by flea-bitten I mean the colour, not covered in flea bites as one might assume. She was great, Moyse and I, Aria and Lady (her chestnut horse) would be able to continue our adventures together. We covered nearly every street in Tarragal, and often dangerously bareback with no bridle and no helmet, dodging traffic as we looked for places to canter. Speed at our age was our friend and we weren't afraid. Now I look back, I wonder how we survived as we galloped along the main roads taking any jumps we could find with gusto, and probably frightening most passers-by. Aria and I would take the horses to the beach for swims in the ocean. We would often lose track of time as we basked with our steeds in the shallows of the water, coming home with sun-kissed skin and a big smile. Sometimes on our way home, we would even stop at McDonald's to buy Big Macs, not just for us, but our companions loved them too. They did cart us everywhere so well deserved I would think. Don't know what the vet would say!

Regardless of our crazy horse adventures I always found solace in my alone time with my horses. I somehow felt heard, and strangely their friendship gave me a feeling of strength and harmony. I would eventually find this bond to be so powerful in my life and in tackling my adversities.

On one of our many trips away with the family to a country suburb called "Sutton Forest Lakes", in the middle of winter I was able to convince my little sister Sky to join me on a ride. The place we were staying had a paddock full of Shetland Ponies. So, I took the job of saddling up. Mum, Dad and Caprice stood at the end of the paddock awaiting our arrival. I gave Sky a leg up and jumped on myself, ready! I rode ahead first, being the more experienced of the two as Sky followed closely behind. Trotting along I heard her go into a canter. Most ambitious Sky, I thought. Next, I looked ahead to see my family waving their arms vigorously. I gathered there was something amiss, so I glanced around to see my crazy little sister riding upside down, under the horse's belly, legs wrapped as tight as her small frame would allow. I didn't know if I should laugh or cry as this could have been my fault. I could be in a world of trouble, so I maintained a concerned big sister look. The reins were gone and I think from the fear there was not much of a sound coming from her, only far distant moans! Then plonk, she hit her mark on the ground and everyone came running.

Sky stood up, winded, leaving the pony to gallop away. Her face flushed and her body shaking just a little she promptly received a big mummy cuddle, a quick check and an assurance that all was well.

The attention turned to me. "What happened?" everyone yelled. Well, I started to ask myself the same question until I heard Sky cry. "The saddle was loose and started to slip as soon as we trotted," she whimpered. Oops, that had to be me. I was the saddle doer-upperer. Let's just say I wasn't the most popular cookie in the jar that day! I'd say from that little adventure that's why Mum and Dad didn't book any more holiday resorts where there were ponies involved—I'd done my dash on that one!

My primary school days were made up of generally good times. Roller-skating in the playground, Hide and Seek, Bullrush, Flying Horses (a well-devised role play involving all the horse-mad girls which were acted out nearly every day), and Tip during our breaks. For lunch, frozen oranges and Elanora specials were the winners (named after the school, it was Devon and salad on a roll). In winter, meat pies and soup.

I liked school but I wasn't overly academic when it came to my studies. Not bad at reading and art but average at math and comprehension. At times it would upset me to be at the bottom of the class and genuinely struggling, but in general, I was pretty tough and let things go. I tried my best when it came to school but some things just didn't make sense to me. I wanted to fit in but being bottom of the class did not lend itself to acceptance from others.

I was the quiet one in my year, and happy to sit and take it all in as I was a still a tad shy. Unlike preschool, where although I had a tendency to be on the quieter side I went through a stage of maybe slight paranoia and anxiety, especially at sleep time, when, if I felt unwell as I became frightened to venture into sleep, I'd scream and yell every time making it impossible to let anyone rest. The aftermath of that was the poor teachers had to change the kids sleeping arrangements to none at all. The other kids would just have to rest at night-time. I don't know when I developed my hypochondria, but I do remember being petrified to vomit. Mum would always say I was a bit of a nightmare, running from room to room leaving a trail of mess. She could never get me to stay in the bathroom as I tried to escape the sickness by physically running away from it. Poor Mum.

I remember my continued shyness clearly, especially from Kinder to about fourth class. I was worried my friends would judge me and I didn't want to take the risk of saying or doing anything that would make me feel picked on. I assume now I'm older that some kids feel that way too. One day my mum bought the class some mice in a cage, and I most proudly took them to school. Wow, was I the important one? It felt great, and I might become super popular. The teacher had me speak at the front of the class about these cute little vermin and explain where we got them, what they ate, and what we needed to do to care for them. Then the whole class decided on names. Honey and Vanilla. Most original kids. The mice were handled a lot and I was the leader, passing them out to whoever was deserving. Oh, the power! Then one day Honey was running up her little plank in her cage when she just stopped and dropped to the ground, dead. The tears from a few girls in the class were contagious and everyone in the room started to sob, including the boys! We buried the little one at the side of the classroom in the garden and Mum came and got Vanilla. My days of stardom were over. Poor little Vanilla didn't last too much longer either. When handling her at home she escaped and ran under the house, never to be seen again. My days of class popularity were finite! Kids were fickle, and if you didn't have the latest gadget, top marks, coolest hairstyle, or in my case the class mascots, then you often fell by the wayside. I felt disappointed and sad all at one time.

During my growing years, I also found another talent. It came in the form of my voice. My mum took my neighbour and I to see the latest film that was out—Xanadu. We had a choice to see Superman or this, and my neighbour Narelle won. I didn't realise I had a voice until then. The movie was an inspiring one for me and opened my vocal cords to new heights and ambitions. We bought the soundtrack, which back then was on a record, and I played it and played it. Not only that (to my parent's shock), but as we had a cement platform like a veranda on the outside section of the house that sat perfectly like a stage above the neighbourhood, I sang those lyrics to the world, every day, all day and if possible into the night. My personality was finally emerging, although I'm not sure the neighbours throughout our valley were overly impressed, as many could be seen poking their heads outside to check where all the ethereal sounds were coming from. Ok, ok, that was my word choice guys, they may have just been checking out the noises that reminded them of cats fighting, none the less they nor my parents could stop me.

Poor things, as an adult I can see how that would make you cringe but I was on a roll. Look at me, look at me, look at me! I wanted to be a star, a singer, an actress. I wanted recognition, appreciation, and attention. Children on the other hand can be more forgiving—and lucky for me the neighbouring kids were.

One afternoon my parents came down to my makeshift stage to check on me and laughed out loud to see a group of about eight youngsters gathered in a bunch below me, clapping along with cheerful sways to the backup music I had playing. They shook their heads and walked away rolling their eyes with a look that only said, "What's next Zoe?" … seriously.

The late part of primary school was tough, and maybe that's what helped me get tough too. I became more of a confident person and not such a wallflower. Kids can be mean, both boys and girls. If they weren't making fun of your name like me, they found other things to pick on you about. Or they would just decide they didn't want to play with you anymore, and all gang up! No particular reason why, other than kid victimisation which is horrible and hurtful. In fact, I remember clearly one particular afternoon as school finished, getting a phone call at home from a boy who I fancied, Michael. He was medium height, although obviously hadn't fully grown yet only being around eleven, and had dark, wavy and longish hair and was, well, rather dreamy. He asked in his high pitched, undeveloped and unbroken voice if I would like to go to the park near me and meet up. An offer too good to refuse. I ran to Mum, begged her to go, and hurried up the street. Waiting for what felt like an eternity I realised I'd been stood up. I was devastated. How could he, and why would he? When I arrived home, I soon received another call. This time with giggles on the other end and "Ha, ha! Michael wouldn't want to meet you, why would you think he would?" It was some girls at school, bitches even at that age, and they had set me up. It had been them on the phone, not Michael at all and I cried to my mum for ages. I know reading, hearing or even telling the story now to someone sounds age appropriate but being young and vulnerable, it hurt. Growing up can be rough but character-building, I guess. So many kids go through similar experiences, and some kids if bullied repetitively can cause damage to how they see themselves in the world. Thankfully these days we are more aware of what victimisation can do and I feel we are heading in a better direction to curb it.

High school years were approaching. I had made friends with all the local kids from my primary school; trying of course to leave out those bitches, most of which were going to the public high school in town. Mum and Dad hesitated on which school to send me to, and apart from me stealing ponies from the community regularly, I had started to go a little off the rails in other ways. Well, it depends on personal opinions, and that I guess was my parents' take on it. Not over the top or anything, but I'd gotten in enough trouble that after being found out hanging out with local friends, kissing the boys in an abandoned water tunnel up the road, and smoking with them in a nearby park, I was soon packed off to go to an exclusive private girls school in Portland where there would be no boys to distract my learning. I thought it was going to be the worst experience of my life, and I hated my parents with a passion. I couldn't understand how they could be so cruel and take me away from my friends, but parents did know best (most of the time), and I was to meet bosom buddies and have lots of fun without boys. Well, not at school anyway! All I knew is that I was excited, not sure what about, just that I knew school was going to be good. I was older and possibly going to be taken more seriously, and gosh maybe those kids at high school didn't play the silly pranks or call you names.

My first day brought with it a lifelong friend named Tammy. She sat next to me in English. She was quiet and wore rounded silver glasses that she would often adjust as they fell slightly off her nose as she looked down. She had the blondest of blonde hair and wore her socks higher than most of the girls and folded them neatly back on themselves. Tammy smiled at me and introduced herself, and before long we were chatting any chance we could get. She mentioned she had her own horse and that to me was irresistible. Mia was to arrive halfway through our first year. She didn't like her first school and requested a change. I think Mia found Tammy and I pretty quickly as she probably heard us gossiping about horses loudly and passionately. She fitted in perfectly with her opening line to us, "I have a horse too." Mia was more talkative and a little taller than us but also had extremely blonde hair as she was part Swedish. I would often be asked to judge who had the blondest hair, not a job I wanted, as they squabbled about it regardless of who I had chosen. I still hadn't got my very own pony yet, but at least I had more people to live through vicariously. In fact, Tammy and her younger brother Owen were lucky enough to have their horse property in a leafy suburb nearby. She had a little bay quarter horse called Mistique. Mia had a chestnut thoroughbred called Harry. Not to forget Aria and Lola. I had introduced them all too as Aria was a year ahead at the same school.

I never really felt like I caught up with my schoolwork, which I was hoping to do when I finally reached high school. I struggled in most areas but as time went on, I did manage to excel in some subjects. I just wasn't the strong academic type.

Throughout Year Eight I worked my fingers to the bone to show my parents I could do better, and to try to convince them to let me have a horse.

When I reached Year Nine, my persistence paid off. My parents called me into their room for what appeared to be a serious conversation. Thoughts ran through my mind on what I may have done as I sat waiting anxiously at the end of their bed for "the talk". Instead, it was announced that a pony was to be bought! I won! I couldn't believe what I was hearing.

I felt like the king of the mountain. Nothing could have made me happier. I jumped up as if on springs and flew into my parents' arms sobbing with sheer joy. I did it, I would have my dream. I couldn't wait to tell all my horse friends, and rang as many as I could, chewing their ears off with all my excitement.

Now, as to what pony to get. I had spent years daydreaming about this special day. I would often find myself lost in horse books circling my favourite to least favourite colour, breed, and markings. Imagining what it would be like to spend every day grooming, braiding and riding my very own horse. My absolute top choice would be black with white stockings, a white blaze and a long flowing mane. Second to that a pure white one. When it came to reality I was happy with anything that had four legs and that I could ride but let's start with searching for my first choice. We looked and looked but didn't find what we were after. I had to satisfy Mum as well, as she was sort of fulfilling her lifelong pony dream too. Mum had lived as a child with a big paddock behind her house full of cows and horses. My grandparents knew she had the desire to ride and own her very own horse so one day my grandma visited a nearby farm and saw a small, grey Shetland pony for sale. She made an offer to the farmer and had arranged to have it delivered to their home. Unfortunately before this happened it fell sick with colic and was tragically put to sleep. My mum and my grandparents were devastated. Mum never really got over the fact so was always interested deep down to re-live this dream. No worries Mum, Zoe to the rescue. Dad didn't mind what we got, he was more concerned about paying the bills and keeping the peace. Let the girls figure out the details Dad, especially if it keeps them happy!

Tammy was to visit the stud where her pony was from. They had a full sister to Mistique on the farm and it was for sale. Might be perfect. So I ventured there with high hopes and a racing heart. But I wasn't overly wrapped with her. My heart sank and I lost a bit of hope. She was nice enough, but just not for me, so we thanked them and left. This horse was going to be important to me, so I had to get it right. Just before we got into the car, the owners told Tammy that their neighbour which was also a horse stud had Mistiques' dad who was a sire there, so off we went to check out her ponies relatives. As we arrived, I wandered over to the stables where the foals were. A cute chestnut-coloured beauty poked his nose through the stable fence to me. As I got down to his level we started to kiss, or what seemed as close to that as it could be. He and I were nose to nose for ages. We had a connection. The owners let me into his small fenced-off yard and the chestnut tagged behind me like a puppy dog. It reminded me of following the leader, I always enjoyed being the leader. I was thrilled, and I looked out to the others and waved to Mum. I heard her sing back, "Oh Zoe, I think he is the one." That he was. It turned out that he was also Mistiques' sibling, sharing the same daddy. Unfortunately, he was only one year old, and couldn't be broken in for another year or so. I was just going to have to wait a little longer before I would have the great pleasure of riding him. The good news was, boys were also on the horizon and in our sights. Something to surely keep me occupied for a while. We didn't have to look far, there were plenty of boys that lived in the same area as us that we regularly socialised with. I introduced Tammy and Mia to my boy mates, and they reciprocated in introducing me to theirs. One day in Year Nine, another friend stopped by me at the traffic lights near the bus stop home.

"Hi Zoe, this is my boyfriend, Jim". I said hi, but didn't think much of him. He was just a guy, and was ok I suppose. Little was I to know what role he was to play in my life! Mia had brothers. The eldest, Chris, and a younger brother, Tom. As we got older, we hung out with Chris and his mates. He had many friends come over to their place, including Jim. I, along with many of their friends, often went with Mia and her family to their horse farm. I got to know all of their friends, especially the boys, but didn't have any big crushes on them. Lots of flirtatious fun, but nothing else. We all mostly hung out with the horses. Everything revolved around the horses and our love for them. They were great days, and while I had originally cursed my parents for sending me to the private school, I thanked the heavens they did. My life was great! I had awesome friends, and a horse of my own on the way, my grades in school had elevated, and everything seemed to be coming together.

Year Ten arrived and so did my beautiful new steed, Major. I wanted something regal and strong. He was so special and all mine. As we reached the end of high school, I became closer to Mia. She was my best friend. Not only did we ride together, but we spent many nights out. She was as adventurous as I was. We laughed and laughed together to the point of almost wetting ourselves. She was fun and quick-witted and we were on the same page life-wise. We enjoyed riding together, studying together, meeting new people together, and going out and having a ball. I could talk to her about almost anything. I trusted her, as I felt she trusted me. Tammy came along too a bit, but she had become closer to a neighbour of hers, Peter. I kept Major at his stables for a few years and met many of his mates spending time there as well. Two of the boys, Luke and Andrew, became fast friends and whenever I wasn't riding I would be with them. Unfortunately for me, it was at the expense of my studies and high school certificate. My grades began to plummet, spending every spare moment with Major or the boys. Mum and Dad kept trying to tell me to pull my head in and focus. But me being my unruly self was living my best life and didn't really care. My parents tried to reign me in since I wasn't getting the message. They would drop me off at the stables to ride and muck out and pick me up straight afterward to curb my social tendencies in a bid to make time for school work. Too many times they'd arrive at an empty stable and no sign of me. To my little sister's disgust, my fuming Mum made them clean the stable and wait for me to trot back. Then the day I'll never forget. I pushed too far. After a report card stating "Zoe talks too much, could work harder, and shouldn't daydream so often", coupled with the fact I went missing with the guys one afternoon and left mum waiting with my horse for over an hour, I'd done my dash—Major was to go. It was the straw that broke the camel's back. Resentment was building and like a bottle of shaken soft drink, it wasn't long before Mum blew her top.

"We warned you, and you didn't listen!" they had said to me. My legs turned to jelly in a split second leaving me feeling weak and speechless, I was crushed! What could I do to turn back time?

I wasn't involved in Major being sold. My parents arranged it. I wanted nothing to do with it or them for that matter. I was livid and devastated. They made a few calls and found a horse dealer who found them a buyer. Major was to leave for his new home just weeks later. I wondered how they could do that to me. How could they do it to him? We had a connection I thought could never be broken—ever. My consequence was swift and reflecting it probably had to be because I was heartbroken and they didn't want it to drag out. The day Major left I cried to my grandparents on the phone for an hour. They also didn't think it was fair (grandparents are allowed to take your side, that's their job), they listened to my sad plight in between sobs and tears. I didn't think I'd ever been as sad as I was that day. I still don't think they should have sold him. Maybe put him out to pasture for a while or leased him out to teach me the lesson, but not SOLD him! He was my friend, my joy, and made me feel proud. But he went. I felt deeply betrayal by my parents, and had a lot of regret for not showing them I was concentrating on my school work still. In a way, it brought on a niggling feeling that you couldn't rely on or trust situations that in your heart you believed to be stable and secure. Things can change quickly. The only consolation was that the new owners were lovely. Lucky for me he ended up close by, and they said I could ride him any time. It took years for my heart to stop hurting, but knowing I could still go see him, and that he was with a family who loved him as much as I did, seemed to ease it somewhat.

It's funny how life goes as that afternoon I went for a walk through my local horsey area. As I passed a usually empty paddock I heard the thundering of a horse in full gallop. I turned to look. A magnificent silvery grey steed was standing waiting for me at the fence, his head arched, his mane blew gently in the breeze, and the sun hit his coat highlighting his metallic glow perfectly. He extended his neck out so he could nuzzle my cheek with his velvety soft nose. I smiled as we looked each other in the eyes, I felt calm and maybe not even as sad as I had after losing my beloved Major. He nickered quietly as if he was trying to tell me something. I knew deep in my heart what it was. Have faith Zoe, and keep strong. My journey with horses was far from over. I just knew it. I walked away with a renewed sense of energy. This unknown creature had reset my heart and mind once again.

CHAPTER 3

THE BOMB

The HSC came and went, with its fair share of stresses. It was like pulling teeth. Very painful. I was so glad when it was over, and the reward was "Schoolies". The end of high school party on the Gold Coast in Queensland, Australia. I was becoming more and more confident as I entered adulthood right in the middle of holiday time. A group of friends I'd been catching up with from another high school in my area offered me some drugs. I hadn't done anything like that before but everyone around me was giving it a go. I thought "Why not, how bad could it possibly be?" People were trying all sorts of things around that time, marijuana, magic mushrooms, etc., and the main one, and drug of choice for those I hung around, was LSD. I had a friend of a friend who had sourced it a week before leaving for Schoolies.

Mia and I thought it was smarter if we tried it at home first to see what it would do just in case it all went wrong. On the first night we tried it we cut them in half, and we were a little apprehensive! It was a big dance party at a local venue. Mia and I turned up, ready to have a big night. We had taken the so-called mind-altering drug and were awaiting its effects. Soon after we arrived Mia felt strange. She described feeling like she was surrounded by spider webs, entangling her body. I didn't feel anything like that, all I could feel were tiny pin pricks all over my body. I'm unsure if hearing about her strangeness conjured up mine, but regardless it felt very real. I had to wonder, why on Earth do people pay to feel that? Surely there was something we were missing. The night went on. Lots of dancing, flirting and fun, but not much more to report in the way of extra side effects. Well not then anyway.

Soon after that big night out, our HSC results arrived and we received our much-anticipated marks. Hmmm not great... Maybe Mum and Dad were right! Can't dwell on the past, onwards and upwards I'd say!

The day before we left for Schoolies, we tried the last half of the LSD drug we had. Mia didn't feel as much this time, but I on the other hand certainly did. We had gone out in a large group to a pub. From the moment I arrived, I started feeling very odd, and not in a good way. I had a deep burning in my stomach and my heart was pounding. I mentioned it to my other friends who hadn't tried anything before. They calmed me down saying they were sure I was fine, but they would also ask someone we knew who was a bit of a regular drug taker to see if what I was feeling was normal. If I had known what she told them at the time, I wouldn't have taken it. Well of course, to an absolute hypochondriac panic merchant like myself, telling me that it burns your stomach lining and does other crazy scary stuff was a recipe for disaster. I was brave enough to take the drug I thought, but hearing the gory details, and feeling the drug's affects sent me into a panic attack. I made everyone leave, and begged my girlfriends to take me to the hospital. Unfortunately, they wouldn't. "What would we say to the doctors?

'My friend has taken drugs?' Oh sure, no way!"

"Yes," I said, "please!"

"No," they said. "We will take you home, and you can rest."

Now I look back, I realise how some poor kids can die. No offense to people who take them, but drugs and I just aren't a good mix! I know my kids might try them at some point as I did, but I've already got it drilled into them that some drugs will be ok and others won't be. It's not worth the gamble to test the theory. I was lucky, I survived the night, obviously, but not without its panic and, as you will see later, its aftermath.

In the morning I was fine and went on my merry way. I would just forget the whole experience and fly to Queensland to have fun, which we did! Nights out and days on the beach and in the pool. We met amazing people, including a lot of friends I still see regularly even today. Jackson and Harry, who were brothers, were great to spend time with, and we all continued to hang out in Queensland to live it up and take in the sun. With only a few nights left of Schoolies, something strange was happening to me. I began not feeling great. I felt spaced out and would have these moments of fear, and an overall weird sensation. It reminded me of the LSD but on a smaller scale. I was not coping too well with what seemed like flashbacks but wasn't about to call my parents as they did not know about my recent LSD incident. What would they think? I struggled through but only just. The worst was yet to come when it came to my health. While I counted myself lucky, two of my friends weren't so fortunate. Around the same time, Peter, I guy I had dated briefly for a time, apparently had some depression problems, and had started taking drugs just six months after we broke up. He was found by his family in the shower, deceased. Trent, another friend, slightly younger than me, had just turned fifteen when he experimented with some pills. Unfortunately, he too had an underlying condition and was also found in his home by family, deceased. Their deaths rocked us to the core, and it was a heart-breaking time. So very sad. Back then, there weren't the warnings we have these days. If only there was, and with it more education and money spent on preventing youth suicide, drug abuse, drug awareness and depression in general, we may not have lost these boys—good people, dearly missed.

When we arrived home after Schoolies to Cape Bridgewater, everyone had to decide whether to proceed to university, take the year off, or get a job. I decided the local pharmacy would be a good place for me to start. They were on the lookout for staff, and it was easy to convince them they could benefit from having me on board. Before I started that job, I had joined the gym to get fit and well, so my interest in health proved to be an attractive quality they were keen to have. I still went out with my friends (minus the drugs) and continued to have the weird sensations of disassociation and feeling not quite with it.

One day as I was driving over the local bridge I started to feel an overwhelming haze and confusion along with a very strong smell and taste of burning feathers. It engulfed me, and I almost felt paralysed, like it was making my body go rigid. I thought I was going to crash the car. I tried to tell my passenger that I felt like I was going to have an epileptic fit. Her reply made complete sense, "But have you ever had one before?"

I couldn't last on the road any longer and to my friend's surprise swerved to the side of the road.

"No, you can't just stop in the middle of the bridge," she exclaimed. Oh yes I could, something bad was happening and I was scared to death. The major symptoms of the smell stayed for a few minutes and my friend jumped in the driver's seat and drove me home. When I got there, I still felt strange inside, just not myself mentally, but I was so worried I decided to tell mum about the drugs. Oh God, beam me up Scotty. Although Mum was a sensible ally and that's exactly what I needed. The panic that had set into my body had given me a burst of adrenaline which made me feel like there was no escape. I had to just push through.

Mum was very worried, but not overly surprised. I think she knew what most of the youths were getting up to. I thought she would kill me! But she was very understanding and called a neurologist straight away. Love my mum, I knew I could rely on her. It was late Friday afternoon and the only doctor who could see us was over an hour away. Mum and I got straight in the car and drove into a huge storm that had hit our area with flooding and to top it off, peak-hour traffic. We arrived eager to find out more and set my mind at ease. With my active imagination, I kept thinking I would be the next kid listed in the obituary column. The appointment proved interesting. They picked up something odd on the EEG. It cleared me of what was first thought to be an epileptic fit but showed something abnormal. Bloody drugs! I'm sure it triggered this was my initial thought. My family sat down one night soon after my doctor's appointment to discuss it all. Only to find that my grandma had similar feelings throughout her life as did my mum, Sky, and Caprice too! Not one of them ever mentioned it, and none of them had ever known anyone else to experience the same. For some reason, my symptoms seemed a lot worse than theirs and more debilitating. Each one of my family members was a little different from the others but all not your average sensations. Dad was the lucky and odd man out. Normal Dad. He was the rock again. No one had had an official diagnosis up to this point, but with mine being so bad, it was time to find some answers.

The following months were awful. I turned into a baby. I was so scared of these horrific events that I would barely leave the house. I would cry at the drop of a hat over anything. I wouldn't have been surprised if I was on the edge of a nervous breakdown! And when I did go out, the slightest abnormal feeling in my body would send me into a collapsed heap. Unfortunately, part of my role at the pharmacy meant I had to make drug deliveries to the nursing homes. How ironic. I was now surrounded by the one thing that was paralysing my life. And I was scared to drive. I was still legally able to because the tests didn't result in straight epilepsy, but I was nervous in case another episode happened. The fact I didn't have a choice if I was to keep my job pushed me to get out and at least give it a go.

I seemed to be doing just fine when one day I was driving to one of the homes in a nearby suburb. I was coming into the street when all of a sudden my vision started to blur. I had that strange sensational sweep through my body and felt absolute impending doom. It was completely terrifying. I stopped the car, sitting in it to steady my vision. I'd had slight sensations, and different ones too since the first episode, but hadn't had a bad one like the one I was having since the first time. Panicked, and already feeling my body stiffen and seize up. I got straight out of the car but felt unable to move. "This was it," I thought. I had to be dying. What the hell was happening to me?! I dragged myself up someone's driveway, the car door left open, and the keys still lodged in the ignition. I managed to get to the door, quietly beginning to sob, I reached for the doorbell and rang it. The stiffness engulfed me. What would have normally been a thirty-second walk from my car to the front door felt like an eternity. Not sure how long it took me in truth, I was already well and truly entering another world. A lady answered, and I uttered "Help me". Shocked, but concerned, she took me straight in. I muttered what I could to her to give her my mum's number and any other information she asked for. Carefully putting me on her couch, she offered me water. I was not unconscious, so I guess she didn't feel the need to call an ambulance. Instead, she waited with me for Mum to arrive. Mum didn't take long and in no time we were off to the doctor again.

More answers were needed! More tests were done. I was prescribed many medications in hope that they would help this mystery illness. The doctors knew about the drugs and thought that the LSD had triggered something that possibly could have been lying dormant. We had no idea what it was. In the years that followed, we were still no closer to finding out what the mystery condition was. I played it safe. I changed my lifestyle in the hope it would prevent any further episodes, limiting any alcohol, increasing my exercise, meditating, getting lots of fresh air, and good food, and staying the hell away from any drugs. It seemed to work because while I still had symptoms here and there, I rarely had any more big ones that rendered me paralysed. I played it safe.

My chemist days were fun, all twelve months of them. The owner Mr Bell was great and tolerant! Even though I had pulled my head in considerably, I was still a bit rogue and your stereotypical blonde. I was really good with the people aspect though. Happy to have a chat and make most customers feel at home and well looked after. It was the more handy, practical, and mathematical things I couldn't cope with. My days of failing maths came back to bite me on many an occasion. How many times could I give the wrong change out? And when it came to building things, forget it, I just couldn't get my head around the maths to do it.

Once poor Mr Bell gave me what seemed to be a very simple task. "Zoe, can you put together this hat stand?" The hat stand was already where it needed to be. It just required screwing in the prongs onto the pole it stood on. Although it was time-consuming, it was a pretty simple task, or so it seemed. It probably was for most people, but not me. After over two hours of fiddling around with it, I was finished and proudly brought it over to him and the staff to demonstrate my work.

"It's good Zoe, but what you have failed to realise is that you have screwed every one of those prongs upside down, and unless we all start living in a topsy-turvy word, it's just not going to work!"

I was so embarrassed. I had put it all up the wrong way so the prongs that held each hat were upside down. All forty-five of them. A nice blonde moment I'd say. I don't know how Mr Bell held a straight face so as not to hurt my feelings sometimes. The rest of the staff gained great entertainment from my antics, giggling wildly behind him.

One of my other more memorable moments was when at Christmas time I was to hand out our pharmacy Christmas calendars to all our regulars. Again, simple job. Yes, you would think so. But regrettably not. I managed to give all our patrons (which were mainly the elderly) kid giraffe growth charts. What a lovely little surprise for them as they arrived home and unwrapped their gift. I can only imagine the looks on their faces as they stood confused flush against the wall for their final measure-up! Yep, poor old Mr Bell had his hands full with me.

If he wasn't fending off or righting something or other that I had unintentionally done, he was running out the door with another staff member to retrieve the pharmacy car I had randomly dumped, keys still in the ignition, drug deliveries still sitting in it, after Mum had yet again raced to my rescue.

It wasn't surprising that the poor guy after twelve months of putting out my bushfires came to the end of even his tolerance level and called me in to have "the talk".

"We are so proud of you, and love you being here, but the corporate world is missing you (missing their prescribed amount of stuff ups, I think he was trying to say). You have so much to offer (roughly equated to him saying just not here). and we think you should try your hand at something bigger than this."

Gosh, imagine my stuff ups in a bigger world than the one I had been in.

I couldn't blame him and took his wise words with me and tried not to take them to heart. I was excited for a change and to move forward with my life. Maybe I could find a more exciting career.

During that year at the pharmacy, I started to make lots of new friends at my local gym. There was only one girl there I had known beforehand—a primary school friend. She was three years younger than me, I had been in her older sister's year. Her name was Lara and she was one of the fitness instructors at the gym. Lara was a cutie. Full of energy like myself, we revelled in our gym obsession together. I then met another girl, Penny. She was a couple of years older than me. Penny was much more conservative, coming from a strict and well-to-do suburb. Penny was a rule breaker. I suppose she had grown bored by all that proper behaviour she had to live by growing up. She wanted to bust outside the square, live it, and have some fun! The three of us had an absolute ball together. Some of the local boys also joined our little tribe. We were into fitness and all things healthy but with a big dose of playfulness thrown in. I would walk to the gym from home in the morning to do a class. It would take me an hour to walk there, I'd do an hour of class and then walk to work. Often at the end of my workday, I'd walk back to the gym to do another class before walking back home. That's youth for you! Like one of those little pink Energizer bunnies—I had the energy to burn.

Eighteen was a great age. In my new group, we went out to bars and clubs but were probably not as crazy as others our age because we were trying to keep fit and stay away from trouble.

My vocal talents had been laying low, not having found an outlet yet. So, I searched to find a place where I could expel my lungs. "Verado" was perfect. It was a small Mexican bar and restaurant opposite our gym and that was where the gym goers would often meet for dinner, right on the oceanfront. Beautiful! Aldo was the owner, lavishly homosexual, and a ton of fun! He was only young himself, but full of life and so lovely. He agreed straight away to my appearances. And we decided I would sing every weekend. I was getting good money too. Gosh, it was a great time in my life. I had the attention any Leo craved, and I genuinely loved singing and performing, I was in my element.

I sang Madonna songs like Hanky Panky, Whitney Houston's I will always love you, Black Velvet and my favourite Perfect by Fairground Attraction—"It's got to be perfect", and that life was—perfect. My positive outlook was transforming into my physical world. I met lots of new people there including many cute guys to date. I started to introduce my other friends from the Jackson and Harry group to my gym friends, and we would often all go out. Sally, Paula and Jackie and her cousin Gabriella were amongst my favourites.

One night Jackie and I visited the local hotspot Devina, in the city. It was one of those places that you had to be chosen from the line to go in. Well, Jackie and I decided that we were not going to do that, and started to just walk to the door, smile and stroll on in. You wouldn't believe it, but not once were we ever stopped. We figured we oozed confidence that said, "We're owning this joint!" and it worked! I think they thought we knew the right people and didn't want to stop us for fear of being told off! It wasn't long before we were let into all the VIP sections in the club, and of course met the owners, the Canning family, who owned many clubs and bars. Paul seemed to head it all up, and lucky for us, he liked us a lot. We quickly became friends, and he even asked me to join the Devina band a few times to sing at the club as a guest. What an honour! One night I appeared right alongside Chrissy Amphlett of the Divinyls! Rock and Roll royalty. It was thrilling, and it only inspired me to think "What else am I capable of?"

Our hard days at work and long nights out didn't faze us and we all kept on going. Sleeping was for the dead.

CHAPTER 4

JOB AFFAIR

I soon left the comforts of the pharmacy and started searching for the big time. They had been great and while I had made mistakes, I still managed to get built up from their kind words. I was pretty confident! My mum was again by my side, helping me to take the next step, and she came to me with an ad for a person to work in tele sales. I was unsure but decided to give it a go. I had no experience but I did have the enthusiasm and lots of energy. "Easy!" I confidently thought.

I turned up for the interview at a large publishing company and straight away I knew it was somewhere I would like to work. I became like a dog with a bone and chased this job down. I had to have it. A guy called David interviewed me. He was lovely. I gave him my twelve months of experience and fabulous TER marks (not), and we had a little chat about my history. It's amazing how you can embellish your experiences. I think I had him confused with all my rambling on and big-noting because he was silent for a while before pointing out the obvious to me—I had no experience. To add to that, he said there were people five years older than me and from Vogue and other similar publications with years of talented work in this area who were very desperate for this role.

"Why should I even think of giving this to you over them?" he had said to me.

"Well..." I began quite quickly, "I would be better at it than them, and I would prove that to you straight away. I have fantastic people skills and could sell ice to Eskimos." I said enthusiastically. I wanted this roll, and it showed. Oh, my goodness, David was sold! I was elated when he told me he would give me a go. He loved my gusto and thought I'd be good in the role too. "No way!" I thought, "I got the job! Yeah!" Note to self, embellishing and rambling on, combined with confidence does work!

At nineteen, my life felt like it was moving in an uphill mostly positive direction. I had learned how to control my emotions around all the symptoms of what was my brain malfunction and made sure I just tried to focus on the good things.

I started my job as a tele sales rep. It was the first-ever colour newspaper to hit the streets and I was a part of it. I was proud as punch. But, it got better. Within one month of being in the role, I was offered a position as an account manager handling my very own pages. I was the chief! I was boss, well, of my little part of my world here, but good enough for me! I was very happy about it. My job was with a top company and my business card title was account manager. I felt very special and very important. They were so impressed by my sales, energy, and attitude, they told me I wasn't to be wasted and they promptly replaced my job as a humble telemarketer. I was thrilled. It just kept getting better and better. I had found my niche. This is what I truly excelled in I thought, talking to people and selling them something they didn't even know they needed or wanted. Nifty. I can truly say this time in my life, and the next few months to come were like a whirlwind of exploration. It was a time of huge personal development, and I loved it.

I felt like I was on the biggest, best, and the most thrilling roller coaster of all, and the boundaries were none. I felt superhuman like I could do anything, tackle the world, and still keep soaring.

Within months I decided I wanted to write as well. This was the time to beef up my resume! I asked my editor if I could write something.

He agreed to let me start doing some food reviews and if they were any good he would publish them. Fair enough I thought. I didn't have any experience with that either, but hey I'd try anything. After a bit of training they threw me in. I ate out at the most amazing restaurants and wrote all about the experience and the food. I put them all together and handed them in. Low and behold, my articles were published in the following few editions. Gosh, I didn't know what I liked more, writing or sales. It was incredibly cool having options. Unfortunately, I didn't write too many more, because before too long the paid journos had a gripe about it and wanted their job back. That was ok, I had plenty more things to do. I was soon put in charge of the wine section. Again, I wasn't an expert by any means, but wow I learned a lot fast. I was trained by our wine reviewer and soon invited to launches, sent amazing pressies from PR companies, taken out to lunch and wine tastings, and generally schmoozed. This job had to be a dream! I then started a column called Coffee with Zoe. I wrote stories and sold advertising in this section. It was all about the local café scene and was very fun to write.

In between times, the staff grew larger and I met so many different people. The good ones and the bad eggs. There were a few nice girls who I hung out with at lunch and various others who sat close by. There was also one guy who was older than me around twenty-eight (I was still nineteen at the time), Mario was his name. He was married and had worked with me in a similar position for a good six months or so. One day as we got out of my car in the car park after coming back from a meeting, I felt his eyes firmly on me. "Zoe, you look hot in those pants". Was I hearing that right? He was married, he had to have meant temperature hot, didn't he? Ahh no, he certainly didn't, and though it may seem naïve I didn't think that committed attached men cheated! Oh, so young and stupid. He quickly grabbed my bum and tried to kiss me. I was so shocked! I pulled away and walked to the lift, my mind ticking over as to what to do. When we got in the lift, not a word was spoken. I thought to myself, just ignore him and he might leave it alone and not try it on again. No harm done right? Nothing happened and I was ok. Yes, I guess nothing did happen, but I felt so uncomfortable with it all. This guy was married. I didn't like him in that way at all, so I can't imagine he ever got that feeling from me.

As time went on over the next few months, unbelievably, he kept trying. Under the table in meetings, he would rub my leg, and in the coffee room, he would try and pin me against the fridge. And to make matters worse, he would treat me like a dog in between times. Making fun of me in front of others and putting me down. I assume it was his way of coping with guilt and covering it up. I was over it. I had let this go on for way too long. I was a little apprehensive of what to do but decided the best tactic was to go to the Director and tell her. She acted fast, picking up the phone to make some calls straight away as I turned and exited her office. Walking back to my desk, the more I thought about what he was doing, the angrier I became. Who did he think he was?!

The next minute there were security guards at the office door watching him like a hawk. When I got home in the afternoon, they were even at my house, watching me make sure I had arrived and entered my home safely! Mario was pulled aside and got a serious talking to, which resulted in him resigning on the spot. The next day my mum received a phone call from him begging her to ask me not to tell his wife. He couldn't lose her too. Mum was great, but she wasn't about to let him off completely, and gave him a good lecture on my behalf before promising him I wouldn't tell. He was relieved, and thankfully I didn't hear from him again. The whole experience was a eye-opener into the real and sometimes seedy world. Nothing is ever what you might think it is, I pondered. Clearly, I shouldn't be so trusting. Life lesson at its finest!

For the next year or so, I worked hard. I was doing alright moneywise and had just purchased my first sports car. Next on my list was to save for a horse. I missed Major so much and felt life just wasn't as perfect as it could be without a trusty hoofed friend. A new editor called Tracey had started at the paper. She was a horsy gal too. We became very friendly and started socialising together.

I had only just started looking for a horse when I fell upon Reunion, a relative of one of Australia's most famous racehorses—Kingston Town.

She was a real beauty, with a gleaming black coat. I bought her to do some show riding I was interested in doing. The owners said she wasn't fast enough for the track but with her elegant manner she would be perfect to parade around at a show event. It wasn't long afterward, I discovered she had a problem with her feet. She had some type of disease that was slowly becoming apparent the more I worked with her. We had barely started when she became lame and had to be rested. A vet check had been done by the previous owner's vet at the time I purchased her, but they had said she had a clear bill of health. My vet, however, said there was no way they could have missed it. The previous people wiped their hands of this beauty, and wouldn't take her back, or take responsibility.

I was gutted, but Tracey helped to keep my spirits up, and kept me busy giving me lots more tips on writing. I enjoyed my writing and she even published a few more stories for me, which gave me a buzz. Soon after, the publication closed its doors. The competition was high, and there were just too many similar magazines around. All the staff, including me, were moved to other positions within the company.

I wasn't overly impressed, but as far as the universe goes in looking out for me, it was doing its job. It knew I had more interesting things to achieve, and fabulous people to meet. In a matter of weeks, I was offered a new job via a head-hunter—Tina, who worked for Anderson and sons. Tina and I became friends, and she later joined me and my new team at yet another magazine. I moved to a prestigious group of fashion and photography magazines, and because of the people around me this turned out to be one of my favourite jobs of all.

Romeo was the owner of the business, and Claire headed up the sales and marketing team. I started with her and a character named Fran. I was put in charge of the sales and marketing on the women Collection magazine, and the Men's Collection, and was to share the job of the Bridal magazine as it was one of the biggest publications around and took lots of people to put it together.

As soon as I met Claire, I knew she was special. Claire was ridiculously good at what she did and is to this day one of the most inspirational people I know. Apart from the great job my parents did, Claire was the single biggest motivator in my younger years. She was also a local Cape gal. Originally from the UK, she found her way to Oz and didn't look back. Claire oozed what I wanted more of. She was larger than life and the funniest, most caring, and fair person I had ever worked with. She was also an incredible friend. No seasonal friendship with this one—she was a keeper! And wow, did this girl have style! She was always immaculately dressed, and always carried a small mirror to check her appearance, talk motivating words to herself, or just banter on at her reflection to the amusement of us all. She loved her wine, and all the good things life had to offer. I think she felt everyone was deserving of whatever their hearts desired. She adored luxury, was excited by power and had a beautiful, loving family life. She had it all! A great job, money, husband, two kids, two dogs, and a rock star house in one of the best streets in Victoria. I wanted to follow in her footsteps, which I did willingly.

We had built up a fantastic little team environment in our office. Being in the fashion field, we were fortunate to be the first ones to hear of any new trends and were spoilt at the numerous events we were invited to. We were as thick as thieves and loved every moment of it.

I had met Jackson previously at our Schoolies trip, and we had stayed friends since. Ironically, he also worked for the publishing company I had been with but in a different department. When I told him about my new move he asked if there were any roles there. Claire invited him to join immediately as we knew he would fit in perfectly. Jackson was very funny, as in laugh until you almost wet your pants funny. Kind of silly funny. He was good looking, charming, and had the gift of the gab, just like us girls. Like me, he was also accident-prone, and his antics would often have us on the floor rolling around in stitches. Jackson took over the Men's mag. The four of us worked hard long hours, but we found our balance by playing just as hard. Claire was the one who really taught us the art of work hard play hard. Even at the office or on the job, wherever we were and whatever we were doing, it was always accompanied by lots of laughter and fun!

Our days began with morning meetings to discuss our prospects and plans for the following editions. They were not your normal sorts of meetings with us three in attendance. We laughed, joked, and generally had a ball. There was always something we would find amusing. If it wasn't Jackson dropping his full plate of bacon and eggs on his lap, it was Fran providing the laughs. Her amusing potty mouth cursing to someone on the way to the office or dodging the hypodermic needles on every corner of the street. We were based in the heart of a slightly crooked area at that time. We had a very tight team who could always find the joke in each other's life to giggle about. One day Jackson came into the office and said I smelt like dog poo! The stench seemed to get a thousand times worse in just minutes to the point where we were all wrinkling our noses. I was getting a bit paranoid and wondered why I smelt like poo when Jackson casually plonked himself down on a chair and lifted his clod hoppers onto the coffee table to stretch out. The smell nearly knocked us off our chairs. A quick search led to the bottom of Jackson's boots which were caked in poo that led out the office door. "Thank god!" I thought, for once it wasn't me, which before he came along it would be highly likely I'd be the source.

It was great to have someone else around that did as many weird and wonderful things as I had done. I was happy for once it wasn't me! I'd already had my share of things occur over the years, now it was Jackson's turn, and I was more than happy to hand over that gong!

I was like a walking medical journal. One day Claire and Jackson said we should list all the things I'd had wrong with me medically. They'd never heard of anyone so young that had so many medical issues, mind you neither had I! From Temporal lobe epilepsy (of sorts), carpal tunnel, irritable bowel, migraines, polycystic ovaries, and parathyroid issues, I kept writing and they kept laughing. By the time I listed number 35 we were all in hysterics! I didn't have a problem with them laughing at my expense, especially as I knew it was just a bit of fun and they loved me.

We lunched out together and every Friday if we excelled in our budget, we could take off early to begin our adventures we planned to have on our weekend. We always smashed our targets with time to spare to join the fashion parties and showings with our associates. The designers and socialites we knew were many. The models, the actors, the photographers, and of course all the other well-known editors and CEOs of the magazine and fashion world. We held our own parties for work too, and we always put on a no-expense amazing shindig. One such memorable party we had we opened with waiters serving champagne, caviar, and Swiss chocolate in masquerade costumes. Our boss had set up a catwalk in the middle of the warehouse and all the members of the magazine came down the centre isle one by one dressed up as certain top fashion designers in Australia, strutting to individual songs we felt suited each person and all glammed up to the nines. Most of these designers were attending and as you could imagine they were tickled pink. We were a total hit, and many laughs were had as to how close we were at being their look-alikes. I often attended many events where I was photographed and appeared in the social pages of several newspapers and magazines. Mixing in these circles was certainly esteem-building and intoxicating, albeit sometimes a little shallow and self-indulgent if you weren't entirely grounded. The amount of socialising we could do was endless. Fortunately, they were all truly wonderful people which only served to be a bonus. I loved the environment, the glamour, the people, the life.

Claire knew I had a talent with my singing, and also found out that I was keen to become a TV presenter as well, so she booked her and I in for private lessons with TV radio guru Max. He took Claire and I under his wing and trained us. All the experience you can get helped, and he certainly provided that. Claire constantly encouraged me to record songs, which I had started to do. I was eager to get a role on the box as soon as I could though. I was lucky enough to meet Maura Faye, one of the leading casting agents in Australia. She was best friends with Fran's beautician. She was fantastic and was happy to lend a helping hand sending me off for roles. She was super down-to-earth and a talented woman.

I had been keeping my horse in the same place as a well-known TV personality. She had left her job on a lifestyle show. Maura came straight to me with the opportunity to try out for her role. I went with bells on.

They had asked us to come up with our own script of funny stories. "Gosh," I thought, "I had a bundle of those!" I started with the time my mum and dad had dropped me off outside a café to pick up some lunch. They had waited out front in their car, motor running. When I had finished, I ran straight for our white Holden Statesman, opened the door, got in the back, handed the food to the front seat, closed the door, put on my seatbelt, and looked up to say something to my parents. Umm, no parents to be seen! Just two strangers with very awkward looks on their faces. There was a white Statesman parked in front of ours and without looking I had jumped in the wrong one. What are the chances?! I apologised rather flustered and got out as fast as my legs would carry me. As I glanced my parents' way all I could see were tears of laughter.

It was great being put up for these fabulous roles. Hard work though, as the competition was always very high. I went along further in the process, but unfortunately, I was beaten to the prize by another newcomer. And she did a good job too! I was a little disappointed because I had thought it was my turn to shine, but the universe had something else in mind or so it seemed.

Back on the jobsite, our team was slightly changing. After two years Jackson wanted to try his hand at real estate, so off he went to gain some more skills and possibly add some more accident stories to his repertoire. Tina who had originally head hunted me, always knew how to spot a good job when she saw it and promptly took his place, she would also fit in nicely. She was very in tune with herself, and a calm centred person and after many conversations she told us of her own paranormal stories and all the studies she had done in this area.

"At last," I thought, "someone who could relate to my world as a child in a very paranormal environment". At a young age, she lost both her parents which sparked this curiosity about other worlds. She wasn't as crazy-natured as most of the people on our team but she was lots of fun and she fitted in perfectly. I had developed more of an interest in the paranormal because of all my families sightings and because of Tina and her studies so I asked Claire to do a parapsychology course with me. Off we trotted every week to learn more about the spirit world, angels, auras, fairies, and lots more! It was amazing and taught us most importantly how to meditate properly.

I met wonderful, gifted people. Margaret Dent, naming just one. She was the founder of the spiritual Enlightenment Society, the Spiritual Enlightenment Church, and later the college that would pass on many of her talents to others, dispel the fear of death and encourage all to make the most of our time on this planet.

One spring afternoon I decided to take Reunion for a ride up the road to a public riding area to practice some dressage. She was pretty frisky as the new season was kicking in and the sugary pastures were giving her that extra bounce. I was feeling on top of the world with my new found adventures. Maybe a little too cocky as instead of being aware of her mood I forged through with all eagerness and no care taken. Big mistake. As I walked from the roadside into the bush, Reunion spooked at a bird, twisting with speed and force 180 degrees dumping me hard on the track. I winded myself but was ok. She calmly stepped to the side and looked at me with dishonest dismay reminding me to rein in my ego, be in the present and never get too far ahead of myself. Point taken Reunion.

CHAPTER 5

LOVE SICK

While life moved on at work, it also did on the home front including my love life. I was still living with my folks so I guess you could say life was easy as I had somewhere to live almost rent-free and a cook AKA Mum most nights. I could also save my money for when it was time to move out. Back at Mia's place, we had developed a small more intimate group of friends that included Mia, her boyfriend Tom, Chris and his girl Jane, Phil, Johnny, and of course Jim.

On many occasions the gang would try and set each other up with people, playing matchmaker. Jim to a girl called Mindy. And me to Johnny. Both were not to be compatible. It's hard to meet someone you click with. Just stick to being friends, I think. It wasn't till Mia's birthday, around Halloween that I had a realization! We were all celebrating and getting on well.

I had sat with Jim most of the night and got to know him a little better than I had over the many years we had been friends. The next day I developed the photos I had taken and while viewing them with Mum I started feeling something, a tingle, a spark, something different from how I used to feel about him. "He seems lovely," said Mum as she flicked through them. He was, I thought. Over the next few weeks, we focused on each other a little more, flirting, teasing, and chatting about our jobs. It felt so right. Jim and I were just friends but something was happening. It's so weird how that works but he appeared to feel the same way. It wasn't long before all the matchmakers of our group stepped in. Mainly Chris.

"I think Jim and Zoe would be perfect for each other," he announced one day. Somehow, I agreed. Although we had years of just being friends, all of a sudden I was falling for him very quickly. I had never felt this way. Was it Love? No, it couldn't be, or could it? One day Jim bought a new car and even though he wasn't letting anyone else drive it, I asked, and it was a swift yes. Everyone's eyes widened in surprise! You always knew a guy liked you if he let you drive his new car. I was in like Flynn!

Soon after we went to another dance party, a Jackson and Harry dance party. Jackson and his younger brother Harry had become celebrities in their own right, becoming well-known party organisers. It was there that Jim and I had our first kiss. And boy was it special. He was special and I was smitten! Afterward we went back to his parent's place where he was living at the time. They were away so he had the place to himself. I was driving, so he asked as I pulled in if I wanted to come in for a coffee. I nodded with a big warm smile. When we got to the kitchen, he piped up that he didn't drink coffee. "Me either!" I said, and we both laughed. It broke the ice a little, we were so nervous. We started pouring tea but soon forgot, as he drew me to him and began finishing where we had left off at the party.

I was getting a little anxious because I didn't want to go all the way with Jim. Well not just yet anyway. This guy was very possibly the one, and I wasn't going to ruin it. The rules, the rules everyone! Apparently don't sleep with a guy on the first few dates if you want it to last. I was always told this in my early years so I wasn't going to risk it, and to be honest I wanted to take it slow. It was getting rather intense, so I spoke a soft, "Ahh, I'm not going to do anything with you, in err Ummm that way." He jumped in with an "Of course not, I didn't think we were." Although some would think that was a typical guy response when they were thinking they were actually going to score, I felt Jim was being truthful. He was nice, and I could tell he liked me. Our kiss had sealed the deal. We were then without a question boyfriend and girlfriend!

Time seemed to stand still. I was in the bubble of love! The affirmations I had been chanting, living and breathing almost weekly had worked. My guy had arrived. I clearly remember each time after being in his presence, thanking the angels above. The universe was the best. They had delivered him to me. We socialised in a group situation mostly but found our time alone almost every day too. I was so relaxed around him. I didn't think that sort of feeling existed but now I know, I was in love for the first time in my life.

The saying is correct when they talk about seeing each other in rose-coloured glasses. We were perfect in each other's eyes. I'm sure we were perfect together to the outside world too, but that didn't matter to us if we were or weren't. It wasn't long before it was time to meet the parents. When I arrived at Jim's I met his sisters, Leanne and Rebecca, and their kids and Jim's parents, Anne and Steve. Anne and Steve seemed almost excited to see me, reminding me of young children about to visit Disneyland. They embraced me with open arms and added that they knew I was the one when he started to talk about someone he was seeing and called me his girlfriend. He had never brought girls home or referred to them as his girlfriend.

I was over the moon. I wasn't surprised though; I knew he was the one for me too. They liked me a lot, and from then on included me in all their family do's. They were his adoptive parents as Jim and his brother Tony had been adopted out as babies. Anne and Steve were really into family. My parents and sisters reciprocated and loved Jim as much, and we took turns in dinners and secret smooches at our folk's places. Happy Days!

Within a couple of months of making out, if you get what I mean… I missed my period. I was even on the contraceptive pill so not sure what happened there. Unfortunately, the pill didn't do the job! I was devastated. We had only been dating a month or two and I was only twenty-three at the time. Too young for a baby I thought. I wasn't the only one who was upset. Jim and my parents were too, as was my little sister Caprice who cried. Maybe she felt sorry for me or was simply just embarrassed. We never actually spoke about it. After the initial shock, Jim was a gem, so supportive of my feelings and my decision on the matter. Even though it wasn't what he wanted at all, he said he would have it if I wanted to and would marry me. I didn't want any of that so soon, but it was nice to know he would stand by my side and cared not just about himself and his feelings, but mine too.

I went to the doctor for a blood test to confirm the dates. I was a wreck. I passed out during the blood test and had to rest in the surgery for an hour. Two days later the results came back. It was negative. In the week or so of doing the urine test and blood test, the baby was gone! I was sort of relieved but also a little sad, but it wasn't the right time. Jim confirmed he was serious about his commitment when he thought I was pregnant, but he had been faltering a little because a woman who worked with him (ten years older) had said don't commit to her, she is trying to trick you into marrying her. I was so insulted. How could a woman who didn't even know me or the situation say that? It had never crossed my mind. I certainly wasn't that sort of a desperate person, I had a career I wanted to fulfill. Jim wasn't sure, I think. Did women do that? Maybe Jim questioned that too. I'm certain they do but I wasn't one of them. That woman should have butted out! I was a little insulted that Jim even entertained what she had suggested if I'm honest. It made me feel he didn't know me at all. You want a partner who backs you all the way and who knows you are a good person through and through and trust, well even more than that, know you wouldn't be capable of certain things.

Well, with that little hiccup over, life continued. The sting of the woman poking her nose into our business still annoyed me. I made a mental note to avoid those kinds of people at all costs—who needed that? Not me.

My life was busy. I had my number one, Jim. My fab job. My horse. My friends. My hopeful career in the entertainment field and of course lots of love, parties, and life experiences to deal with. Although we both still lived at home, Jim and I were getting very excited about our future times together and decided we should extend our family! No, not what you might think after what we had just been through. Our next family member had to be a puppy… or two. We were on a mission. The bubble of love could be extended, couldn't it? We were able to squeeze one more in, I was sure. What type of canine would we get?

Jim had his heart set on an American Staffy. I hadn't grown up with dogs, so I was unsure what personalities they all had. In saying that we decided on one dog each. He had his chosen, and my choice was a Doberman. I always loved that breed. Regal, intelligent-looking, and great guard dogs. We searched for a while for both dogs. Eventually, we came across some breeders out in the country. They certainly were characters! Derek and Linda. Derek was tall, gaunt, and very wiry. His companion Linda was short, plump, and had a hard look about her. Unusual pair. And with the language consisting of many a swear word, spitting, "bushman's", which I later found out was disposing of snot from your nostril into the wide-open space around—and no tissue involved, lots of yous, geez, did ja, gunna and similar true blue Aussie expressions, it became a bit of an experience being around them. They bred English Staffies, American Staffies, and Pitbulls. We met the pregnant mum Millie and fell in love with her. Soft and affectionate, she was what they called a blue fawn. A gorgeous combination of light brown and silvery blue. She was gentle and somewhat timid. Then the big dad—Thunder, came strolling out to see what all the fuss was about. Amazing to look at, tail wagging and jumping up for cuddles, strong and very athletic. He was silvery blue all over and so cute. Yep, these were the ones that would bring our big blue boy into the world. The wait was on. We were excited!

Next, we headed off to see the Dobermans. We didn't have as much luck with these. Although there was one thing in common. The breeders. Not sure if all breeders are weird but so far this was proving true. One guy we saw introduced us to his "bitches and sires" and gave us a little show. I nearly died when he began tickling the poor dog's privates. I'm assuming to stir up feelings directed at males and females. But if you ask me, it was a tad too pornographic for our liking, and in fact it turned us off altogether. I then convinced Jim to let me get two cats instead. Although we decided to wait until we moved out together to get them. Our little pup was to live with Jim's parents until we left home for good. The plan to leave was soonish but no date had been set. Polo arrived and wow was he a cutie. Although he was a sickly type of a dog, often did little vomits around the place. Just extra stuff to clean up really. He looked like a mini hippo. Like most of the litter of puppies, Polo also was blue which was very rare back then. And we paid the price literally. Wow, he was expensive! But gosh, so, so worth it.

Well, he was naughty that's for sure. Full of beans as lots of puppies are. Dragging off Anne's shoelaces as she walked through the house, stealing pillows, plants and shoes. Jim's parents weren't over the moon excited about Polo, they had a preconceived idea that American Staffys were vicious killers. Every time he growled or nipped he'd get a good yelling at. That type of breed is tarred with the same brush, which is a shame. It's such a generalisation. Anyhow, he was certainly a pampered pooch and as any new couple with a puppy will tell you, your life often changes a little from parties, late nights, hangovers and the like to delight in taking your newfound friend to parks, the beach, friends' houses, cafes and pretty much anywhere you could. Having Polo was a good trial in seeing what having a family together would look like.

CHAPTER 6

HELLO INDEPENDENCE

Jim attended many launches with us including one of our photographic magazines—or you could almost say book as it was such high quality and was a stunning visual arts masterpiece showcasing the world's best image makers. In this particular edition we focused on nude Olympians. The party/auction for the charity began. Jim became a little over-excited and then got busy getting involved in bidding on a nude photo of an Olympic swimmer crush of his, forcing the other bidder's boyfriend to bid higher and higher. I wasn't overly impressed as I was possibly wanting an engagement ring in the future. One had not been purchased yet and this was surely taking these funds. Come on Jim you could have me to yourself, naked or clothed, you don't need a picture of her. I saw no choice, you had your prize right in front of you. It was all fun, especially when he missed out. Phew.

It was getting rather crowded at Jim's parents. Because Polo was living there, I was expected to be at their home too, taking care of the puppy's every move. It got quite hard, so we decided the time was right, and we would make our leap into the big, bad world alone. I think Jim was also waiting for the right time to propose as well, and still living at home just didn't match! He knew how I felt, and that I would love to get married, but probably knew Mum and Dad were a little funny about me moving out before we were committed. Then of course throw Polo into the mix and it was time to make the move.

My parents were kind of old-fashioned when it came to relationships and marriage. They liked the tradition of at least being engaged before you moved out together, and I wanted to have happy parents, so I tried to oblige.

Our move out was inevitable, but timing was involved, so before we told anyone about leaving home Jim came to pick me up for a night out at a small Thai restaurant on the beach. "Zoe", he said as we walked through the car park. "I love you!"

"Yes, I love you too," I promptly replied.

"No, No, I love you so much that… will you marry me?"

I was so happy, car park or not. I have to say I didn't expect it then. He had a lot of opportunities in more romantic, special locations away together, and I clearly remember looking for diamond rings in my champagne, caviar, or desserts but obviously to no avail. I'm sure Jim knew I would be expecting it and deliberately didn't use those times. Very stubborn my Jim, and he liked to be unpredictable. Like any man I guess, he wanted to do things in his way when he was ready, not when he was told to, and rightly so.

We planned to get married in late February. We had our trusty friend Claire on our side to help with our first big move together. She promptly offered to buy a home near her and her hubby and rent it to us at a slightly cheaper price. How lovely and so kind. She found one almost immediately on the next street to hers, bought it, and we moved in. It was beautiful. It had a nice feel to it and lovely gardens, fountains, and all. And the greatest thing was, we were together!

We soon met our neighbours. Very funny story. Polo had escaped from the house one day while we were inside. After noticing him missing we ran out in a panic. It was a new area that he didn't know, and he had zero ideas about roads and cars. We soon heard laughter coming from next door. As we ran to their house, we saw Polo bounding towards us sucking a dummy right way in and everything (photo moment). We were beside ourselves. What had he done? He had the most excited look on his face, wagging his tail like a crazy thing. Worried, we yelled at our neighbours asking what he was doing. They were in stitches. They had a one-year-old girl, and Polo had come over to say hi to the family and thought the dummy looked like a good thing to take as a souvenir. Mindy, the little girl, was not upset, just fascinated by this hairy fast creature who softly stole the comforter from her lips.

Luckily these guys were not highly-strung or we might have been in the bad books, but no… this was our introduction to our very laid-back, cool (Dutch) friends Katy and Richard. And wow, what amazing neighbours they ended up being. The best ever. We all clicked from that day on.

Jim and I liked to keep fit. I ran, and Jim liked his triathlons and road bike races, and so did Katy and Richard. Katy was shortish, with a slight build, dark hair, and a cute mole on her cheek like the model Cindy Crawford. Richard was tallish, with brown skin, handsome, and had a very large muscular frame.

We fell into a daily routine that consisted of coming home from work, buying dinner at the local shops and putting it on the stove to cook. Katy and I would go running with the dogs up in the national park above our houses, and Jim and Richard would either ride, swim at the beach or do their run. Although a couple of times a week, mainly Friday afternoons we would all hit the beach, dogs, kids and all. Bodysurfing the beautiful waves was the best. When we would get home, we would check our dinner to see if it was ready, and Jim and I would go over to theirs (because they had kids) to share our food. They ate fairly differently from us, morning and night. But it was good. Katy taught me many a recipe including a favourite snack of theirs, blue cheese and baguette for brekkie! We would all sit on their deck laughing the day's worries away. And they were always certain to finish it all off with a strong coffee and port, either on the deck in summer or around the fire in winter. Great times.

My new kittens arrived soon after we moved in, but not after lots of very hard work convincing another slightly odd breeder.

"I choose the right kitten for you," she explained.

"You will not see the litter," she would say in her snobby voice.

"I will bring the ones I believe would suit"… Gosh was that a normal thing?

"I will interview you first and see if you are ok."

We sat in her waiting room and were quizzed, intensely! Luckily we both had skills in sales, I dread the poor unsuspecting buyers that didn't, don't think they would have passed the test. It was a true interrogation.

Both kittens she presented us with were gorgeous! We named our new additions Chino, who was a cream point Himalayan, and Rumpole, who was a black Persian. They arrived at our house and we carefully introduced them to Polo. All good, safe and friendly. No killer in our Polo! Unfortunately, within a week I started to notice some funny things happening between the two cats. Rumpole seemed to be beating up Chino. Why? It continued and I got worried. When I took a closer look at Chino, I noticed his eyes appeared not quite right. They seemed to be reflecting the light and looked orange/blue. I felt something was just not the way it should be. So, I started what was to be a run-up in vet bills that would unbelievably continue for decades.

The first trip was to Jim's family vet, the one Polo attended. He was a nice vet and had a look at Chino. Straight away he saw he had cataracts. I didn't understand, he was a kitten. I just got him! What did it mean? What was going to happen? I phoned the breeder to explain the story, but she blamed us saying it must have been exposure to chemicals or the like. But no way was I taking that. I was a huge animal lover, and very responsible. I know how to take care of a kitten for goodness' sake! And, Rumpole was fine so that made no sense even if there was a miraculous chance of it. I then made a hard choice. I gave Rumpole to Fran from my work who was overjoyed to have him. I couldn't let my sick one get beaten up every day.

I took Chino on and decided to try and fix this issue as best as I could. I love my animals, and when I commit to one, I go all out as to lose them is too heartbreaking. Trip after trip, test after test, and even double whammies of normal vet to specialist centres! Money, money, money, or soon-to-be a lack thereof. Polo and Chino became the best of friends over the following months. Sleeping together and generally hanging out. Polo was still throwing up, and we decided, hey let's try and provide our vet with a mansion and possibly a Ferrari! We took polo in for testing. More money! Nobody seemed to be able to give us any real answers for his issues either, so the vet suggested the specialist centre for Polo too. "Sure, why not!" He obviously could do with another Ferrari too! During all of this building lives for the rich and famous, Chino escaped and after a day of looking outside we found him tucked under a large pot, covered in ticks. We rushed him to the local vet who happened to be a friend of mine. She was really worried about him. Apart from the ticks, he had many other medical issues emerging at the speed of light. We took him back to the specialist centre who told us he would have to have an operation on his cataracts which would cost a fortune, we sadly had to put him to sleep. This on top of all the other bills we'd already forked out for tipped us over. We just couldn't afford that and all the other medical expenses he would need to have as well. It was gut-wrenching and I cried a bucket of tears, but the expenses were completely out of our reach. It was probably a godsend with all he had been put through already, but with the vet not promising he could get him through it all, there was no other choice. It was such a sad, sad day. Polo was sad too, he missed his pal. I called the breeder to tell her what was happening. I was in tears. She kindly offered me a deal, if I bought one kitten from her (of her choice of course), then she would give me another one free (of her choice). Why not, I thought. I was so upset, I had ended up with no cats at all! Things had to get better.

Polo was consistently sick, and it was becoming more frequent, with up to ten vomits a day. We had also found out during this time that the rest of his litter passed away from something days after we took him home so maybe this had some bearing on what was occurring now? The stress from all the animals being sick or deranged was high. I have no idea why on Earth I would want to put myself through more, all I can say is that my love for my animals was greater than the stress of it all. More tests for Polo resulted in the now Porsche driving specialist vet diagnosing him with stomach disease. It appeared our Polo was allergic to meat! Beef, lamb, pork, and all the classic foods dogs eat. And we hadn't known, continually feeding it to him was making him worse. There didn't appear to be a cure other than changing his diet. Still having done that, he would never be free of his vomiting, not even one day of his life.

The breeder of the cats had made a condition upon taking more of her kittens—I had to ensure all care for them was put through her nephew, a local vet. I agreed. On the day of pickup of my two beautiful creatures Cubbins and Crumpet, we went off to her nephew. On first look, they seemed ok. But after a closer viewing of Cubbins' eyes there was a very familiar appearance and believe me, I had become a bit of an expert by now and spotted it just as quickly as him. He was scared, I think. His aunt was a nightmare and very controlling. Would he agree with what he saw? Yes, but, I didn't care. Off to more vets! This was heartbreaking. It seemed we were on a merry-go-round that didn't stop! And all I could think about was how many Chinamen I had killed in a previous life to be put through this karma now.

It was soon confirmed by an ophthalmologist we saw—yes, cataracts it was. I decided to go straight to the best. This guy was the top in his field. If he couldn't make them see again, nobody could. We worked out that Cubbins was the worst. He had them in both eyes, and could hardly see anything, and Crumpet had one eye nearly completely covered, and a slight one in the other. But poor Cubbins also suffered from bad asthma and would jump on my bed often in the middle of the night wheezing terribly. It was like he was letting me know when he needed his meds. The Ophthalmologist was amazed as I retold the story of all the cats, and I think he felt for us and decided to help by reducing the bills for consults and operations. Every bit helped. But mount up they did, and Jim and I were feeling the pinch. It wasn't just the financial burden; it was a huge emotional strain. I'm sure a lot of people would have given up at that point, but I'm not like that, I was determined to see it through and win the battle! Good or bad, this was who I always have been. I decided to take the breeder to the courts through the Department of Fair Trading. I was not going to roll over and die. And breeders like her should not try and put the blame elsewhere and leave everyday people paying with their pockets and heart.

Next was the time-consuming and expensive research to prove our case was genetic-based, and not environmental. I mean the thing was that the three Himalayan cats in question were related by parents, but Rumpole was not, as he was a Persian. Of course, as timing would have it, I was changing jobs from my fashion magazines to a fitness magazine. So, I had to master managing that, and all my feline investigations. I was becoming quite good at juggling. I thrived being in a stressful situation, I think it was the whole live by the seat of your pants kind of thing. I almost felt I could have studied to be a solicitor myself and taken it in my stride. I'm sure some of you think, like me, in that the busier you are, the more energy you have, and the more you achieve. It was hectic. Every moment I wasn't selling or writing in the mag, I was phoning and seeing more vets, breeders, cat societies, the head of the RSPCA, and high-profile people including politicians. I received letters, affidavits, facts on cataracts in animals, and general comments on the situation. Soon there was enough to be used in the case against her. Claire was great during this time in my life too. She was strong and egged me on to prove my case and help our poor puddies. We caught up every few days and she would give me a big pep talk to keep going.

I had decided that amongst this hectic time of my life tackling legal cases, weddings, and new jobs I needed to visit Major. I was invited up to the new owner's property to go for a ride and have a much-desired cuddle. When I arrived I was greeted by the family and taken to Major's stable. Major came up to the gate and nickered happily. I was so glad he seemed well. I went into his stable to unrug him to prepare for a ride, when I heard a noise coming from the corner of his box. I walked over to check and Major followed. I looked up and a possum was struggling to keep upright as he tried to wedge himself back into the corner beams where he had tried to make a small home. As we stood there he fell to the ground, and almost vanished in the sawdust beneath us. Before long he resurfaced looking more alert. Major to my delight lowered his head to the ground to meet the little fellow who jumped quickly on board. Major straightened back up and moved gently toward the corner beams. The possum jumped off his back to scurry to his hidey hole, but not before leaning forward to Major for what I could only describe as a grateful kiss. What a sight! I was later told by his new family that the possum had been injured and was recovering in his stable. At night they were spotted interacting and on occasion Major let him rest on his back for warmth. I knew then restoring justice to the animal kingdom was the right thing to do. All creatures great and small, Major and his unlikely relationship reminded me I needed to do my best work in protecting them.

CHAPTER 7

BRIDAL PROMISE

While we were returning justice to the world on behalf of the animal kingdom, we searched to buy our first house, whilst booking wedding venues, flowers, the photographer, and stationery. Jim had lost his beloved grandfather and he had ever so generously left him an inheritance that was to become our home deposit. I had enough savings to purchase a whole house full of new furniture and belongings. Jim soon came across a cute little fibro cottage next to Bridgewater Bay. A perfect first-time purchase. We had our loan approved, and our offer on the house was accepted.

It was not as nice as our house, courtesy of Claire, but it was closer to the beach on a flat, large block. Most importantly it was ours. It makes all the difference when you know you worked hard and it becomes yours. A real accomplishment. It was never smooth sailing, as being out of home and doing everything for ourselves off our own back took lots of money. We had good jobs, but still, you need to learn how to handle your finances and life in general. It took time, learning, and sacrifice. When we finally got it all together, we were super proud of ourselves.

Unfortunately to start paying for a mortgage I had to give up my beloved horse, Reunion. She was still lame and the vets had told me she was untreatable. Yes, I know what you are thinking, another sick pet?!

She would only ever be good as a broodmare or pleasure horse, not the show-stopping sensation I planned on her being. She was moved on to a family in Queensland that would love and pleasure ride with her without too much pressure. Losing a horse felt like losing a part of me. Saying goodbye to Reunion was tough.

Over the years, my horses have given me such happiness, strength, and company. They have always been a big part of my world. I missed Reunion greatly after she left.

The house move wasn't too bad, although no move is easy, always hectic, masked by the fact you are so excited about settling into your new residence. We brought with us Polo, Crumpet and Cubbins, oh and a couple of fish in a big round glass bowl—a parting gift from Katy and Richard. The wedding plans were coming along and I was filled with anticipation. I had all my connections from the bridal magazine which helped.

Planning a wedding was one of my dreams. Stressful but fun. Not sure about the guys though, they didn't seem to be coping that well with it all. Too many questions about what seemed to be in their eyes trivial decisions. Oh well, boys, you know the drill, you can't say you weren't expecting it. At least Jim didn't have a total bridezilla on his hands!

As we settled into our cottage, we attended many of our friend's weddings. We were at that age that a lot of people around us were getting married. I was a bridesmaid for Lara from the gym. That was good practice for when it was my turn to stroll down the aisle. And I had recently met one of Jim's childhood friends Paul and his fiancé Samantha. Sam and I clicked straight away and started to see a lot of one another. As Jim's special lady in his life, I was then invited to their wedding where I met many of his other friends from school. We were in that new couple phase you get caught up in when you become one yourself. It's nice. Lots of dinner parties, trying new wines, BBQs, and doing the normal things in life that families get up to. It's just growing up, and we seemed to move effortlessly into this new way of living. It was a bit of a novelty doing adulthood. We still went to parties, and I was still being invited to work functions, as was Jim. I was still meeting Katy for our runs in the mornings along the beach and the waterfront at the lake. Also, my friend Claire and I started meeting a personal trainer to share a session or two each week after work. Living on the beach promoted such a healthy lifestyle. You feel so alive and ready to take on the world. We loved to be active people.

Being a small village, everyone knew everyone. Even the shop owners knew your dog's name and would stop for a cuddle with Polo. Everyone was so blasé in that neck of the woods that even when Polo pulled me up the street, over the road with such force I went splat in the middle of a courtyard next to an outdoor restaurant, seeing me land face down, skirt flipped up over my head, and bearing my behind to all the patrons, and not many a local eyebrow was raised. Nothing phased our beach crowd!

My friendship with Mia was still as strong as ever. The group still hung out, and we continued to socialise with them. Jane and Chris were still together, and Mia and Tom were an item. Jim and I had been together a year by this time. But it was a little weird. There seemed to be some kind of shift happening. Siblings Mia and Chris had been used to having Jim around at their place constantly. Because I was with him and we had moved in together, that didn't occur nearly as much. I'm not sure whether the events to follow were any indication of that, but after a night at a function there was a falling out.

We were at a party for Mia's work and being a new couple we were holding hands. Then I went to use the bathroom and Jim said he would come with me. He waited outside and when I finished, I came out to see him chatting with some people who he then introduced me to. We stayed for about twenty minutes before walking back to Mia and Tom. When we approached them we got a bollocking, being told how dare we go and have sex in her work friend's bathroom!

Now maybe some people might have done that (more power to you) and as much as Jim and I were loved up we weren't those sorts of people. Sex in the toilets—not for us. We denied such behaviour but it didn't seem to be accepted. She had a bee in her bonnet and we were in a firing line. I'm a fair person but when someone accuses me of something I haven't done I fight back. At least if I had had that sort of fun the bollocking wouldn't have felt so harsh but no, no such wild behaviour had taken place and there was certainly no past behaviour she had seen from either one of us that would ever suggest that.

Well, it was on like Donkey Kong. Tom tried to keep the peace, but to no avail, and an eleven-year friendship of being the best of friends was over. Just like that. No amount of talking could convince her and I stood by my story too. She also threw in a couple of comments about how Jim would rather buy a new bike than spend money and go on a holiday with me, and that we weren't meant for each other. Knowing Jim, he may have said that he would rather have a bike, little bugger he was, often making offhanded comments to joke around. I didn't think he would have meant it, and he denied it in any case. Unfortunately, the Scorpio sting of Mia was alive and kicking. God love her!

If it wasn't enough that I was fighting with Mia, her brother Chris decided to join in too, saying he thought Jim and I would only be a fling and he didn't expect we would stay together and even marry! I wasn't happy with this new found hate for us, what the heck was happening? Jane didn't agree with the negativity towards us either and it seemed the two siblings were causing waves. Jane was standing by him as a girlfriend, but I'm not so sure he was doing the same to her as there was talk of another girl on the scene in some capacity. It wasn't long before Jane and Chris parted ways. Unfortunately, the bad blood continued.

I found out after the engagement party was over and all the presents were unwrapped, that Chris had given him a football jersey and a note saying, "You're a braver man than I". I was really upset, and I wondered why Jim had let him get away with this. Soon to follow was another family member, Mia's mum. I'd always liked her but she took a swing in a gutsy phone call to me stating that I had tricked Jim into marrying me and that his parents Anne and Steve hadn't even liked me and were not happy I was joining the family! I'm not sure the origins of this info, but I felt it couldn't be right.

At all of that, I just exploded big time. I was ropeable! I called the wedding off, there was no way I would take this from them, and no way I would let Jim allow them to say and do these things. "Back me, Jim!" I screamed silently in my head. Jim was non-confrontational in general but come on get some balls and stand up for what was right. I was angry, and Jim was distraught. Anne found out from Jim about the comments Mia's mum had made and phoned her to set her straight and demand that no lies were told again. Anne and she had never even spoken before that day, and certainly not about me. All very strange, my tears were never to come, I felt only anger. I was so upset. I didn't look back on my decision but sat and listened to his emotional plea. It was one of the only moments in our lives I saw him cry. But unless he drew the line with Chris I wasn't budging. I couldn't go into a marriage having my partner not give his 100% support to me. What sort of a marriage would that be? It wasn't right he was allowing his friends to make stuff up, be rude, and treat me like poo. Not a very respectful relationship in my opinion. I even saw a counsellor as I was that cut up about it all. They said your partner should always have your back. You should feel supported, and respected and your feelings considered.

Gary, Jim's smart, older and married work colleague and now close friend, stepped in to share his thoughts on the matter. Gary also knew Chris as they both worked at the same local car company. He spent a long night explaining to Jim that it wasn't right for Chris to be doing this, and the best move to make was to put an end to the friendship unless Chris could get over it and treat his ex-friend and best friend's wife-to-be with respect. Thankfully the pep talk worked and Jim ended his friendship with Chris and wedding bells were ringing once again. I think if Jim hadn't made that decision, I may have missed him immensely, thank goodness it didn't come to that.

Jim ended the friendship and Chris thankfully stopped stirring the pot but Mia and I still had issues from a far. Although we had been so close it was sort of a blessing for both of us to have time away from each other. Things change and so do people and your relationships with them.

I didn't think Mia and I would ever have those sorts of issues, but life sometimes blindsides you. People make mistakes and have different ideas from one another but that's life and that's ok. People come for a while and people go.

Our wedding day was making its way into our reality. Whoopie! With the excitement, we forgot about all that drama and it all went off without a hitch. It was beautiful and the most perfect wedding I could have imagined albeit a little rain but good luck they say. I spent the morning with my bridesmaids at my parent's house having my makeup and hair done while sipping champagne and being snapped by our photographer. My bridal party and my dad and I were picked up in silver two-tone vintage Bentleys. We arrived at the church in perfect time. An umbrella was held purposely over as I got out and prepared myself to marry Jim. I stood at the door with my father as close as he could to my side as I wore a huge tulle skirt that had an ever so slight blue pastel appearance coming through. It took up half a room. Well, a slight exaggeration obviously but it was big! A matching lace bodice, hair tied up with roses, and a beautiful diamond cross fell delicately around my neck. I was ready to walk down the aisle. My heart was racing almost faster than before I sing on stage but the excitement that I was to be married spurred me to forget the jitters and enjoy the experience. The music began to play. Shania Twain's "From this moment". It had just been released that month so we must have been one of the first to use it. I think now it could be the most played wedding song around and a bit kitsch but back then it was ours and ours alone. The bridesmaids followed in a stunning teal gown with tulle underneath picking up the blues of my dress' crystals. I managed to arrive next to Jim safely and we got through our vows without a hitch. The reception was just beautiful and set on the wharf on our Bay. I remember it was such a social evening I didn't even get time to eat as I had so many family and friends to catch up with. Jim and I barely saw much of each other at all, only on random times to get photos taken. The wedding came to the end. I sang a song to Jim and our guests just before we cut the cake and we danced a bridal waltz before saying goodbye to our guests. When it was over, we had a little honeymoon on the cheap a few hours' drive into the countryside. Not a lot of money was around at that time, well not with all those vet bills and our mortgage but love doesn't need resorts with crystal-clear waters. Just us and those rose-coloured glasses.

CHAPTER 8

ZOE'S CRUMPET

Back home to the real world and our new house, sick animals and all. We had some nice neighbours at the new place, but nothing could beat Katy and Richard. There were street parties that were friendly enough with BBQ invites and talks over the fence which was nice. One guy was quite a character and amused himself and others at street gatherings we had by telling lots of wild stories and many a joke including one that left me wide-eyed! He announced he had "seen Zoe's crumpet walking along the back fence" that day, much to the laughter of the neighbours. I was like "What, my cat walking the fence?" What's so funny? "Crumpet" for some here in Australia is slang for your hoo-ha, and Crumpet was my cat, and voila a perfect joke. It gave us all a great laugh.

Jim and I started the whole nesting thing and began painting and decorating our new pad. It was so much fun. Gardening, buying ornaments and we had even more parties. Being in Bridgewater Bay was free and easy, almost none of us ever locked our doors, and would head to the beach or down the street with everything left wide open.

With Polo looking like a killer guard dog, we always thought we'd be safe anyway. Some people used to jump across from one side of the street to the next when we passed him as he looked so fierce. We would have to be super unlucky to have someone rob us. But as we soon found out, robberies were not the only things to happen. I arrived home one afternoon to see a note as I got to my door.

"Don't worry, come next door we will explain."

What did this mean? I came inside to find the place trashed. Oh my gosh!!! My back room was a mess. There was bird poo all over our white lounge and lemon walls! And to top it off a few of the leftover offenders flew aimlessly around our room. My neighbour saw me and came over with her mum.

Her mum explained that while on her veranda she spotted a crow or two balancing inside on our huge candle sticks. She asked her daughter if we had pet birds flying free in the house. She said no and peered over the fence to look. At closer inspection, she noticed that there weren't one or two birds, there were at least thirty birds of all different types flying around in our house! Starlings, Indian Minors, Magpies, and Crows. And our fabulous watch dog had let them all pass him. He was laying in amongst all the mess, happy as Larry in his bird aviary! I wasn't expecting our two blind cats to be alerted by it, but Polo, come on! What a disaster. The only thing we could think of as to why it occurred was the fact that Polo's food sat outside near the back sliding doors, and the hungry little birds may have wanted more. The last bird took us two days to finally catch as it got into the roof. They stained the walls, and the lounge never really returned to normal after the aviary party.

The court case date was looming, and Cubbins seemed to be getting sicker and sicker. It was terrible. The breeder even tried to use Polo in the case saying he frightened cataracts into them. You have to be kidding! They even turned up at our door camera in hand before the case unexpectedly and tried to capture Polo in some sort of aggressive way, and always in letters he was referred to by them as a Pit Bull. They tried their hardest to use any excuse under the sun. My mum joined Jim and me on the day in court, we had handed in all the evidence a week or so prior for the judge to read. The only thing left to do was re-state our case. We were concise. I was nervous but with a feeling like I had it in the bag. The breeder and her son sat upright at the end of the table also looking confidant or maybe I should say arrogant.

I presented real, compelling, and medically backed information. I even impressed myself. The very hard work had paid off. I had seriously been a wealth of information with this one, thorough through and through. I think I could have written a paper on cataracts with all the knowledge I had gained. The breeder must have known it wasn't looking good for them so she scrambled to find more evidence to add.

The thrill of feeling so intelligent filled the gap of no university attendance! Life experience can be just as informative. I felt empowered, and pretty smart to be honest, as I was presenting a pretty airtight case. Anyhow it seemed we had by far the stronger lawsuit but would have to wait a month for the final verdict. We had only asked for a little over half the money for the vet bills we had already outlaid, which I thought was more than fair. I could have asked for more, but I just wanted to be reimbursed some not make money. A couple of days before the result, I was sitting in the lounge room at home after having my dinner when I saw Cubbins sitting with these huge magical orange-gold eyes, staring intently at me. It was eerie. It felt strange, and I spoke to him softly asking if he was ok. He soon vanished in the house, and I went to bed.

In the morning I was due to visit Major and let the animals out before I left. I was gone most of the day but when I arrived home, I felt an overwhelming tiredness come over me, one I hadn't felt before. I went to call the animals in, but Cubbins never came. I was not worried by him not showing up, it wasn't out of character for him to be missing in action curled up in some nook in the house. I fell asleep and slept all that afternoon and that night, and only woke up late Sunday morning to find there were still no Cubbins to be seen.

I searched all day and night, and the next afternoon. I decided to pull the back shed apart as he loved to get in there and sleep. It had a very tiny gap under the floor, and I just had to check if he was there. I had to find him alive, he couldn't be gone. But within minutes of Jim and myself shifting the timber, I saw him. He had his mouth open just like he did when he would have those asthma attacks and his eyes were wide open. He stared into space, but this time not at me. He was gone. I was inconsolable. I cried and cried and cried. It seemed as though he had had an asthma attack and gone under the shed to pass. Had he tried to come to me for medication? Had I not heard him in my weird deep sleep? Was I not meant to save him? It tore me apart. Surely the universe wouldn't want to take more animals from me. I was consumed by horrible guilt. If they had been 100 per cent indoor cats this wouldn't have happened, or would it? Was it asthma or some type of breathing issue, or his bad genetics? I just kept thinking of so many reasons that could have taken him. I would have done whatever it took to save him.

We buried him in the backyard under his favourite tree. I didn't sleep very well that night and was rather flat as I left for work. On my return, I checked the mailbox. It was the result we had been waiting for. We won. The money was to be returned. It was a bittersweet moment in time! My boy had gone, but together we returned some justice to the world. And with that, I went inside to have a weep only to find a little surprise on my back doorstep. I half laughed and half cried. I wasn't sure how I felt about it, but Cubbins was sitting upright on the doormat! Polo it appeared had missed his mate so much that he dug him up, carefully pulled him out of the black plastic he was wrapped in, and put him on the mat. In his eyes, he probably thought that could bring him back to life. Crumpet on the other hand was totally freaked out. He wouldn't go near him. I buried him three more times. Polo was persistent! While out of his grave for the third time the vet asked to do some final tests on him which we agreed to help future studies. After they finished, he was cremated and eventually he rested in peace forever. Goodbye Cubby, love you boy.

Jim had been offered a role with a large fleet vehicle firm. Claire had written and tweaked his resume to help him score the role, and it was a success! Little embellishments can get you everywhere. It was a role that would lead to numerous experiences in our lives, some the best, some the worst. The most positive was Jim's rise in the industry and his pay cheque. The worst, however, would bring our family to its knees.

The journey to work every day in the city drove both Jim and I crazy. It was close to a two-hour trip in, and one and a half for me. Jim's was a little less but still, out of control travel time that took up the better part of our life. After careful consideration, we decided to make a move closer to the city. We hated the thought of leaving our beloved Bay and all our good friends, but you gotta do what you gotta do. I wished they could have all come with us! So, house hunting it was again. It was time-consuming, but fun!

Finally, after a lot of searching, we found a beautiful federation semi near the city, just thirty seconds from Portland CBD. Very handy. It was tucked up in a most unique spot above bushland and the water was so close it was right at the end of our road. It wasn't our Bridgewater Bay but it was a great compromise. The most amazing walking and riding trails surrounded us, and the house overlooked the beautiful suspension bridge. So peaceful. It was unrenovated and we had work to do on it, but that was ok. Plenty of time to do that.

Life was great. Jim and I were still madly in love. He would often pop home with the most thoughtful gifts like a teddy bear, a bunch of roses, or a month's worth of beauty treatments! I was one lucky gal!

We added a little kitten to our family to keep Crumpet company. I thought it was only fair as he had been through so much. We found a new breeder, brought a Cubbins look-alike home, and named her Lamington. We seemed to have a real food fetish with names. I can't blame Jim for that entirely, I was the one who named all our cats. He did however originally want Polo to be called Spud. I said no to that. Luckily, but also to be expected, Lamington was perfectly healthy. Again, proving our case that the breeding line from the other breeder was flawed. Lamington easily fitted into our family. Together, we all began a fresh phase of married life.

My interest in TV and music still played a big part for me, and after randomly meeting a producer from a major TV home and garden show, I was asked if I was interested in appearing on a few episodes. "OMG yes!" I exclaimed. In one episode, they even had Jim involved in the background.

It was just what I wanted, and I was able to add that to my growing and healthy-looking resume.

After the stint on that show, I was then put up for a job on another show but just missed out as the person I was due to replace didn't want to move onto the new show they had suggested for her. They decided to keep her in the role and the new position became redundant. I was used to getting my hopes up and having them drop, so it didn't faze me. Next was an offer to host the fitness section of a lifestyle show. I would have been a shoo-in for that one, but I hadn't completed one of the fitness courses required for full qualification for the job. Kind of important I guess, can't be leading people astray with dangerous fitness moves, can we? Next was an introduction and meetings with a huge talent. A man who launched Australian lifestyle shows on TV. He was lovely and as I sat with other known presenters he liked to work with in his studio office, he offered me a role as a presenter on the new show he had pitched to one of the channels. That was unfortunately soon after put on hold. Back to the drawing board. In between times I thought I would jump back to my singing and see how far I could move along in that department. It was all so cut-throat out there in the TV and Music world, but I was still determined to give it a crack. I'd bang on some more of those doors of opportunity, I knew one would eventually open.

I had a few songs I had recorded, so I went shopping for a deal. I had a connection with a South American singer-songwriter who had taken an interest in my talent and asked me into Warner Chapell to record some more songs. I was happy. Some extra tunes to my repertoire. I also got to meet the team there, and I was soon offered many amazing songs by very famous writers all around the world. I chose one to record—By Heart. I took my sister Caprice to Melbourne where we met up with a well-known producer to remake and record the song. My sister did the backups. Both of my sisters could belt out a tune by this stage. Seemed we had great vocal cords in our family genes! Caprice had no desire to be a singer, and Sky favoured singing in choirs, but I wanted to hit the stage. After the song was complete, I came back to present them all to the who's who of the industry. I was lucky enough to get a hold of a well-known promoter and manager, and he asked me over to his offices to hear me and have a chat. The world of the entertainment business is funny. It was all go, go, go, super fast-paced! I was invited in with open arms, which was nice. A few people sat in on the meeting and I played my stuff.

"Amazing," they said. "It's great. So, what do you want?" they asked me.

"A deal!" I said promptly.

"Yep, I don't see that being a problem," he replied. I was beaming! I was all excited, then he said he needed me to give him one or two more songs to work with. I felt a little deflated, as that took money to produce songs. I had to consider Jim and our new mortgage, etc. I couldn't be selfish as it was not just my money, it was ours. Unfortunately, after talking with Jim he felt that the recording and cost involved may never stop, and we couldn't afford it at the time. I knew it too, I was sad but ultimately gave in to logic. I was so close, but oh so far!

Burning the candle at both ends had wearied me. I felt wrung out. I was pushing my limits at my job and felt like I was about to hit burnout. I was hoping my brain issues wouldn't return so I took heed and I thought to myself I needed a change. Fresh energy. I had a talent in the PR side of things so decided to look down that road. Gabriella, my girlfriend, had her own PR company so after a chat, we joined up and started working together. "Show Pony Publicity," it was called. While I was still in my current position I worked on PR in my spare time. It was different and hard work. The buck stops with you. I learned a lot doing it. And it was nice to have a friend to do it with. Gabriella gained us a few clients, and so did I. We sailed along fairly smoothly and I was thoroughly enjoying it when my maternal clock clicked in.

I had begun to feel a little clucky—and the need to have a baby was racing up the list of my priorities. It was strange for me. I'm not what you'd call an overly maternal person, but I had the feeling of having my own would be different. It would be such a big change for us. Life was great. Jim and I had a healthy lifestyle that we loved and spent every night together relaxing. We had a double income and lots of spare time to do our own thing as well. Jim had started training for triathlons with the guys from the Jackson and Harry group. They were all incredibly fit, and they loved the training. The girls were always left behind though, we didn't share their intense training regime. The girls grew close, spending lots of time together. In particular with Harry's partner Izzy.

She was beautiful and full of fun and laughs. Although not an exercise freak, she took good care of herself and looked amazing. Harry, like Jackson, was also a handsome guy, not so accident prone as Jackson had always been, but very funny. The two boys were such great value. Izzy and Harry were not married as yet. Izzy was divorced and had a gorgeous little eight-year-old daughter, Ali. After her divorce I knew she wasn't overly in a rush to walk back down the aisle until she felt the time was right. In saying that, they were very close, and heading in that direction.

Almost all the boys were getting completely obsessed with their exercise. Jim always watched what he ate, but this was about to turn into an obsession. He would get up at the crack of dawn to cycle and kick off his five hours of daily training scheduled in around work. He spent his lunchtimes swimming at the pool and hit the home trainer at night before bed. If passing a large or small shop window the boys found delight in appreciating their gorgeous new physiques, lingering a little as they cycled past. People thought the boys were wasting away, but they seemed happy and proud of their new lean, whippet-like transformation. With the diet, exercise and work, Jim would be shattered, leaving little energy for anything else. He and the other boys would even fall asleep watching TV at night, and sometimes during the day as well. It was taking it out of them that's for sure.

Molly, Pete's wife, began getting very annoyed he was not spending enough time with her. She would make him go to the movies on the weekends, only to look over at him fast asleep within fifteen minutes of the screening. She was ropeable. Kind of amusing now but then, not so much. Calculating everything that went into their mouth, and pretty much no alcohol. Yes, it was admirable, but getting a little old. I felt unhealthy next to Ironman Jim. He would playfully rib me at restaurants saying "Oh, are you going to have dessert?" with a glint in his eye, challenging me to pass on it. Once home, he'd say "Oh, are you going to have a glass of wine now?" I don't think he appreciated me not getting into fitness like he was. Either that or he didn't want me splurging when he couldn't. Maybe it was too much of a temptation and he didn't like knowing what he was missing out on.

I would say to him, "That's your little thing Jim," not mine. I loved fitness and health too, but I wasn't obsessed with it like he was. It was taking over his life. I'm pretty strong-willed, so his comments here and there usually slid off me like a wet duck's back. I'd be lying if I said that was always the case, the constant digging away at me, eventually began to penetrate and sit in the back of my mind when it hadn't done beforehand. I didn't appreciate where these comments were coming from when it was him trying to reach elite fitness, not me. I think it began making me wonder if he thought I had some kind of a weight problem. I was totally fine with my body and never had body hang-ups. I'd always been active, and still attended my gym daily, and ate healthily. But his remarks began to cause me some insecurities about my body I had never had before.

Izzy and Harry were often around at our place. Usually helping us decorate or renovate. Jim, God love him, was pretty hopeless when it came to anything domestic or handy, and it would regularly get left for ages or ignored altogether. He even turned a blind eye to light globes that needed changing for six months at a time. They would sit there annoying us until I would do it or hire someone else to do it if it was a complicated task. Jim didn't mind that, as long as he didn't have to do it, he gladly handed the money over to anyone that would make his life job free. But Harry, Izzy and I thrived on doing work around our house. It provided me with one of my biggest pleasures in life.

Painting, planting, pulling apart rooms and redecorating, choosing ornaments and art, we even laid tiles and pavers! If I wasn't doing it alone, we had our two neighbourly comics around to help who would often giggle at Jim's inability. Amusing, but sometimes frustrating. If he wasn't hammering nails in the wrong way, he was stepping backward onto sheets of fibro snapping them clean in two, making us start from scratch. We paid Bunnings Hardware rent I think! He was a bit like America's Tim the Toolman in full swing. It was always easier to have a laugh when there were friends around. It was much harder to get angry at him in their company. The frequency of his antics cost us a bomb financially. I could understand his lack of knowledge about basics, but it was the lack of drive to do anything that began wearing thin.

I was beginning to feel the uncomfortable absence of horses in my life. I'd been used to having them around and visiting them often. Reunion was in another state, but Major was not too far from me and much more achievable. I craved that warm nuzzle they gave, their funny personalities, and of course the challenges of training them and working towards a goal together. To gain their trust, to find trust in myself, to maintain my confidence and to work as a team. I had spent years taking my horses to hacking shows. I'd jumped too but never had I accomplished a full eventing competition where horse and rider compete against other horses and riders across dressage, jumping and cross country. Eventing tests the horse and rider's fitness and the winner is the one with the least penalties. The horse needs to be agile, hardy and skilful as does the rider. This sounded perfect and something to work towards. Major's owners were so relaxed and did not fuss over when or where I rode him so when the opportunity to train him up and compete in my first eventing competition near where Major lived, I jumped at the chance.

I had to visit frequently and train him to jump a little higher than we had done when I was younger. It was nerve-wracking as jumping scared me a bit but it was exhilarating all at the one time. His owner had another horse and she used to come out to a nearby field to practice with me as although her expertise was in endurance, she was open to teaching her other mare a few new skills.

I was focused and disciplined and felt I was building a stronger connection with Major than I had before. We were on fire, jumping logs at a gallop, perfectly executing our dressage moves and clearing rounds in the jump arena.

The big day arrived, and to be honest I was nervous, to say the least, but I had a great group of horse friends around me which without a doubt helped. The dressage test was up first. I walked Major into the arena and gave the judge a salute. We made sure all our lines were straight and forward moving. We finished circle after circle of the walk, trot, canter, figure eights, and simple changes. I found myself holding my breath most of the test and as when I exited the arena I felt pretty faint but satisfied I had done my best.

Cross country was next and as I was warming up, I whispered to Major, "Be brave," and we took off and up over the first hill leaping over the log and turning a sharp corner to continue the course. We sped up and slowed down at all the right places and he was steady, just how he needed to be.

Lastly the show jumping. We had walked the field prior so I felt confident we knew the course. I stayed as calm as I could and we approached the jumps with confidence. Almost a clear round, just knocked one down.

The results came in later that day. My score for dressage was 65 per cent. Amazing, I was thrilled! Cross country clear and within time, and jumping only one down but within time. Although not a win I ranked fourth and I had to be happy with that. It was our first comp and we had done well and worked together perfectly. There was no better feeling, so we came home to the horse paddock to celebrate with champagne. One challenge was over, our determination got us to the end. Friendship, trust, and communication had strengthened and made it a day to remember.

CHAPTER 9

MY LITTLE DARLINGS

Before Jim and I started to try for our own little family, I suggested that we might track down some medical history about Jim's natural parents. I think it's good to know a background like that to see if there's anything your kids may inherit. Just in case. He readily agreed and signed the docs to permit me to search. I promptly began the little investigation. It didn't take long before we found his birth mother, Dee. She was just the most beautiful, soft-natured lady. And when we finally found her, she cried tears of joy. She seemed very shy. She told us of her many years of living in the very same suburb as Jim while he was growing up just to be close to him, even though she had never met him after he was adopted. She had managed to find out where he lived and would drive past Jim's family home often, just to catch a glimpse. Never knowing if Tony, Jim's brother was her son or Jim. She was ever so keen to meet us. And finally, after a month or so she phoned Jim's natural dad. They had ended up together after Jim was adopted, but they were not suited to long term.

Dee eventually married a lovely guy called Brett who we met at the meet and BBQ. I think it was very confronting for Jim and his dad Fred. They were both super nervous, and you could tell that they were watching what they said and listening to each other like hawks too. All in all, it was an amazing day. We were shown photos of Fred at around twenty years of age. Both he and Jim were like twins. Really identical! We found out all the history we ever wanted and stayed in touch with Dee and the extended family. To this day I see them every year. I wouldn't like to lose touch with such gorgeous people. Fred wasn't interested in catching up again, as he had never told his family of the child he had out of wedlock. It was such a shame a relationship hadn't resulted.

With the family history known, Jim and I began trying for our babies. It wasn't easy. I thought I'd fall pregnant quickly but after five months I wondered what was happening. The doctors said it may be harder than normal with the polycystic ovaries and endometriosis I had, but it still should happen. Izzy found it laughable that I was stressing after such a short time and told me to just chill out and let it happen. I think she was right and we, or me, really started to forget the apparent rush, instead, I just enjoyed the trying part.

Then it appeared, the pink line in the home test. I was pregnant! We were both completely elated. With the pink line came nausea. Blah! Yuck. Morning sickness is the worst. It reminds me of being way out in a rough ocean, a boat rolling back and forth, sea sickness building, and no way off to escape it. That pretty much sums up how I felt. Sometimes if I was lucky, I'd throw up, get five minutes of relief and then back to feeling sick again. It was better than constantly feeling it like I did some days where it persisted on and off throughout the day and night. I had cravings and gave in to all of them. That's probably why I put on 22kg! I thought I'm pregnant and had an excuse. I wish I had known that my body would struggle to get that weight off afterward. Maybe I would have second-guessed giving in to them so easily. But I went with the need for salt and vinegar chips, lemons that were eaten like oranges, green apples, and vinegar poured into a cup. Talk about ripping your stomach to pieces! For the sickness, I tried ginger tablets for relief, but what the doctors forget is your gag reflex is out of control, even brushing your teeth causes problems often bringing up your breakfast in the sink. That's if you got it down in the first place! So, when that huge tablet touches your tongue, you have little chance of getting it down. I tried ginger snap biscuits. Better than nothing. I have to be honest; I wasn't one of those women who enjoyed being up the duff. I hated feeling fat, tired, sick, and emotional. Oh, and the swollen feet toward the end were terrible! Cankles to the enth degree! Not a good look. But that's the price you pay.

We had begun antenatal classes at the hospital. There were eight couples including us. Everyone was nice. We sat in a room weekly and discussed our worries, did exercises, and talked about what essentials we may need. I was the queen of the essentials. A little OTT. The class would giggle wildly as I would constantly announce the latest gadget I had purchased in anticipation of our arrival. I had everything, most of which I probably would not even use. But I was prepared!

Soon after the classes started the eldest couple dropped out, and seven were left. In no time the girls named us the G7. I know geeky really. But hey we were mums to be, and we didn't have to be cool all the time. The group consisted of lovely girls. Antenatal classes usually don't stick together we were told, but obviously our group didn't get that memo. We had enough compatible personalities to hold a gang together and make the effort when needed. Plus, we got on well. Later the girls never really stuck with their mother's group; they were all allotted, instead, we chose to stay in our G7 group. Meant to be.

Now I was getting a little upset as time grew near for the big arrival. Many years ago, I visited a clairvoyant to give me an insight into my future. From memory, all was not too bad except for the fact that I was most likely not going to make it through childbirth! What?! Who says that to a mother-to-be?! Although I grew up around the paranormal and do have a firm belief in most things, I wanted to take this reading with a grain of salt. I know they can be slightly off, and with this reading, I was hoping she was going to be way off! The reading was that I would have major complications, and she was unsure if I would pull through. Not good. Ok, I had to take stock, or I was going to have a meltdown. She shouldn't have told me of such things. I thought it was against all rules of clairvoyance, but she slipped up on this one. Mum was always trying to tell me she didn't feel any such thing so I placed my trust in her instead. I had to this time, no turning back now. Mum, always had the gift, so I calmed down a little and trusted it would all be ok.

Our baby was due around the 15th of March, the day of Jim's birthday. He had signed up to compete in a birthday marathon. The run finished and he was hanging out with his friends when he received my call that I started to experience some pretty bad pains and to meet me at the hospital, but after a couple of hours on the monitor it wasn't quite time and I was sent home for what they expected to be another day or so to wait. No baby gift for you Jim. That's my mum's talent!

A day went by and I was fed up. I didn't want to wait anymore, so I begged my obstetrician to induce me, which he did. I sat like a beached whale on my hospital bed as they gave me the drip that was going to bring my little one into this world. And did it ever work! Within minutes I was dry retching and in some serious pain. It didn't take long before I asked, or yelled, for an epidural. It came pretty fast and finally there was a reprieve from the pain. Ahhh peace. And perfect timing too, I started feeling the need to push. The doctors were ready to go. I tried but after 10 minutes the feelings disappeared, and there was nothing. It seemed the baby was stuck. So, it was decided that if we waited any longer, we could have issues. That was the last thing I wanted to hear. Issues!

Without further ado, I agreed to a C-section. Mum, Jim, and the doctors joined me as I was prepped and given another dose of anaesthetic. Because I had the epidural, they seemed apprehensive about what dose to give me to ensure there was complete pain relief while they operated. They played it by ear and kept asking if I could feel anything. I was so nervous about the pain. I waited until I was certain, before letting them top me up.

The incision started. Unfortunately, it began to go wrong. All of a sudden, I felt uncomfortable. I was unsure, but it almost felt like I couldn't breathe. Was I just scared and having some sort of panic attack? Or was it more? As a minute or two went past I started to feel worse. Sharp pains in my chest and my neck were escalating and yep, I couldn't breathe, for sure this time. I made the announcement and looked quickly at the clock on the wall. I was distraught. I was going to die at 2.05pm. The clairvoyant reading was right. It was set in stone; this was my fate. The time is imprinted into my mind to this very day. The doctors started to panic, but calmly as not to worry us. They worked fast and tried to reassure me as they pushed and pulled to get the baby out. They told me they would be looking at putting me on life support if it got worse, and it would all be ok. No, no, no it wouldn't! I was so scared. Life support?! This wasn't good.

They injected me with something they mentioned to reverse the anaesthetic. It must have helped because it stayed at the same level. They held my baby up quickly, declaring it was a boy, then just as quickly cleared everyone from the room. I was left alone. No baby, no husband, and no mum. The doctor was by this time massaging my shoulders vigorously, and there were still things going on around me. They were persistent about the questions they ask me, about my symptoms, and how I was feeling. I was sort of drowsy, almost in another world. I tried to relax and sleep it off. An hour or so later when I was a bit better, they took me to another room, and there I lay for hours because of the doctors. It was a shocking emergency, and one they didn't expect, so I think they wanted to make sure I was 100% before I was sent to meet my new baby boy.

When I came completely to, they gave me a basic rundown of what they thought happened. Although they were not certain, the explanation was sort of simple. I had an epidural, and when they topped it up for the c-section, they put too much in (although they watched their words as you can imagine). Because of the overdose it crept higher than it should have, froze my lungs, and began creeping up towards my heart. I never asked what would have happened if it completely reached there. Not sure I want to know! Anyhow, they caught it in time, and again I lived to tell the tale.

We named our boy Max. Born on the 16th of March on his very own special day. And wow was he always into mischief. His room was picture perfect, and he had all the mod cons. Although, the comfy bed, lounge, soft relaxing baby music, and massage oil I put on him didn't work their magic in helping me to calm him. He was an unsettled baby. And he certainly let everybody know it. He was a sickly one too. Always vomiting. If it wasn't Max's vomit we had to deal with it, it was Polo's or our blind cats running into the furniture knocking out teeth or bumping their heads on a misjudged leap. Very eventful it was in our house!

After the first week of trying to breastfeed Max, I gave up. He just didn't seem to get the whole sucking thing. I did get help from experts but to no avail, so I expressed for six weeks so he could get all the goodness he needed. The crying was fairly constant with Max, but on the 11th of September I woke to what was a day I'll remember for a few reasons.

It started with Jim announcing America was under attack. Then the crying started. From both mother and child. As I sat in front of the TV watching the beginnings of the news and the horror unfolding, and Max for no apparent reason at all cried regardless of the fact he had slept, been fed, changed, and was being cuddled. Then the phone rang. It was Caprice, she had been taken to the emergency suffering excruciating stomach pain. I wanted to go down straight away, but Mum and Dad said they had it covered, and I should deal with Max who they could hear in the background. They would keep me posted. I was crying at what the world had come to. What had we done? Bringing a baby into a place where World War 3 appeared to be starting. Jim went off to work but I kept waiting for Max to settle and for Mum to phone to see how Caprice was. Five hours later, Max was still upset. Exhausted I phoned Tresillian, an amazing group of qualified women who assisted in teaching settling techniques. I was at my wit's end and needed some rest. Some mothers had said these ladies were a godsend, and the fact was, they were.

They took me in before lunch, and I stayed a few hours, before being sent home by four in the afternoon. The ladies assured me he would stop any time soon. But he didn't. Ten hours had clocked up, and no sleeping was to be had, no ceasing of him belting his lungs out either. By six that night, I called them again. They were worried and asked us to go to the emergency. So off we trotted back to the same hospital we gave birth in. We were greeted by what was to become nurses and doctors that knew us by name. We sat in the waiting room, and I still clearly remember holding our screaming baby boy, only one-month-old, and watching a mammoth world event on the hospital TV, with tears in my eyes. I guess the Emergency staff were not too worried about the headache-inducing cries because they let us wait there for almost two hours before seeing us. The doctor took off Max's nappy, examined him, picked him up, and within a minute he stopped, and fell asleep. It was unexplained. The doctors had not a clue but we, me in particular, were exhausted and just grateful he had stopped crying! We had tried everything that day including specialist help and still nothing. I think we might have had a sensitive soul among us .

Max had a few crazy things happen around him growing up. One day in the first six months we arrived home to find black flies and black spiky spitfires everywhere in his room. Lots of them. I was a tad freaked out, thinking the ghosts of the house I had grown up in had followed us! But after I got rid of them, they never reappeared, and our place seemed to be spirit free.

Max was really hard work, and I was pretty much-doing it all on my own. Jim was so heavily into his fitness, he was barely around, so I was always being left to do it on my own. He did a few things like feed at night when he was a baby, but the work during the day was left up to me. It was a lot with a baby like Max. I didn't want to admit it, but I was not coping. I eventually told Jim and Izzy. She had Ali and knew how hard it was being a mum and what a nightmare it would be not having Jim around. Harry had not been a dad of a newborn before either, only entering Ali's world when she was three. But he was up to speed on what being a dad was all about. The rest of our friend group was so far childless, so they were no help to me, and had no real understanding. I would have been the same pre-Max. You don't understand what you don't know. If anything, in my emotionally exhausted state, they were a hindrance. Pete told me one night at a party to lay off Jim, as he was just doing his own thing and needed time with the boys. I was overreacting! He very sensibly apologised a few years down the track when his very own child entered their life, and the truth was to be seen. Good of him to acknowledge it regardless of the fact it was years later.

Jim and I decided to renovate our little semi and moved to my parents while we did. We lived with Mum and Dad for twelve weeks while the reno was being done. I think Jim found it hard being in someone else's house and probably was a bit uncomfortable and unhappy, but for me it was great. I had help from my parents and sisters who were still at home. Towards the end of our stay, Jim's Iron Man event was on. All the training he had done was leading up to this one event. I hoped when it was over, he would be around more, I could only hope.

When at Mum and Dad's, Caprice, Sky, and I tried to help Max deal with his eagerness to grow up fast. He seemed to be in a hurry to do everything. At nine months our mighty boy took his first steps. He was so happy with himself and ran around investigating all he could. I knew it wasn't the best thing for a child to walk early, I'd read that crawling was important in developing their brain skills and coordination. But as Caprice pointed out in a conversation we had about it in later years, we may not have been able to stop him. The little bugger was adamant in doing it all himself, as fast as he could.

Max also had developed debilitating allergies, and we had a hard time finding food for him. He was allergic to everything but oats, corn, vegetables, fruit and meat. He was even allergic to rice! He had so much reflux as a baby that the doctor ordered us to start him on solids early. It seemed it had done something to the lining of his stomach which was causing the ongoing sensitivities. Poor kid. We stuck to his new diet religiously and crossed our fingers that one day he would grow out of it.

The big day for Jim arrived. Iron Man was on. I knew Jim was anxious. Mum, Dad, Max, and I travelled up the coast to watch. We stayed at Steve and Anne's place, which they had recently purchased to retire in and was only twenty minutes from the action. The day was just a perfect reflection of all that training. Gruelling. We were up at four, and in the dark, we stood preparing for the start. After they took off, we followed around the prima donnas to watch their bodies move in ways that would make you sick. Pushing themselves harder than ever and contorting their bodies to try to fulfill what was required of them in the race. It was a long day. By the halfway mark their faces were grey, and there was foam collecting in the corners of their mouths. Ghosts of their former selves, in my opinion. They started the race almost parading to the audience as they went by, but now their eyes told the real story. No energy, or expression whatsoever. In a trance, their entire focus was on dragging their bodies through the course like a well-programmed robot. Night fell once again, and Max began getting restless, not to mention everyone else. But we were there to support our boys. Good wives and girlfriends, I say! Jim completed the race in twelve hours. I was proud of him but tired, and I went to collect him for the drive back to his parents. He didn't want to talk to me or come home. He was with his mates reliving their shared pain. Steve agreed to come back and get him later that night. He was happy, and at least it was all over. I was hoping we could celebrate and reward ourselves with a family holiday to Queensland's sunny Port Douglas to bask in those glorious rays and try for our next bub. Max was nine months old now, and we had always planned to have our children close in age. Having had such a hard time with Max when he was younger, we weren't ready beforehand to try, but had discussed it recently and knew we had to begin trying again soon. A holiday in between would be perfectly positioned.

The getaway was lovely. We had a great time as a family. Our first trip away for all of us. We lazed around the pool, took Max to the zoo, and went for long walks. It was just so nice to get away and take a breather. It wasn't too long after we returned from Port Douglas that another pink line emerged on the test. We were pregnant again, with number two!

Our house was now ready, the renovations looked amazing, and it made such a difference. We moved back in to enjoy our clean, fresh, fabulous abode. We had extended, and now had three bedrooms, not two. Two bathrooms, not one. A larger living and dining and a pretty, formal hedged garden and courtyard. Perfect for our growing family. Jim was still doing his triathlons, but the regime had lessened thankfully so we saw a bit more of him. Max and I in turn were happier too.

The only thing missing was that sense of excitement we had always created. My routine was regular day in and day out. There wasn't much time we had to ourselves. During the day, I was completely flat out looking after a very busy Max. One day I put him in the highchair with some milk and let him watch TV for five minutes while I escaped to the next room to have the fastest shower on Earth! Looking back, I can see it wasn't my finest moment. I'd barely gotten wet when I heard what I thought was a cat howling in distress. I stopped to listen and get a better idea of what it was. It sounded awful like the cat was dying. Or was it a baby's cry? Oh god! I bolted out of the shower rushing naked and wet to check what was happening.

When I got to Max, it almost stopped my heart. The straps had not clicked into place properly on the highchair, and being the active child he was, he had squirmed out and put both legs in one hole. He had got down to his neck but because the space was only for one leg his head was not going to fit through. His face was turning a strange colour, and the cry sounded not like a normal distressed cry anymore. He was in serious trouble and no matter what I did I couldn't free him. He was being strangled and was losing breath. God, he was suffocating!

I reached for the phone which luckily was close by because I had to support his body or else the ambulance wouldn't have made it on time. He needed to have his head held a fraction higher to help him get what little oxygen he could into his lungs. This was crazy! How on Earth did he get stuck so badly? I phoned the ambulance and sobbed the story to the woman on the other end. Then while I waited, I called Jim to come home right this second. He arrived at the same time as the emergency services but not before everyone, the ambulance, fire and police all stormed through. Of course, I was naked and drenched still from my shower, but my little boy's life was at stake. All inhibitions go out the window. Jim got me a towel and the ambulance took over. Followed by the firemen and then the police interview.

They must have thought we were criminals, or I was suffering postnatal stress and was trying to kill my baby, I guess. Well, none of the above applied, and it didn't take long for them to figure that out. The ambulance held him and wrapped him in bandages so as not to get hurt while the fireman cut his head and neck free of the highchair. The cat-like cries had stopped, but the sheer horror of the situation left Max shivering in shock. His eyes told the story. I stood by helplessly although with an overwhelming sense of guilt coupled with a nervous demeanour, hoping Jim would not judge me too harshly. Everybody, including Jim went back to work, leaving the house empty, and I was left with Max alone to ponder the event and recuperate. As Jim left he hugged me and said all was ok. I breathed a sigh of relief. The highchair sat in the hall. A reminder of the stressful, potentially fatal event. Another lesson learned for me, and Max too it appeared.

Soon after I had a scan and found out that our second child was going to be a girl. I was elated! A perfect pigeon pair! I only had a couple more months to wait to welcome her. The pregnancy had been pretty much the same as Max, but the sickness was worse. The only consolation was I knew this would be my last baby, and I'd never have to endure pregnancy again. During my doctor's consultation, I was told the pregnancy was that of a placenta previa. One where the placenta sits in front of the cervix and can cause deadly bleeds before, during, and after birth if not managed correctly. Great I thought, more complications! So, a C-section was scheduled to avoid any risks, especially given the drama that had occurred with my first birth. No one was taking any chances. I found I was more nervous than before, just letting each day come and kept busy with Max.

One night about six weeks off from my due date, I was lying in bed asleep with Jim when I awoke to hear an almighty scream of a cat. Not another child emergency? In terror, I leaped out of bed. No, Max was sound asleep thankfully but Polo wasn't in the house though, and because he had a dog door he could go in or out, and I feared the worst. He was great with our cats, but not others. We were paving some more out the front of the house, and as I flew out the door in the dark, I fell over all the pavers onto my stomach hard. I didn't even think about it at the time, all I could hear was him doing terrible things to this poor unsuspecting visitor.

"Where were they?" I panicked, looking around wildly. I hadn't turned the lights on because I had rushed out the door so fast and was falling over everything. Jim, not being as in tune with noises in the dark as I was, was still in bed, maybe waiting to hear the result, or sleeping through it all. I picked myself up and approached the side gate, just in time to see Polo's head, and a ginger cat in his mouth. I opened the gate, carefully feeling my feet on the path so I didn't trip over again. I reached out, grabbing Polo's jaws, trying to prise them off the poor cat who was groaning at this point. The cat leaped forward, grabbing at my face in fear, trying to hold onto anything to escape Polo's grip. It clawed wildly, and I could feel my face rip open. I didn't have time to consider it, all I could think about was getting this cat out of Polo's mouth alive. As I finally did, I looked at it to see if I recognised it. It seemed to be Woolly, our neighbour's cat, so I hurried up the street two doors away carrying this poor cat and holding back tears. I could hardly see a thing. But within seconds I heard one last growl and its tongue fell out to the side and it went limp. I thought once I got him from Polo, he would stay alive, but he was obviously too stressed and hurt and couldn't pull through. I sobbed hard as I dragged myself up the street to my neighbour's door. It must have been a sight, eight months pregnant, see-through nighty, face torn open whilst holding a bloodied deceased cat and crying to them that Polo had killed Woolly. Well, we had a rather laid-back but tough neighbour who poured cement for a living and when he saw me standing there he roughly stated, "Zoe don't worry that's not Woolly, he is inside with us." And promptly grabbed the cat and threw it in the back of his Ute. I didn't think to look for a collar, as our neighbour steered me quickly back home to Jim. Jim, in turn, took me to my other neighbour who was an anaesthetist and could repair my cut face and sliced open ear. I was a mess about the poor cat being killed by Polo. It was horrible to think about someone's loved pet meeting his maker like that and ending up in a deep cement grave on a building site somewhere. I was emotional thinking about it for months afterward.

With only three weeks left of the pregnancy to go, Jim wanted to attend the boxing day sales in the city. I was still feeling down after what had happened but reluctantly agreed. We got into the car and drove. The day started badly when we got a parking ticket out the front of the department store, then it quickly headed in a downward spiral from there. We were nearly home when I spotted a beautiful lorikeet that was stunned from being hit by a car in the middle of the road. I begged Jim to stop. He did but insisted we should swap places from there to the vet. He wanted to hold the poor thing and said I should drive in case I caught something from the bird, being pregnant and all. He picked it up, wrapped it in his t-shirt, and got in the car. "I'm just going to put him on the floor, he won't go anywhere," he said. I quickly butted in that if he put him on the ground he would try and get away by jumping up and under the flooring near Jim's feet. But no, he insisted it would be ok, so with the bird wrapped up, we headed to the vets.

Well, you guessed it, I was correct, within minutes of driving, the bird broke free of its wrap and vanished. But where to? Jim looked everywhere. Jim, just believe your wife next time! Quick as a flash, it had escaped under the dashboard of the car and was hiding among the wires. I didn't want to act as I knew it all, so I sat there with a neutral look on my face until we got to the vet, but I was cranky. Max however was intrigued by this little bird and where it had gotten to. We got out of the car and Jim tried to retrieve it, but, as it always seemed to be with us, the situation got a little crazy. Its head had been caught between the wires and we were finding it impossible to get to. I was not impressed. If he had listened and held him, this poor little bird would be safe to recover in the hospital. We called the vet out to the car to see if they would have any success at getting it. The vet soon realised that he had now broken his neck and needed to be put to sleep right where it was tangled in the wires of the car! That was it. I broke down in tears. This bird had a better chance of being left for a Russian roulette on the street than getting in the car with us! Out came the dreaded needle, and it went to bird heaven. Now to pull it out. Oops, it still wouldn't budge. I'm sorry, says the vet, we have to decapitate it, as it's not coming out. You have to be kidding! I was so upset. Being pregnant, loving my animals, and of course the cat saga recently, now this, it was all too much. I just got up in anger and a flood of tears and started to walk home, leaving the headless bird and vet team to do their job. Jim, who seemed a little sheepish, soon pulled over in the car and picked me up. When I got home, I cried and cried to Mum on the phone. What a shitty week!

That night I went to bed, sad and exhausted. Typically, and understandably, I woke to labour pains. Baby two was on the way, three weeks early! I woke Jim, but he didn't believe me, repeatedly saying, "But you are only thirty seven weeks." He wouldn't get up and take me, as he didn't think it was going to happen and didn't want to wake our Max. So off I drove, myself, to see where I was in the labour progression and check if Jim was right—was it just a false alarm? A quick check from the nurse confirmed I was right. The baby was coming! All the stress and events had brought the labour on early. Come on Jim!

It didn't take a rocket scientist to figure that one out.

The hospital said it was slowly progressing, so the obstetrician decided he could arrive a few hours later because I was in the early stages according to his diagnosis. Jim and my family sat around waiting for him, in fact, we all waited for most of the day. My labour pains got worse, but they were still slow. We had the doctor on duty come and chat with us and made sure he knew about the placenta previa, which he did, but he was hoping to hold off until my Obstetrician turned up. When finally he arrived, he grunted hello, and I got wheeled into the operating room. I had intense pain. A nurse had told me he had been playing golf with his son-in-law on the public holiday as he had received it as a gift at Christmas and didn't want to be disrupted. He thought I could at least hang on for another few hours until he had finished. Nice! By the time they got my little girl out and laid her on my chest, it was four in the afternoon on the 27th of December. What an ordeal! Thankfully our little India arrived safely, and that was the main thing.

CHAPTER 10

LEAVE OF ABSENCE

Jim and I, who usually got on like a house on fire, began to bicker and fight. It was out of the ordinary for us. I thought it may have been all the stress at the time with two kids to look after, and the fact he had to step up more and be accountable for helping out. He couldn't just do his own thing anymore, and I believe that affected him.

It puzzled me, and I just wanted our relationship to go back to normal. There was only one positive and that was he was well and truly climbing the ladder of success and the money was amazing! He had been given a promotion at work, and when asked if he could participate in managing the social committee with a few other employees he accepted to show his commitment to his new role. I was always a little unhappy with the fact that Jim had so many work functions. I hated him leaving me at night so often to do them. When he started managing the social role it became even worse, and so too did our arguments.

I'd ask him how his day was or where he was going as you do in a simple exchange about the day's events, but he hated me asking. What was once a normal query that I could ask and get a simple response to, now had become something that aggravated him to no end. I couldn't understand why he needed to work three and sometimes four nights a week. One or two yes, but four, consistently? Surely his work could understand he was a married man with a toddler, a newborn, and family duties? In the beginning, I was invited by his workplace to accompany him to things, but they seemed to be involving the partners of their workers less and less. Maybe it was to save funds? At least that's what I had assumed. I did on occasion wonder if Jim was just using work as an excuse to get out of the house, to avoid any jobs or activities with the kids, but as soon as the thought came into my mind, I'd discard it. I loved him and couldn't imagine he would think like that let alone do it.

I'd met and become friends with Jim's boss Mick and his wife Haley. They had two beautiful kids born at similar times to ours. Mick had been at the company a little longer than Jim and was moving even faster up the ladder. Jim liked him as he seemed like a good guy.

Then there was William. He became the CEO. But I hardly saw him at work functions, and only later when our kids ended up at preschool together did I see him around more and get to know him. Again, a nice guy I thought.

One night when baby India and toddler Max were in bed after dinner, Jim and I argued. I had a go at him for two reasons. The previous day he had locked Polo in the bathroom as he was doing something around the house that Polo was bothering him with. It was a hot day and when I arrived home, he was still in the bathroom without a water bowl and panting with heat exhaustion. Not responsible pet ownership that's for sure. The day before, I had come home with a week's worth of groceries. I packed it all away but after a function he had left the fridge and freezer door wide open spoiling almost everything in it. All the groceries down the drain and a wasted shop, not to mention the other food that had to be tossed out. He was becoming careless. He didn't drink much so I couldn't put it down to that—I didn't know what was going on with him. I know accidents happen, but the frequency of these things was driving me insane.

Now after the fight, I thought we would come to an understanding, but it wasn't the case. Whenever we disagreed or had a discussion in the past, we always tended to work it out. But not this time, Jim just sat there for a minute with a sad look on his face before announcing to me he didn't love me anymore. What??!!! I was sick to my stomach. In total shock, I didn't know what to do. He went on to say he didn't want to be with me anymore. I felt sicker and felt like I was going to throw up. Tears sprung to my eyes and I cried. India was only one, and Max was two and a half. How could he do this to us?

I remembered at that moment that Jen had called the week before to tell me she had left Mal, her husband. I had told Jim about it that night, maybe he was jumping on the bandwagon? Surely he wasn't serious?

Incredibly he was. He left straight away and spent a few nights with his sister Rebecca, leaving me in total disbelief. She had a talk with him about her issues in their marriage and convinced him to see a marriage counsellor and come back home to me. Together, we chose one that a friend had recommended and went every week together to work out what was wrong and how to fix it. Jim, it seemed, just wasn't interested and had begun treating me like a second-class citizen, and a piece of dirt. And I was acting like one. At his feet waiting at his beck and call and doing everything for him, and treating him like a king, but to no avail. I was desperate to save this marriage I genuinely valued, but he was acting like he didn't care at all. It was completely out of character for him. He was constantly out with whomever he wanted. Living a single life. He gained a new friend, a guy from his office who was only twenty-one (Jim was thirty-two) and began hanging out with him and his girlfriend and their mates more and more. On the occasion he was home, he didn't lift a finger to help with the housework even though he said to the counsellor he would. It seemed the counselling sessions weren't working because I could tell he wasn't interested, he'd look at his watch counting the time down to when he could get ready to run out the door and escape.

And after nearly twelve weeks the counsellor was about to give up, telling me that she couldn't work with a couple if one party wouldn't participate properly. Our friends desperately wanted us right again. We had an abundance of supporters around us, but I was suffering emotionally and physically, and weight was dropping off me from all the stress. I'd lost ten kilos in less than two weeks. I barely touched my food. I ran on sheer adrenaline. I also lacked the energy I needed to go to the gym, even though I tried to keep up with my classes, I felt dizzy and faint and had to leave them early which I hated. I wanted to maintain a fit-looking body for Jim. I did whatever it took to try to sway him to stay or feel differently about me.

I still didn't understand why he wanted out. He avoided the details whenever I asked him. He had been living his dream life, as he used to say. He had a job he loved, great money coming in, a beautiful house, amazing kids, and a wife who adored him. He used to tell me all the time how lucky he felt. What had changed? I thought I had been doing everything right. I loved him with all my heart and would always tell him how proud I was of him (except for shit-stirring him about his handyman prowess). I thought he was amazing at his job and would tell him. I always bought him little pressies and the latest fashions and always cooked him amazing meals straight out of the latest cookbooks. I made sure, as did he, that we spoke every day on the phone. I read that couples stay together longer staying in touch during the day. And in the bedroom, well put it this way, he would never go without, ever. I was often more toey than him for most of the relationship. So, it couldn't have been that. Had I done too much? Not been aloof and mysterious enough? I had always been an open book and that was what he said he loved about me. Maybe it was the pressure I had recently put on him about working most nights. Surely that wasn't a marriage deal breaker? I spoke to other women and they agreed, it was a completely normal request to want to see your husband at night. Was it the stress of life and kids? Or was he having an affair?! I asked him this, he assured me he most certainly was not having an affair. So, what was it? He wouldn't say. I loved this guy and believed everything he said, but the issue was, he wasn't telling me what the problem was! If I didn't know, what could I do about fixing it?

I trusted him, always had. But something somewhere just wasn't right, and it got even worse. He began lying to me and became even more closed off and secretive. With no answers from him, and at the end of my rope, I booked in to see Margaret, a friend who was a clairvoyant. Margaret didn't muck around telling me straight away to go home, pack his bags and tell him it's over and to leave. So brutal! I sat stunned. She said he won't leave you, but watch what happens, she had said. I honestly didn't know what to do but I figured I'd tried everything else.

I was keen to see what was to be, so off I went home to do a little packing! When Jim arrived home, I said verbatim what she had told me to say adding, "You have made no effort to resolve this so I'm letting you go." It was hard to say, but for some reason, I knew I had to trust in what Margaret had advised. At that, Jim moved fast around the room, mumbling something. When I asked what he was doing, he said he just had to fix Max's three-wheeler, and he was not leaving till he did. So odd, I thought. I didn't argue and left him to it. I really should have watched him, it may have been the only household job he ever initiated. Probably should have got it on film! But I left him to it. Later that day friendly nice Jim re-entered. It was like he had a split personality—what a turnaround! The kids were sleeping, so Jim asked me to join him on the lounge. He started to cry as he held my hand. "What was I doing? I'm so sorry," he sobbed. "I love you and never want to leave. I don't know what came over me." The emotions were also too much for me, and I burst into tears. I loved him deeply and never wanted him to leave. I was willing to compromise if need be, he just had to tell me what it was he needed, as I still didn't completely get it. Unfortunately, he never really did. All he said was that he didn't know what had come over him. I took his apology but felt something just wasn't right. I had started to suspect that something had not so much come over him, more so, something had come under him. Was there a third person in this relationship? I prayed not and pushed it far away!

We made love right then and there. It was kind of special. Almost a surreal moment, but maybe that's because the passion was running high. And when you hear people say they make love not have sex, there is without a doubt a difference. That's what it was. Emotions can be very overwhelming. We trotted off to what was to be our last session with the counsellor to tell her the good news. She was amazed. She didn't understand how someone could do a complete turnaround practically overnight. All she could do was quiz Jim in a bid to understand what had happened, and wish us well. Love has no rules, it's authentic and raw and everyone has a different take on it. That's what I thought, and I was pretty happy—my marriage and family unit was saved! For the moment anyhow!

The next year was perfect for us. More love and more affection. After about a month or so, in a quiet moment at home over dinner, he told me he would never do this again. He would be with me for all eternity. That he promised. And like before, I believed him. He would often have tears in his eyes as he spoke. It had to be true. I could feel he was being authentic.

It was a renewed love for us. Like being in the honeymoon phase all over again. They say that the initial bubble lasts only up to about the first year, but we had been super lucky getting a second bite at the cherry. We were back on track! Being in love like we had been was incredible. Nothing except starting your family beats it in my opinion.

We hung out more with and without the kids. He would come home for lunch and a little extra loving! And there was still more of it again at night. We were on fire! Breakfast on the weekends together, walks in the park, and lots of nice dinners out. He still exercised but it wasn't as excessive as before. And even if he had continued exercising, I may not have minded because I was back in the bubble of love. Love is great, but it doesn't stop life's stresses and sadness. It just helps ease them when you have a wonderful partner to help pick you up and dust you off.

The kids were growing up and with it came all the regular stresses that follow bringing up a family. Soon after all our drama, India thought she would add some of her own. On a lovely afternoon waiting for Daddy to arrive home, India and Max were walking in and out of the house with a sandwich in hand and as I turned to India who had finished half of hers already, I noticed she was bending down at our sliding bi-folds intently focusing on something, her sandwich close to the floor. At a nearer inspection, I was horrified to see a funnel web spider balancing on her hand, up on its haunches, fangs out ready to attack. I screamed and in turn, so did she. I shook her hand and pulled her back as quickly as I could. But she kept screaming. Had it bitten her? I phoned the ambulance and then ran straight next door to get help. Our neighbour came over and caught it. It was jumping at the walls of the glass he captured it in. So aggressive. I was then more scared at what it had possibly done to her. The ambulance arrived and examined her. There was one fang mark on her hand, so they assumed it was possibly a dry bite. But after fifteen minutes she stopped crying, and they told us it didn't inject its venom. OMG. Lucky escape. We quizzed her after to find out what she was doing with it. Her innocent reply was she was feeding it her sandwich.

Great. For once it wasn't Jim or I causing drama, the wand had been handed to our kids! Max was always a little quirky, and he had shown us that by doing some unusual things like licking shopping centre floors, eating creepy crawlies, and the like, before displaying his new talent—turning blue and blacking out! Not a nice sight for a mum, I can assure you. It began when he was around three and a half with one of the worst incidents happening at my mother's group. We were all meeting at our local park for a play date with the kids and had been letting them all run around in the dog park and socialise, when Zali, one of the little kids, latched onto Max's arm. Now I didn't get too upset because it was usually the other way around. Max had left his bite mark on others before. But Max getting a dose of his own medicine didn't cope well with it. He cried for a second, then to everyone's horror, he stopped breathing and began turning blue! People came running from everywhere, and literally, no one was calm at all. I was screaming "Max! Max!" What was happening to him? Had something else been going on? Why had he stopped breathing? Before I could think straight, someone had already called the ambulance so I called Jim to tell him what had happened. He was worried and came straight to us. Everyone stood on edge waiting for help to arrive and looking at Max in my arms with horror, willing him to breathe. It took almost one minute until finally Max sucked in air and began breathing again. Colour came back into his face. Ten minutes later the ambulance arrived. They took him aboard and examined him. He seemed ok, but they wanted to take him straight to the hospital to run some tests with a neurologist. This sounded familiar!

It was an interesting consultation. While he ran tests, we filled the doctor in on all of Max's rare achievements and quirks. The doctor agreed—he was one very interesting kid indeed. "They are the best people in the world," he said. The test results came back and he told us Max also had a medical condition called Infant Transient Dystonia and asked if we would mind him being included in a study, as he hadn't found a case like this before! Of course he hadn't! Typical of our family history.

Photos were taken, and many words were written, which would go on to be included in a book for all to see, and doctors to study for years to come. The Infant Transient Dystonia, as it turned out, was a neurological posturing condition. It was incredibly rare in adults and even more so in infants but he should grow out of it. The blackouts were known as Blue Attacks and were more of the common sort and ultimately not likely to kill you. We were sent away with a schedule of regular consults and instructions to keep him checked out, and for now just had to endure the breathtaking attacks!

One day Max was laughing and running down the hallway away from me because he had taken something he was told not to, and I was chasing him. As he flew round the corner of his bedroom he slipped on the carpet and went sliding head first into the wall. I saw it happen and was worried more about the damage to his head more than anything else. He started to cry for a split second, then took his last painful breath, stiffened his body in an arch, and started to turn blue! He was out cold, unconscious. I ran holding my boy up the hall unsure of what to do even though it had happened before. I laid him on the lounge to see where this was going. It seemed like an eternity, but after a minute or so he came too. A big lump on his head and another fright for me. God this child was sending me grey!

The kids were now a nice age of about two and four. Our life was pretty good and mostly in control. Our finances were looking better than ever, but most importantly there was lots of love, particularly with Jim and I. I was now a stay-at-home mum, which was lovely. Jim was happy because he was never a fan of me working if we didn't need the money, and that suited me fine. I spent my days keeping busy with the kid's routine and didn't think about a career or anything else at that time. I would wake up early with the kids be out the door by 8.30am, walking to the gym in time for my class at 9.30am. The kids loved to play in the creche with their newfound friends, and I loved the opportunity to catch up with some of my girlfriends. It was a win-win. I got my exercise and social time in, and the kids did too. We'd walk home, have brunch, then the kids would have their mid-morning sleep, and sometimes I would join them. The rest of the day was spent either shopping, having a coffee catch-up, champagne luncheon, cheese and bickie picnic with friends, picking up groceries, or a multitude of other activities we found to do.

I had met a lot of new wonderful people in my life and am blessed to have them in my life to this day. Sue was my champagne mid-week buddy, with two kids the same age, and Jan was my going out and tagging along-to-watch hubby triathlon friend. Jan had one child the same age as Max and a husband into his exercise as well. We would often accompany them to Noosa for the Noosa triathlon. It was nice to have a friend to go off with as they all went crazy running themselves into the ground. Rose was a gym friend. All my girlfriends were gorgeous, but Rose looked like a beautiful ballerina. So convinced she was, I asked her the day we met. I remember her laughing at my question and replying that she wasn't but her husband would find that amusing, and thanked me for the very flattering compliment. Always humble Rose was. She too had kids of a similar age and we all got on so well. Rose was also into my love of parapsychology (the study of the psychic phenomena) and we would often sit for hours talking about it. A great friendship—kindred spirits.

Now don't get me wrong, I loved and could have kept up my lunches and coffees going on forever, but I did miss my GG's. You may remember,

I had to sell my last horse Reunion to help buy our first house. I asked Jim if India and I could get one each. India was daddy's little angel. Girls often are. So, the answer was a very quick yes. Oh, the joy of buying ponies again! Max liked them but was a tad afraid. India, however, was a mini-me and couldn't wait to have her pony. She was at the perfect age to train up as my riding pal. We purchased a beautiful Chestnut mare for me called Amber, and a 10-hands high pony called Stuart Little for India.

Stuart was great and so easy-going. India and Max could get his rugs on and off and even sit bareback on him as he ate his dinner, he was so placid. Amazing for kids and he never put a foot wrong. India couldn't ride him alone, as she was still too young, so I used to lead her which suited her fine at the time. My horse was slender and very pretty, but you wouldn't believe it, again I had chosen a horse that suffered problems. She and Stuart moved into a paddock not too far from a rubbish tip. It smelt to high heaven and I'm not sure if it had anything to do with it, but after time in training preparing her for shows she developed a cough that never went away. She became unwell, and we got vets out who gave her injections and ran some tests but eventually we had to take her back to the breeder. The cough went away as soon as she went back, so we thought she may have had some allergy to the paddock she was in near the tip. Sending her back to where she was well again, was without a doubt the right thing.

We purchased another to fill her sad gap with a big boy called Paint, from Queensland. He had done a lot of showing events and was to join Stuart in the now bare paddock. But again, things didn't work out well. I hear you yelling! Why get more?! There was a recurring theme here wasn't there. Yikes! I know. I just kept thinking no more could occur and Stuart was well, so I tried yet again. How can a person who loved animals so much have so many animals who became sick?! Talk about a run of bad luck. This was now thirty-odd years of it. I tried to convince myself it was all just unfortunate coincidences. Anyhow the next minute I received a phone call from the man who was trucking my new horse to Victoria for me. "I'm sorry Zoe there has been an accident. Your horse has come down in the truck and he's done quite a bit of damage to himself." If he had only told me how much, I would have had him put to sleep straight away as the damage he had was shocking. Torn from head to tail, including his legs to the bone! He was taken to a local vet in Queensland and the vet bills started pouring in. I hadn't even met the poor boy yet!

A month later he arrived. And even that far down the track, my vet was horrified looking at the damage he had received. Horrendous! It was inhumane for him to have to go through that and deal with such terrible injuries. We soldiered on trying to repair him as best as we could, again emptying our pockets. Over the next few weeks, we were with him every single day. Treating him and giving him lots of love and care. It was all we could do, it was a long road to recovery.

Well, if it wasn't one of the animals, it was one of the kids! Paint, who was feeling a lot better now and healing, had been tethered to his hitching rail standing quietly taking in all of Max and India's antics. The kids wanted to sit on his back which to me was no problem. He had kids back in Queensland that he had grown up with. They would ride him around their property, so I knew he was fine around children. I sat India on his back first, holding her firmly, while Max stood clinging to my leg awaiting his turn. When India's turn was over, I helped her off and scooped Max up and swung him on, while India was to wait by my side. As I looked to Max to give him a big smile, India decided to venture a few steps away to what I can only assume was towards Paint's injured back leg. Before a second had passed, I felt a sudden movement from Paint, and out of the corner of my eye saw India fly through the air and land about five meters away. Grabbing Max off Paint's back, I ran to India who was sprawled out on the ground. OMG, why hadn't I been holding her hand?! Sick to the stomach was an understatement of how I felt, it all seemed to happen in slow motion, and my legs felt like lead racing up to her. As I got to her side, my heart was in my throat, she was so silent, I thought for a second that she was dead. In the next moment, she opened her eyes. Thank God! My baby was alive!

Immediately I could see a hoof mark appear like a bright red beacon on her very pale little face. The mark covered her entire forehead. Oh god, had she suffered any brain damage?! I literally couldn't even bear the thought of it. I mean it when I say I just wanted to die at that moment. I couldn't deal with anything more happening to my kids. I wanted to escape, to have the Earth swallow me up. The fact it was because of me that this had happened completely overwhelmed me. It was my mistake, no bad luck or blaming, this was all on me! I picked her up, and there was blood coming out of her ear and nostrils. She was only three! This couldn't be real I told myself. I didn't hesitate not even for a second before launching into gear. I let Paint loose, picked up India in my arms, and dragged Max up the hill, talking to India as though everything was going to be ok. She was alert now, thank the lord, but for how long I didn't know.

I got the kids in the car, and began driving, calling Jim on the phone trying to suppress my tears and keep as calm as I could. I phoned mum next, pushing the speed limit to get India to the hospital as quickly as I could. Everyone arrived at the emergency department almost at the same time as I did. They took her straight in to see the neurologist who said she was lucky! Being only three, she was small and lightweight, the impact pretty much flew her through the air like a feather. If it had been an adult or larger child they said it may have been a lot different. Just to be sure India was definitely ok, we asked for a second opinion from Max's neurologist, he was fabulous. He agreed with the hospital's neurologist and said he saw many not-so-fortunate cases involving horses, but yes India had been one lucky lady and had escaped serious injury. I became super vigilant, implementing safety strategies and procedures around the horses. I didn't leave anything to chance, keeping a better eye on them making sure they were kept safe, and out of harm's way at all times. Yes, accidents can happen around horses as it's a dangerous sport, but I wasn't about to push our luck.

CHAPTER 11

MEDICAL ALERT

Jim had started coming home stressed and would often want to sit down and talk about his current worries with me at night. One of his biggest concerns was he thought his boss Tim and his secretary Karla were seeing each other. We were both pretty good friends with Tim and Sandy, so it shocked me to hear this questionable allegation. I asked him what evidence he had, he told me all sorts of stories about them being caught out in compromising situations. He said they went away together, and that people from other companies linked to him were phoning Jim to find out more gossip. Jim didn't want to know about it, he was scared that if he knew too much he would get into trouble. I was unsure of what to do. I hated knowing this info and having Sandy being such a good friend and person and not knowing what was going on really upset me. I wanted to tell her, but Jim begged me not to. It wasn't certain I told myself. Imagine opening up to her and it wasn't true! That would cause more harm than good, I'm sure.

I remember in the midst of it all, Jim had come home and said Tim and another worker were due to play a regular game of pickleball after work. Sandy couldn't get hold of Tim. Unable to reach him, she then called Jim and me to ask if I had seen him or knew where he was. She seemed upset, and I thought she must have had an idea of what was going on. I knew where he was but was sworn not to tell. It was so hard to hold it back. I questioned it a lot.

These rendezvous had been going on for ages. Maybe two years or so from when Jim had first told me. Innocent or not, I hated that people could do these things to good, faithful partners, especially with kids involved. Things went quiet on the topic and Jim stopped talking about it. Whenever I asked, he would answer that he was not sure it was still happening and would wrap up any discussion on it. I wondered why it was so quiet all of a sudden. Had it ended? Or did Jim have a private conversation with Tim about it? Maybe Jim just decided he didn't want to spread rumours even if it was only telling me? My mind ticked away. I didn't know and there was no one I could ask. Sandy had said nothing, and I wasn't about to just in case it was all just Chinese whispers.

Around this time our relationship was moving out of its bubble stage and back into a more practical husband-wife-family mode. Normal. As you know, bubbles don't last! And that was ok. I expected it to happen eventually. Life could go on as regular. There were more disagreements, and we both weren't as sweet to each other as we used to be. We were getting ready to sell our cute, renovated semi and move to a larger block in a neighbouring suburb so things were a bit tense. I think anything that involves moving, selling, renovating, family being sick, and losing loved ones brings with it a great deal of stress. I assumed this was the start again of more challenges coming our way.

As we prepared the house for sale my grandma also fell ill. She had suffered a stroke and was in and out of the hospital. She would get home, have another one, and be back in there again. The last one would keep her in. We were so close to our grandparents we just adored them. We visited her in the hospital often. We expected her to be released in the coming weeks although she wasn't well and after a long battle we were asked to come and say our goodbyes before they gave her the final lot of morphine that would send her to the spirit world. We said our goodbye, see you again soon, and sobbed at her side. It was so hard letting go. It's funny even after all my studies, and my firm beliefs about what's on the other side, it only somewhat softened the blow of the loss we felt. We just don't want to say that final, most definite farewell, even if it was until we all meet again, tucked up in that vast loving universe, it was horrible losing her. I missed her to the core.

I can still hear my grandma's loving, hard at times, but true words. "Zoe people are only ever lent to us in this world." When I thought about it, I have to say I agreed with her, you can't keep anybody as yours, we don't own anyone. These were such wise words from my grandma. Souls come and go from our lives. Some mean more than others bringing wisdom, teaching, and love, while others enter our lives to bring hope, inspire us, trigger us to encourage change, help us to ask questions, or to give us strength. Some may be in our lives for a fleeting encounter but are to rock our world forever, and some are meant to walk with us side by side to be our companions in it for the long haul. Such is life. I reflected on my grandma's words wondering which category Jim would be in. I hoped it was the forever category. Somehow, I had a feeling it wouldn't be. Our once-strong bond seemed to be disintegrating right in front of my eyes.

When you lose someone of that special calibre, it makes you stop and appreciate what and who you have in your life. It also inspires you to make each day as special and as fulfilling as possible. I tried my best to honour my grandma by making the most of every day and all the people in my world.

Soon after our loss, Max fell sick. He appeared to have the flu. He had had many colds and flu before as kids do, so apart from giving him Panadol to make him more comfortable, he slept to give his body a chance of fighting it off. He was such a ball of energy most of the time, the bed rest would do him well I thought. Unfortunately, after a few days of high temperatures, he hadn't gotten any better. It was a weekend, and my normal doctor was not open so I thought I'd take him to the local medical centre. I tried to wake Max up, but he seemed pretty well asleep, only opening his eyes briefly as I picked him up and carried him to the car for the trip to the doctor.

The reception nurse then put us in the waiting room after agreeing he was sick but still sleeping so would be fine to wait for someone to see him. It was over an hour and a half until finally it was our turn to see the doctor. I moved him in and laid him down. He still struggled to wake properly and with that, the doctor yelled to someone "Get an ambulance here quickly! This boy needs to get to the hospital now!" A jolt of adrenaline hit me. He seemed so peaceful, but I guess that was the problem. His breathing was shallow and weak. The ambulance arrived and took us straight to the emergency section where we were to wait in the hall to be seen. The nurses kept walking past where we were, stopping once or twice to admire his cuteness. One even stopped and started tickling him, saying, "Come on now, don't be a fox, stop pretending." I turned to one of the amused nurses, and with a panicked almost abrupt sound to my voice, blurted out that he won't wake.

Well, the room went into a spin! I felt a rush of air woosh past me from panicking hospital staff pooling around us. They whisked Max away from me and into the resuscitation room. His clothes were cut off with scissors and they pumped him full of whatever they felt he needed. I waited at the door in a hot sickly sweat that reminded me of how I had felt when Paint kicked India in the paddock that day. My anxiety went through the roof watching them madly working on my son. Heart racing, I asked what was happening and what was wrong. They informed me he had a very bad case of pneumonia—the silent killer they called it because most people were never aware of how quickly it can take hold. After one night he was transferred to a special room where he could be hooked up to all the medicine and oxygen he required. It was devastating seeing him so sick, and in a way, he looked half the person he was just days earlier. He had been so full of beans then, but now he was almost unrecognisable. The hospital provided entertainment clowns for some much-needed relief to the children who felt up to having a game, or at least watching one, as they danced their way around the wards. Even though I knew he loved clowns, Max was just not with it, and barely changed his expression.

After a week he started to improve ever so slightly, and we were sent downstairs for another x-ray. Unfortunately, that would be memorable for us both too. Max and I sat quietly next to a woman around fifty years or so in the waiting area. Not far in front of us lay a man hooked up to machines on a bed, waiting for his turn as well. Then all of a sudden an alarm went off, he flatlined, and doctors came from everywhere. I had never witnessed this sort of thing so close up. The room was filled with all sorts of noises from machines that pierced my ears and frightened my soul. I turned to Max who was leaning forward with eyes wide open like a startled kangaroo caught in the headlights of an approaching vehicle. His little jaw dropped open, and he uttered a soft whimper reaching out to hold my hand for security. I couldn't act fast enough to cover his eyes, and the lady next to me started weeping. I turned to her and saw her trembling and I just knew it was her husband. Oh no, the poor thing. My heart broke. I had to be strong for her and Max. I gently touched her shoulder and whispered "Is that your husband?" All she could do was nod and fall heavily into my arms, sobbing hard. I had to extract my hand from poor Max's for a moment, which was hard to do in his state, and console the grieving wife who had witnessed her husband dying right before her eyes. It was the saddest thing I'd ever seen. The doctors continued to use their skills to bring her husband back to life, but it was too late, he had gone. Max and I were escorted away as they took care of the man and his wife. As we sat waiting for the x-ray Max still had to get done, we talked about what had just happened. Max was still shaken when the nurse arrived to take us to his room. He has a deep, wise, and thoughtful soul my Max. In some ways, I thought he handled the whole tragic event better than me!

Two days on, we were sent home as the doctors felt his remaining recovery would be better in the comfort of his own home. Unfortunately, after a night in his bed, he took another turn for the worse, and we were off to emergency yet again. They had begun to know us by name by now, and as we were ushered into triage, they said loudly, "There is Maxxy! Bring him straight in." Amusing if it weren't so serious! The resuscitation doctor that had seen him before was on again, and one of them was appalled that he had been released and was back. After checking the pneumonia, they found it was still there, and it was worse, not better. They informed us there was nothing more they could do as he needed more specialised cared. He was sent to the children's hospital where he had to be tended to more seriously. When arriving we were told he needed an emergency operation straight away, and that a specialised doctor of only three in the state was to be called out of hours to perform it. That scared the hell out of me, it was far more serious than we had imagined. I didn't even know pneumonia required surgery! But it did. They planned to have a hole drilled through his ribs into his lungs, leaving a tube attached to him that would hopefully over the next week drain all the liquid out to prevent him from drowning from the fluid build-up. Apparently, it's also very painful as with each breath the tube moves against the ribs. I sat by Max's side like glue, listening to his breathing and all the monitors he was hooked up to in case I needed to alert anyone of a change. Waiting was not my forte, and with anxiety levels raising to the roof, I found myself constantly checking in with nurses and doctors to hear of any progress. It wasn't until I asked one official-looking doctor "Is he going to be ok?" that's when I truly thought my heart would stop beating. In all honesty, this was such a shock. I truly expected him to reply with a simple "yes". Instead, he answered with words I just couldn't fathom… quietly he said, "We are not sure if he will pull through, but we are doing our best and will keep you updated." Intense fear shot right through my body turning my legs to jelly and seizing my stomach. In my mind, I felt like I was going crazy. "How could this be?! He had the flu!" I screamed inside. "Surely this is a mistake!" I couldn't even process it. My family was there day and night with me. Mum took India to her place as Jim had said he still needed to work and couldn't be at the hospital each day or be home with India either. I didn't have the headspace to even question him why not? If it wasn't enough for him to see Max's monitor going off and doctors rushing in, nothing I said would open his eyes. It broke my heart to see Max and other kids trying to stay strong and resilient fighting for their lives. I, along with all the parents in our ward sat holding our children's hand with silent tears, hoping and praying they would be ok and make it through.

For us, fortunately, our prayers must have been answered. As each day passed, Max began showing an improvement. Before too long, he was allowed to have visits from the clown doctors and some quiet craft time. I did my best to believe it would all be ok, but after the last time, I was more than a little sceptical but tried to think positive and search for a feel-good emotion. A week and a half passed, and he was given a leave to go home. Our boy had made it through! Pneumonia had left him with bad asthma that would require regular respiratory specialist care and preventer medications, but he was otherwise ok and more importantly alive. I could deal with anything, as long as he was still with us.

Soon after the sale of our house, and move to the new house, our marriage took an even greater turn for the worse. Jim was more distant than ever before. There were no more romantic surprises, not much affection, his sex drive was all but non-existent, and so too were our family outings. Receipts that I didn't recognise appeared in his wallet and when I questioned one restaurant receipt for a large sum asking if he had been to that place. He responded promptly with a no, adding he'd never heard of it. To be fair and honest with myself, I think I was fearful of finding out something I just didn't want to know, so I didn't look into it, instead opting to blindly believe him. Maybe I wanted my life to go back to where it was, to the bubble of love we once had. Asking a thousand questions I knew would just drive the wedge between us further. Regardless, I let it go to save my sanity and kept my head in the sand when I saw anything that gave me cause to question.

We soon got onto renovating our new place. A fabulous run-down Californian bungalow was ripe for repair. We lived out in a studio room we had in the backyard while we tackled what was a big job. Living on-site meant we saved money and could watch the progress of our house in real-time. I also thought it may just bring us closer together as well. It did in one way, the room was about 6m by 3m, and it was a cozy squeeze for all of us in there together. It wasn't too bad though, we cohabitated well, snuggled at night, and had plenty of outside things to do during the day. I would speak to Jim while he was at work during the day to say hi and go over any decisions required for the building process. Jim was the sort of person that didn't like any confrontation, and that posed a problem as the builders were always trying to bully me. Telling me I needed to do this or that, and couldn't have what I had planned to have because it just didn't suit them, their plans, or their schedules. Jim would rarely defend me, even to the point where his sister even noticed and said something to him. It wasn't right to let them talk to your wife that way she told him. "I've seen them do it to her firsthand, Jim, don't just shrug it off," she told him. It fell on deaf ears though, and his lack of interest or care just shoved another arrow into my already hurting heart.

Living in the little studio didn't change a thing. There was still a weird feeling in the air, and we hadn't had sex for well over three months. He kept saying he was worried about the kids hearing—it hadn't worried him before! Even so, he did not attempt to come home at lunchtimes or work out other little rendezvous times, and I told him as much. He knew I wasn't happy, and said he'd come up with a plan when we moved into the completed house, which was not far off. Hopeful, I waited. In the meantime, the kids and I went about our normal lives, riding, going to the gym, and catching up with our friends. At the time India had her pony Stuart Little, but she was fast outgrowing him, so we decided to buy a pony that was a little taller and more trained for showing. After looking for a while we found Shimmer, from Queensland, a gorgeous Welsh chestnut roan with a silver mane and tail. The owner said her friend who had moved to Victoria knew the pony well and could help us with India's transition to this glamorous steed. Her friend's name was Kelly, and she lived close by, so we started to catch up and do the pony child training together. I didn't know her well, but she was a tiny poppet of a thing and was small enough to ride India's pony ok. She had big energy and a huge helpful heart.

As we had another month or so to go in our temporary studio, I would often sit looking at real estate pages in the paper for ideas on furnishings, and on one occasion came across my dream home, in one of the finest horse property locations in Victoria. It could have been perfect for us. Jim had promised me that we could move out that way if the right property came along. Now here it was, and I'm sure he felt relatively safe it was a good investment, as most of those properties were worth many millions and were on over five acres. This one was different. Although it was on nearly five acres, it had its very own cute original cottage set to the side of the magnificent property on its own parcel of land on one and a half acres. It was unheard of in the area. Most of these properties could not be split up, but this smaller block had its own title! It was in an amazing position near good trails and had enough room for all our ponies. It couldn't be more ideal I thought.

I twisted Jim's arm, and to my excitement, he agreed to look at it. It was hard to get drawn away from the main residence to the adjoining cottage as it boasted six bedrooms, three bathrooms, two living areas, a home cinema room, a study, a kitchen with butler's scullery, a dressage arena, and five stables, paddocks, a pool and tennis court. In saying that, the timber cottage was gorgeous with blue, red, and green beams of light reflecting purposely from two old leadlight windows that were placed thoughtfully on opposite ends of the living room. The rainbow of colour bounced through the doors and onto the timber floors reminding me of the movie The Wizard of Oz. I was only missing my sparkly red shoes and blue and white gingham dress to be swept up in my very own fantasy moment. The cottage was charming and included two modest bedrooms, one living room, one bathroom, and a kitchen. Its special feature was the all-important paddock and stable attached. Things seemed to be going our way as the people interested in buying the property could not afford the whole property without selling off the smaller part which we wanted. Jim was sort of getting excited at this point as the trails were also bike tracks and would provide him with the healthy lifestyle he loved too, so it suited us both. But within one foul swoop, the CEO of a large company here in Australia bought it, cottage and all. In one secret bid that gazumped the other people by half a million, they had negotiated an hour before we could all sign off on it. So close yet so far! I was gutted as were the family that had missed out. My new life in the magical land of Oz was to be no more.

Soon after I was told about acreages coming up for sale in a bushy area not too far from this last one, but closer to my family home. There were four lots to be sold, just over an acre each, with ocean views sweeping from one part of the peninsula to the next. Jim was still keen to go along to the auction to bid even though we hadn't yet put our house on the market, we knew we would be able to sell our fabulous newly renovated home in a flash.

The bidding on the parcels of land started slow, but we kept our eye on the last one to go to market. The first one went for a fair price, but probably a little over what we could spend. The rest were sure to go this high or higher we thought, but they didn't. Suddenly our hopes were up and we started bidding on the third parcel of land. My dream property was falling in my lap and all I could think of was all the plans for my horsey life here could be answered in a matter of minutes. It seemed too easy, and the smallest of doubts entered my mind. The universe must have picked up on it because before I knew it, the price raced up to close to our limit and Jim stopped bidding. The one we wanted came next, and with no one stepping forward to bid but us, Jim threw out a ridiculous figure and looked my way, with an amazed look as if to say we could get this. But another couple felt the same and made an almost equally silly bid, you could tell they were half-hearted but knew it was a bargain at that price, and too good to pass up. It got close to the end and was way under the price of the previous blocks and a real bargain. I think Jim realised that we might get this, and what it all may have meant for him, our marriage, and another new build, and all of a sudden he pulled back even though it was in our price range. The other party took over, and the hammer went down, bringing tears from both parties. The disappointment of another letdown and the anger towards Jim led my body to open the floodgates. If it wasn't for all the people surrounding us I would have let him have it. The husband who bought it came running over all flustered looking and had a tear rolling down his cheek. He was a property developer and his wife thought it might be nice to buy. Even though he had made it pretty clear it wasn't his thing, his wife was insistent, but he could see the passion in my eyes and was genuinely sorry. In my head I thought, well give it back to us sweet man with a tear! But it was not to be. We drove home in silence, I was too sad and upset to talk.

By this time, we had several real estate agents through our place to get an idea of the listing price for our home. It was higher than we expected but I did think we had done a great job, putting in lots of energy, and no expense was spared. The agents had also given a sneaky look to a few parties already who were thinking along the same lines. So, we knew there were lots of people ready to pay a great price. We would have made a bit of money in a very short time flipping it and could purchase again in the area, or even better purchase another horse property if I was lucky enough. After we moved from the studio to the house, I expected our excitement to lead into our marriage, and bedroom. Jim had promised me. I wasted no time in putting the hard word on him, suggesting we go to bed early, or drop the kids at Mum's to have a night on our own. Maybe a movie, maybe this, maybe that? I honestly didn't care, I threw out all sorts of ideas.

But nothing worked. Pretty much ever. It had been months! He didn't seem interested in me at all and it began bringing back all the bad memories and feelings I had when he told me he didn't love me anymore. Why are we here again? This I feared to my core, so I questioned him about it. Why don't you want me? What can I do? He just kept fobbing me off.

After barely two weeks on the market, we sold our house for a fabulous price. I called Jim and screamed with joy down the phone. I could see this would represent a new life for us. The sale meant we were on the move, and the money would provide us with far greater options than we had ever had. He was on his way back from a work trip and didn't seem overly excited at all which was a bit upsetting. I had the champagne ready and waiting at home for us, but he delayed getting there by hours.

By the time he arrived, it was long past dinner, and he walked in, brushed past me, and barely said boo. I couldn't believe it. I was so disappointed and knew something was up. He didn't even care about the sale or even my feelings at all. He had no interest in anything. When we went to bed, I tried to initiate sex, using the fact we needed to celebrate the sale, but he declined, and I cried.

"What's wrong?" I yelled.

"I think I'd be happier without you as a part of my life," he said solemnly. I was gutted. Here we go again! What was his problem? I couldn't bare it. I repeated what I had said the last time and told him to leave straight away and get out of the house. I couldn't hear another bullshit excuse from him. He sounded like a little boy as he whimpered about where he would go.

"I don't care," I said. "You should have thought of it before. How could you? You promised you would never do this again."

There was silence from him, and I took myself into the spare room and cried all night. In the morning he left for work but rang during the day explaining that he wanted to come home and chat. What was he going to say? He arrived and sat down. He was upset, but who would know what about? The fact he now had to go through a separation, and or divorce, or the fact he had to leave us, I honestly didn't know what his game was.

We cried together, then he said we really should give this a go, but more confusion set in as I'd heard this before. What was he playing at? He said he was unsure if this feeling of love he used to feel would ever come back, but for the kids at least he thought we should give it another go

I didn't feel this same "out of love feeling" he talked about, so I just wanted him to get this seemingly elusive thing back. Or did I? He was putting me through an emotional wringer! In any case, I'm not sure about where people think this love goes. I never understood it properly, as I hadn't ever experienced it before. Love is hard, and you can fall in and out of it sometimes, but in my honest opinion, how do you just walk away for no real reason? Or maybe there was a reason, and I was a mushroom not seeing it, or wanting to let go of what I had, what we had both built and worked for over the years.

I remembered the first time he decided to leave me, and we eventually saved it, he said to his family and I that if there weren't drugs, domestic violence, mental issues, or alcohol involved it just has to work. He believed they were the main reasons for really having an excuse to leave, and I had to agree with him. We had none of those so what was his excuse? I noticed he left out being gay or having affairs, was this what he had been trying to tell me unsuccessfully?

He had EVERYTHING with a family who would do ANYTHING for him, what else could he possibly want? Up until this point, we had only ever had three fairly serious fights. Our marriage was never volatile, from all accounts in our eyes and those around us, we were a perfect couple. It had always worked, almost effortlessly. We had some difficult times for sure, but no more than the happiest couples we knew. We wanted the same lifelong plan. We thought alike. We were brought up in a similar family unit, and from the same socio-economic background, and loved each other's company. We had good chemistry also up until the last time he said he didn't love me anymore, then we rekindled and became like newlyweds again. We fitted like a glove. But human behaviour is complex. Life is complex sometimes. I was confused and completely bewildered.

I needed to let off some steam, re-group, and reconnect, and what better way than to visit my horses? I drove across to do the nightly feeding and rugging and to snatch a little cuddle from my furry creatures. I wanted to get a few odd jobs done so I quickly made up feeds and walked them over and into their bins. They were waiting patiently so as I walked away I rubbed Shimmer's neck as if to say good girl and let her start eating. Back at the shed, I started cleaning their tack, rearranging the shed, and just enjoying the fresh air when I noticed Shimmer was standing as close to the fence as possible to where I was, away from her dinner and very unlike a fat little pony. What could be wrong? Was she sick?

I got up to take a look inside the bin in case I had missed an unfortunate mouse that may have fallen in or even a bad batch of chaff but nothing. I did however notice she had burrowed deep down in the bin. Then I realised in my haste I had forgotten their favourite part, the yummy pellets with a small dollop of molasses that they enjoyed so much. Dinner in their eyes was not complete without it.

I laughed, there she was at the fence communicating to me and it worked. She needs me as much as I need her. I felt loved and relied upon. A symbiotic relationship indeed.

CHAPTER 12

THE SOUL WOULD HAVE NO RAINBOW IF THE EYES HAD NO TEARS

The following day, Jim started to make an effort again. Deja-vu. It was like being with a human yo-yo! But I was willing to take him nonetheless if this was going to be yet another positive turnaround. Talk about changing your mind! I received a beautiful kiss first thing in the morning. Not just a quick one but a lingering, soft and meaningful one. Was this all for real? Thoughtful presents and more time together followed. The sex thing was still waning. He attempted the old, I'll just cuddle you tonight, sex another night. Cuddles are good, he would say. Well, they were, but sex was better! Especially when you haven't been getting it. Well, I hadn't been getting it, and I remember reading a Dr. Phil book once, and in it he had said something like, sex is less than 10% of importance in a relationship if you are receiving it, and of 90% importance if you're not, which rang true! He also said, you need to have sex regularly for a good marriage—I had to agree.

Because he seemed to be in love again, I waited. Again! I'd rather have a marriage go the distance and wait a little longer for his loins to wake up. Gosh, I had real faith, didn't I? Or maybe I was just stupid, I wasn't sure, it was so confusing.

In the meantime, our house had settled, so we had to move into a rental until we purchased another property—hopefully our ultimate dream home! Jim had dilly-dallied around and began having yet another marriage crisis. He said he was now of the opinion that I had made him own a house all our time together, and it was a lot of stress for him.

What! That was not true!

It was he who had pushed us hard, particularly in the earlier years to save and buy a house, then keep upgrading. Sure, I wanted a house, but he instigated it. He always told me it was important to him and what he wanted. Now he was telling me he wanted a break from having a mortgage and less stress. I wasn't overly keen to rent and waste any profits from the sale of our house. I wanted to invest in bricks and mortar as soon as possible. He did not. Well not then anyway, so I found a rental for us at a lower price than he had envisaged. It was pretty old, but similar to the places we had before renovations took place, and ok in my opinion for a year at best, because that's the time he needed before buying again he said. But Jim insisted on spending almost double a week in rent on a renovated federation. It was a total waste I thought but I let him take the lead. If this was our problem, me being too boisterous or bossy, then I was happy to swap roles for the success of our marriage.

We did have a lot of money sitting there, and he was on an exceptional wage. It wasn't going to leave a big dent in our savings I thought, especially as it was short-term.

When we moved in, there was talk of trips away. I never had the travel bug, and neither did he, but his parents were going away on a trip to the US and Jim thought it might be nice to be spur of the moment and meet them. One week it was mentioned, and before I knew it we had booked our flights. This was so out of character for Jim, but I was happy to go along with it. Jen and her husband Mal from our antenatal group were also trying to patch things up and had arranged a trip to Hawaii to visit family at the same time. We decided to fly out with them and stay five days together in Hawaii, before heading to the States to meet up with our family.

With a month or so to go, we got everything sorted quickly. We were busy with arrangements, so I didn't hassle Jim as much for affection. But I did notice there were still odd things happening like him having a new Blackberry phone that he hadn't given me the passcode to. It seemed like it was attached to him 24/7. There were often bills arriving at home from a Visa card with a number unknown to me and when I questioned him about it he said, "Bloody work, they can't keep their accounts properly, it's supposed to be paid by them!" I believed this, along with most of the other stories. He was so convincing. And he was Jim! I had known this man for twenty-odd years! I'd never had a reason to doubt him.

I believed in full trust, it's essential in a relationship, and one can't function without it so I would play my part. I remember once he said work had overseas guests staying a few days in the CBD, and he was to meet them with a couple of others for dinner. He also said he was thinking of staying the night with them as the girl who headed up the social committee had asked him to play his entertaining role in the company and look after these guests more fully. I thought at the time it was rather suss. We lived five minutes from the city, so staying there didn't make much sense to me. A wasted business expense I believed. Weeks away at conferences. No partners allowed of course, or so he said, and countless team building and dinner/bar outings. I'm sure after dinner these visitors could tuck themselves into bed on their own, couldn't they? Why did they need Jim and this girl holding their hands and sharing accommodation with them? I remember at the time we had words about this, and Jim said I was being pathetic and overreacting and that he was declining the offer anyway. Sure he was, I bet he had no intention before our conversation about it! In hindsight, the writing was on the wall.

He had begun to go out frequently again, this time with a work friend who also competed in marathons. He was living in the east, an area I knew he and I never liked so that made me more suss. He would sometimes be gone all day on a weekend. I had the kids full-time during the week, no problem, but hey he was their dad and they wanted to see him on weekends. It wasn't right for him to trip away and not spend precious time with them or me for that matter. It got to the point I had to almost invite him to spend time with them. I asked him, "Want to join me to look after our rug rats on the weekend by any chance?" He replied, "Why don't you catch up with your friends, I don't mind looking after the kids tonight though." He just didn't get it, or maybe I just wasn't getting it! He spent as little time with me and the kids as possible. I just wanted him and our family time. I loved catching up with friends, but not constantly.

The USA trip arrived. I saw it as an opportunity to connect again, or at least I hoped it would be. Hope should have been my middle name! Zoe "Hope" Fanning! I'm not the best flyer, to be honest, it scares me to death. I'm terrified. I had to work my way up to the trip, particularly as it was such a long flight. Jim being the bugger he was, took full advantage of it. We were flying relatively smoothly in the skies when the plane hit some severe turbulence. I froze, genuinely scared. I was seriously beside myself and hate to admit it but I started to whimper a little. I know, sounds dramatic, doesn't it? It's an irrational fear and I have no idea how I came to have it.

We were sitting in the last row at the back of the plane, right near the airhostess who amongst the bumps was chatting to someone on the internal phone. Jim then lent over and whispered in my ear.

"Zoe, did you hear what she was saying to the pilot?"

"No, What?"

"She just said something has happened and we are going to have to make an emergency landing!"

Well as you can imagine with that info, I was nearly hysterical. I jumped up from my seat, burst into tears, and interrupted the hostie blurting out, "Are we going to make an emergency landing?"

"What?" she said with a very confused look on her face. "No, we are just about to serve dinner."

And then I heard Jim giggling like crazy next to me. Hilarious! Yeah, yeah, Jim, good one, you had me going. What a shit-stirrer he could be.

I was pleased to be going away though, what an adventure! Jim seemed happier than he had been in months as well. This was the perfect trip for us—it involved good friends and family, and the chance to have adventures that would transpire into fabulous life-long memories. To Hawaii and to party with Jen and Mal, then to the USA to visit Disneyland, San Diego, and New York, catch a Yankees game and hang out with Jim's family, and stop in Fiji again on the way back for another relaxing week before heading home.

The trip began well. I was thankful we were holidaying with family and friends for most of the time away. Jim had begun being a bit of a bully behind closed doors but was on his best behaviour around others. Now looking back, I would like to nickname him the "Smiling Assassin". He loved to appear the perfect person in everyone's eyes, a real people pleaser, non-confrontational, and easy to get along with. Often without strong opinions or sometimes really any. I on the other hand was up for a good old heated discussion if need be, spoke my truth, and had nothing to hide, open, maybe to my detriment but no secrets here! People either love you for it or hate you. At least I have stories to tell and conversations to be a part of.

I was hoping all his weird behaviour would ultimately fade away with a good holiday, and while he did seem to calm down a bit, he still had some strange obsession going on with his phone. He would walk away from me to check his phone or text messages, and regardless of where we went and what we did, he kept checking it and it didn't leave his sight. It was so odd that I asked him about it. He replied that he still had to take work calls. Work doesn't stop for a holiday, he said. And even tears from Jim as we stopped in at one of India's ex-classmates' house in New York. She had moved from Oz to the US. As we left Jade cried for India. It was a little sad seeing the two best friends having to part ways again. All of us adults felt sad for them, but Jim burst into tears! I'd only seen him cry twice in the whole time we had been together. He was crying harder than

India and Jade! I gave him a big cuddle, a bit taken by his reaction, it was pretty bizarre, but there was more to come.

A trip to see the Yankees was next on our list, so we rode on the subway together on what was an unbelievably hot day. When we pulled up at the station, we had to line up in the sweltering sun with no shade, food, or drinks to get into the stadium, and once seated, we again baked in the sun which drained our energy. Within thirty minutes the kids became blood-red and heat-sick. I took them inside the stadium to sit in the shade for half an hour to cool down and get some relief from the burning sun before making our way back to Jim and our seats to give it another go. Just moving in and out of the tight area was a feat in itself. No one was happy with you going back and forth and pushing past them. The kids became even worse and were crying by this time. They had had enough and I knew we had to get them out of the sun and home. I told Jim we had to go, but he didn't give one iota. He said it was a once-in-a-lifetime experience and he didn't want to miss it for a minute. He told me to go on alone back to the hotel. I was hesitant. A foreign woman with two little kids, travelling alone in New York didn't sound like such a smart idea to me. If someone attacked us, I would have no chance of defending the three of us, but one more look at the kids' bright red faces told me all I needed to know and that was to get them out of there. I left him happily sitting watching the game and got outside of the stadium intending to hail a taxi. With none around, the only option we had was to attempt the subway again. Down in the subway station, it was dark and deserted except for a few dodgy-looking characters. "This is NOT a good idea," I thought, worryingly looking around.

The game was on so there was no need to be travelling from this train station until the game finished, so trains weren't coming by. We looked for the platform that would take us back to the hotel and were followed by a few men. I tried to get my phone and ring Jim but he didn't answer. He didn't hear it, or worse, just ignored it. After all, he was stuck to that phone and would have had to have heard or felt it ringing. I grew scared as the men were closing the gap between us. Just then, the train whizzed in and we bolted on. I sat down shaking and holding my kids tightly. It felt like an eternity, but we reached the other side and in one piece. We walked back to the hotel and I phoned Mum and told her what had happened—she was not impressed with her son-in-law at all. Lucky for me my mum is kind and understanding. I was pretty embarrassed having to tell her about the man I married and how he was behaving. It was humiliating, but Mum said all the right things, and I soon began to feel better.

The next day we met Jim's family in the Empire State Building. It was a surprise to Anne and Steve because only Tony and his now-wife Dee knew we were coming. Anne said she had strolled around the top of the building and saw two kids and thought to herself, "Oh don't those two kids look like India and Max." Next thing she saw us all and it clicked! It was great seeing them, but an hour was enough for Jim. He didn't want to meet up for dinner with them, or any other outings. He made me agree to say that we were busy if they asked. All that way to spend time with them and that was it? A quick hello? The whole trip was about meeting up and spending time here with them! What was all this about? It didn't make any sense to me, but with every odd thing Jim did, I grew more and more suspicious.

Central Park was next on the list. We had a guide who took us to show us the sights on one of those three-wheeler carriage bikes, it was amazing. When we came to the Bethesda fountain, the guy asked to take a family shot for keepsakes. Jim promptly replied, "No, no just on my own."

"What?" the guide snapped, "not together? Why without your wife and kids?"

Yes Jim, why alone? I was thinking, but no sooner than that thought entered my mind had Jim realised the looks he was getting and quickly indicated one family shot wouldn't hurt. We were on a family trip. Family being the operative word here Jim, not a singles trip! Let me tell you it did not feel good. The guide dropped us off for ten minutes to stroll around Strawberry Fields and John Lennon's memories. Jim said to me, "You go on ahead I want to hang here a little to take more photos, but I'll meet you around the corner in a while." I'm not sure he would have known anything much about John Lennon or cared particularly, as I'd never heard him mention his name ever, but he snapped away taking heaps of pics of this legendary man's display. Again, so very strange.

Our next day included a helicopter ride Jim had been keen to book before we even left Australia. Jim was excited, and I was nervous, but it would be nice to see New York from above. Jim wanted to walk down to the Hudson River where we would board although I thought the forty-minute walk was a bit too much for the young ones. But he insisted they would be right, so like a puppy, I followed him, practically half running and half dragging the kids along the streets while Jim yelled he didn't want to be late. Eventually, he put India on his shoulders and went ahead to meet me there with Max later. I arrived a good ten minutes behind him and said, why the rush? We got there in plenty of time and stood with a few others next to the windows to have a safety lesson and see a video on emergency procedures.

After a minute or two, I interrupted to ask how safe this ride was, as there were an awful lot of instructions. The person in charge answered with a confident, "Yes very! We haven't had an accident yet!" And look here comes your helicopter now to land. And with that, we saw terrified faces throughout the room. The helicopter plunged into the Hudson right before our eyes, bursting into flames. The people (among them Australians) were trapped underwater struggling to get free. There was panic. Alarms. The room we were in went into lockdown, and we were unable to leave as there was talk of a terrorist attack. My heart was in my throat. Those poor people! No one told us a word for ages, then after an hour of being held, we were released. I wanted to get out of the room and find out if the passengers had survived. No one told us anything. That was going to be our ride next, it could have been us! How could I have managed to get my kid's belts off and swim them in water, and up and out to safety? We would have surely perished.

Luckily there were no kids on board, and miraculously everyone made it out with only minor injuries. But instead of leaving together to all recuperate back at the hotel, Jim instructed me to take the kids the forty-minute walk back or catch a taxi cab. He would meet us in a couple of hours after he waited for our refund. So, after a disagreement from me, and a roll of the eyes from him, I left. Very unhappy and wondering why he was acting so strangely.

I walked along the street to take a look around. There was not too much to see in the distance. Mainly emergency boats and police. I ran across the road to wait for a cab. But after thirty minutes of standing around, there was none. I thought Jim may have appeared from inside by that time and we could all go together, but no such luck. I was left to take the kids on the long walk back to the hotel solo. On the way, the usual suspects were stopping for a sleazy chat. "Hi, beautiful." "Need a ride?" "Baby come over here a sec!" And a host of other such remarks. Not so comforting being alone with toddlers.

That evening we had a romantic dinner booked so I decided not to cause problems by commenting on the day. I just wanted it to be a nice night for us. We left the kids in the room with a sitter and ventured into the meatpacking district for pre-dinner drinks and then an amazing meal at BLT, a well-known haunt. It was a breath of fresh air being out and watching Jim perk up towards me a bit. Apart from the regular checking of his blackberry phone, it was really lovely. I even dared to hope it would result in a bit of lovemaking tonight. A girl could only dream! So far, the trip of two weeks had brought none, but tonight could be the night I thought, you never know your luck in a big city! New York, New York! But I was out of luck. When we arrived home, we paid the sitter and not only did he reject me AGAIN but told me to go on to bed. He was heading back out to cruise the streets of the Big Apple (at midnight mind you) and see some more of the sights. It was a lifetime opportunity he exclaimed again. I looked at him like he was mad! I didn't want to ruin the night, so bit my tongue, swallowed my sadness, and focused on being grateful for the night we had. It was at least a step in the right direction.

The last leg of our trip had approached and we were off to Fiji. Maybe this romantic island would ignite some romance? We were back on Castaway Island, a lovely destination we visited in our first year together which we both loved! We had such amazing memories here and I hoped he'd reminisce, and maybe even replicate a few of those passionate nights we had spent here before.

I didn't worry about hinting, I straight up put the hard word on him. "Let's just hold hands, cuddle, sit close, talk romantically, or lay side by side on the beach," he said. But no sex. I kept up the pressure and was finally rewarded halfway through the holiday, yay! A win! Not sure it's entirely ok to call making your husband have sex with you a win but hey, still a positive in my new world of crumb-taking. Not particularly satisfying, and not a turn-on, but it was at least something. I always said to myself, it had come back strong and passionate before, it could again, right? Just be patient. Like a dog with a bone, I hung on. Honestly, what was seriously wrong with the man? Was he gay? Was there another woman? Was something wrong down there that he didn't want to tell me about? A thousand questions and no answers.

Then we met some couples on the beach from Australia. It turned out Jim knew them through some sort of work thing. We all hung out a little, including our kids and theirs. I remember once the husband and wife asked if there was something wrong with Jim, noticing his obsession with the phone. The husband said to me that his wife would divorce him if he did that on a family holiday, and she added how inappropriate it was. Yes, inappropriate that's true, but maybe the divorce was what he was aiming for, and maybe it was just that he was trying to get me to leave first so he didn't look like the bad guy. Who knew?! Then it dawned on me, maybe I was going about this all wrong. I had another ally with this couple, and not that it mattered as I should be able to work it all out by myself, but it helped to be able to tell him others were noticing this crazy phone obsession, it wasn't just me! I told him what they said, and all he could say was F off. I was shocked at his attitude, but his gaslighting was on fire.

We got two more moments of half-hearted sex before we left, lucky me! Hmmmmm. Then back home to the daily grind.

Now because Jim's increasingly busy "work" social life was always on the go, I felt a little left out and was losing who I used to be, the woman Jim fell madly in love with, not just the stay-at-home mum. He always said he never required me to go back to work, and always wanted me to have the very best in life, but love, appreciation, and attraction were still high on my list, and those were most certainly missing. Material belongings only go so far. You can't buy love!

CHAPTER 13

STRENGTH IN NUMBERS

"Ask and you shall receive" was certainly a true statement for me when I was most in need of a rebirth of "Zoe." So re-enter my pocket rocket—Kelly, and my other great friend "The Tasmanian Devil," as I liked to call her—Natalie.

Kelly as I've mentioned was a fiery tiny ball of fun and a wealth of great advice with ponies and life in general. We connected quite quickly when we had met previously and knew we would be friends for life. I had also introduced her to my invariable long-term school friend Tammy. We all took to the horse trails together when we could. Kelly and I had the horses in common and after a long chat, men issues too. She had been through two divorces so was able to give lots of guidance which was desperately needed. We talked about life, where we had grown up, and what we did for a living. Kel, as I fondly called her, was in jewellery, running her shop not far from us. I told her I had started dabbling in sales at a magazine again, but the second time around it just didn't feel the same. I think I was just burnt out from it, so she mentioned a friend she knew who was a pearl wholesaler and was also into horses. Her family home was on a gorgeous acreage, not far from a riding school where I rode as a kid. This girl may have been on the lookout for someone to be her sales agent. I wasn't sure of pearls, but hey it was sales that I was confident in. I could sell anything! Now this acreage place all rang a bell. In relaying this info to Tammy, I soon realised this girl on this acreage was Natalie, Owen's girlfriend! And Owen, Tammy's brother! Wow. Small world indeed. She used to talk about this amazing girl Natalie who Owen was dating and her beautiful horse paddocks and stables. Tammy agreed with Kel that his sort of thing would be ideal for me and I should phone her straight away. My first conversation with Natalie was while she was on a buying trip in Hong Kong and she seemed very together and sweet; her natural high energy was not hidden behind the phone and we arranged to meet up the following week for a talk and see if it could all work. I was about to start collecting a few new friends of importance that would guide and support and stand by my side for years to come and I was going to need them all.

Natalie and Kelly gave me that added confidence I needed, both in different ways. Natalie was only twenty-eight. She was one of few in my life who had that true X factor, who could walk in the room and own it completely, specially from the males. She had that special aura that I'm sure most girls crave to possess, and men wanted a bite of. And she loved it. She was like a drug to them and she played it well. It enabled her to get away with blue murder if required. She had the strut, the blonde locks, and these tiny pin legs and her frame was very slight. She had aboriginal blood in her from her mum's side, which she loved. She said it gave her fire and strength in her personality and her dad was Danish. Wow, what a mix!

Kelly was forty-nine. She was slender as well but a little shorter. And with jet black hair. She was also very beautiful and was able to get on very well with all around her. Like Natalie, she had that natural ability with people but was a little quieter.

I also had become closer to Jen from my antenatal group. She was now thirty-nine, with confidence, charisma, and a magnetic aura. She had light brown hair, an athletic figure, and a very sexy way about her. She had a great personality, but it was her sex appeal that was the first thing to turn the heads of both genders—lucky her. These three were so much fun. She was unfortunately like me in that she was constantly in and out of her relationship too. We talked about our marital stress regularly. I was also friends with Mal, Jen's husband, which sometimes made it hard as I related to him on the matter a little better as we were the ones who were being rejected. Jen was a real kindred spirit for me, although I constantly gave her hell as she did what I was afraid Jim was about to do. Leaving her partner, if she wasn't trying to console me, she had no fear of biting back on her reasons for leaving if I dug at her about them. These three girls had a backbone and were happy to say what they thought. No fear from me, I liked up front strong women and they always had a place in my life.

The five of us decided to take a trip together to a group of local vineyards a few hours' drive away. We were looking forward to doing some wine tasting and trying the local produce. We booked into a luxury hotel sitting high on the mountain with incredible views of the area. It was for a long weekend so we only had two nights and two days to make the most of our stay. After deciding the first day should be wine tasting, Natalie suggested the second should be a horse-riding trail in amongst the bushland. We all agreed although Jen was hesitant as she was the only one that didn't ride horses. Obviously, we convinced her it was a piece of cake and we would look after her. We tried to hold back on having too many vinos the night before to have the best balance possible for the ride plus we needed to be fully alert with no hangover to distract us.

We woke to a beautiful sunny day with no clouds in sight. We drove a minute or two up the road and signed in, picking our horses based on our ability. The instructor suggested Jen take their oldest horse out as he was the most reliable especially for a novice. The instructor led the way out of the gates and as we were all confident he arranged to let us go it alone following the well-marked tracks and to meet him back at a particular time.

We started at a walk as we got used to our steeds and worked out the way we would go. We trotted up a few hills making sure Jen wasn't too far ahead or behind. She was coping quite nicely as we started our incline. A canter was next and everyone took it comfortably as we wove in and out of the trees. We took in the views as we headed back down. We could see a little further along that we were going to need to cross a creek and wind along the bottom of the mountain to get back to the farm and the awaiting instructor.

It was a hot day so as we approached the water we decided to let them all have a drink. The horses stopped eagerly and lowered their heads to suck up the clear flowing water.

"Not too much, they will get a pain in their bellies girls," Kelly yelled. We all started to pull our horses heads up ready to start the last part of the ride when Jen's horse— the eldest, smartest, and most reliable horse there—began to pour the water with his front leg, splashing up waves into himself, Jen and others. We all giggled nervously as the horse girls knew what this meant. We didn't let it go on too long as we knew what was about to happen but all too late. Her horse bent one front knee down then the other getting ready for a swim, saddle, and all. It catapulted Jen who was screaming in terror off over its head and into the depths of the water landing with a thud. Before we could do anything her horse picked itself up and took off towards home. Jen stood up completely drenched and we couldn't stop laughing. Luckily it was a warm day and we didn't have too far to go. Jen walked back next to us all vowing she would choose the next activity. We agreed, what else could we say that was only fair? So back home we went, knowing there would be more adventures to come.

It wasn't too long before I found myself in an unloving relationship again. We had already seen a good handful of counsellors and they all had great tips, but Jim just wasn't responding, forgetting important details strategically and pretending all was good and agreeing to see more counsellors and continuing to lead them on too. Questions about affairs were asked and denied with anger. Counsellors also asked if he was gay, but again, angry outbursts were spewed. Every question and scenario ran past us, his only answer was he fell out of love and couldn't seem to get it back! He was given books on love and relationships but nothing sank in. Love was an action word, although he didn't seem to take the steps required to make that action. In fact, a few months back from our trip and on his birthday, he moved out.

"Just for a few nights," he said.

"That's all it took the last time," he sobbed. It may just need a night or two away I thought. Unfortunately, those nights began a regular pattern of escape that would span the next two years. In out, In out! When he was at home, he was treating me badly or having a relationship with his phone and the volatility that had never been there before was building quickly. Anger and sadness was pouring from me and the harsh and possibly not-so-distant terror of being left alone. I didn't want to be left alone, I loved my family life and having a partner. I was losing my once love, my rock, my world. I just wanted normality again. My head felt like it was stuck on a fairground attraction riding on autopilot with no end in sight. My body felt this horrible, uncomfortable feeling of shame and embarrassment that I couldn't escape. What were people thinking or saying behind my back? I bet they were laughing, stupid little girl, wake up and smell the roses, everyone must have seen the crap I was taking from him and mostly because I was scared, but regardless I felt they were saying get out and gain some respect. Should I? Yes! Would I? Could I?

I must say most of my family and friends kept telling me they thought it must be an affair, but I never agreed as apart from marriage being sacred, Jim was not a flirt. I trusted him, he wasn't a sleaze. I pretty much never saw him look at another woman in that way. He had a fairly medium sex drive and at the end of the day he was married to me and only me, or so I thought. I didn't think he would be capable of an affair but maybe he was gay. That would be better, I'd rather him leave me for a guy, not a girl as it would reflect on me. But no, when I asked he said he wasn't, so I sat with that answer wanting to believe him but there was that doubt, and if I put all the things together I'd seen and heard and felt it wasn't looking good. He would let me go to bed at night saying he wanted to stay up longer.

That from a true clock watcher, normally in bed by 9.30pm on the dot. He extended this time later and later to avoid the bedtime expectations, closing the door between the bedrooms and lounge. The door was half glass and I remember following him one time straight after he sat down, peering through the glass so he couldn't see me only to view him texting or secretly peering around the room making what seemed to be forbidden calls. I would sometimes barge in. The jump he would make nearly caused him to hit the roof. He was definitely up to something and I was determined to find out!

We kept our family breakfast going though. Jim would drop us off at the restaurant while he looked for a park that was often hard to find in the busy street we frequented but in any case, he always took ages. After breakfast he would run an hour as we waited on the waterfront, sometimes leaving his phone but it always had a PIN and he never once gave it to me which somehow maybe made me feel safe, as I couldn't find out something I was maybe resistant to discover deep down.

After a stint at his sister's house, he moved back home and suggested a trip to Thailand. Our friends Jan and Mark were already there, Jen and Mal were a day off leaving to go there too and Jim wanted to join the party. So, in swift decision we were off on another holiday, a year apart from the last. The money was whittling away as there was no expense spared. Jim kept saying the trips would only do us good. True, I mean there couldn't be anything sinister about these trips could there? Good old-fashioned holidays, maybe minus the bad behaviour, and surely nothing underhanded?

We arrived at the airport all packed and awaiting our family adventure. When we reached the desk, we were told Max needed over six months on his passport to fly and only had four which wasn't enough. We had no idea of that rule, so, in typical Jim style, he suggested I, along with India, would go for four days alone, as it was Friday and Jim could get to the passport office on Monday for Max. The trip would be cut short, but I didn't want to go alone. Why wouldn't we leave as a family, go home together, visit the passport office together and leave the airport again… together? That surely seemed the right answer. But no. Jim went alone to

Thailand. Leaving me with the two kids to sort it all out by ourselves. I would miss Jan and Mark but more importantly, how could Jim do that?

On Monday we got the extension we needed and flew out. I would have expected he missed us but on arrival, he barely showed me interest. What was I expecting? I wondered. More wishful thinking, honestly why did I do it to myself? The first few days were ok. Jim attended the workout room for an hour and a half every morning, had breakfast, and then either hit the pool or beach with us, before a trip into the hub of town to shop and get massages. One night we even had a romantic dinner, and a stop in at a girly bar to watch a bit of pole dancing and legendary ping pong escapades from the talented ladies. I thought maybe watching another woman would interest him enough to spur those thoughts of sex! And it did! After a dry three months, we had what I'd call very half-hearted sex that very night.

The next day we went on a little water outing on a luxury speed boat to visit an island for lunch and swim in the crystal-clear waters. The ocean was a torrent, and they nearly didn't leave. I got seasick easily, and so did Jim, so I was worried about going. The kids probably did too, I wasn't sure as they hadn't yet been in this situation. As the waves got rough, we almost bounced out of the boat, Jim leaving me with the two kids clinging to grim death at the back while he sat right at the front. I couldn't even see him! My knuckles were white from gripping the seat so hard, the kids were crying, and my hands were numb. I wasn't impressed. Then as we stopped for some snorkelling, I noticed Jim was no longer beside me or the kids. Had this ironman triathlete drifted away or was taken by a shark, or possibly drowned? No, nothing so sinister for him, only a worry for me as I peered into the boat to notice he was on his phone once again. I was determined to find out what he was up to. To debunk my theories I raced closer to the side of the boat to get the three of us up on board but before I could get to him, he hung up. I had managed to get close enough behind him to see who he was texting in the middle of the ocean, without his family in view but as he spotted me, he jumped a foot high and had a terrified look on his face. Pretty much the guilty giggles you show just as you get caught out and try to keep the charade up and keep it light and innocent looking just to cover it. I was fuming.

"Who was that?" I asked as I went to grab the phone.

"No one, just my work, I was sending them pics to transfer on my computer for our trip."

"Can I look?" I asked. "Sure, just let me…" he said as he shifted positions to appear side on to me. I heard many buttons being pressed on his device before he willingly handed it to me. Suss!

"Yep, here you go," he said, and as I looked at the screen, it was gone, just an empty home page remained. Was he joking? I ignored him for the rest of the day. He seemed upset that I was. Why don't you believe me? Why are you angry? Let's have a nice arvo. I didn't believe him this time. How could I? I had started to think I had some psychological issue that somehow I enjoyed all the pain he was causing, almost an addiction.

We still had days to go and on the last day we were to meet Jen, Mal and their daughter so peace needed to be kept at this time, and of course, the trip wouldn't be complete without drama from the little ones. Max this time. As we popped over with all the other people to feed the monkeys at a popular tourist beach, Max decided to get a bit too close to mum and baby. Within a flash, the parents had come running at him full steam, teeth chomping and claws scratching! It would have been a perfect Funniest Home Video moment, although we shouldn't have laughed. It just looked so funny, but Max was torn to bits so really not that amusing and of course, when he did arrive home the poor boy had to endure months of rabies shots! Fifteen needles per go! What a brave kid.

The next day Jim went missing telling me he was just popping to the front desk to get a map or book a moped or other such tasks and an hour later he would turn up again. No other explanation than his original reason. The trip was certainly causing my fears and maybe addiction to become more apparent. On the last day, he said he just wanted to spend the day alone. He sent me and the kids to spend up big on whatever we wanted so he could be Mr. Single again. The dinner that night with Jen and Mal was lovely. She arranged a beautiful restaurant on the beachfront in a secluded part of Thailand. It would have been perfect but because a cyclone had started to hit, the place was closed and we moved along to another restaurant which was still nice with the company and the views. The wind just added a bit of extra ambiance which if I was lucky could have blown away all this shit with Jim I was dealing with!

On our arrival in Melbourne, I began to let him know it was time to buy a house again. If he wasn't having an affair like he pleaded he wasn't, then we should buy a house and save the remaining dollars we had, although it was vanishing fast we still had enough for a deposit. Yes, he said, we would start to look, so I was happy. I craved security and that may have represented him staying with me. If it was an affair, I might forgive him. Could I? Or would the pain be too great? This not knowing made me feel I was losing my mind. Marriage counsellors aside, I think I needed help. He was making me crazy. It's amazing how you change though. When I married Jim, I always made it clear if there was ever an affair, that would be it for us. I meant it at the time too but when the question marks arose, I changed my mind in the name of love or maybe just fear. Right or wrong. I know many friends and acquaintances that have even turned a blind eye to their husbands, knowing what they were up to but ignoring them. I now say you never know what you will do until it gets put in front of you.

Then I noticed another Visa bill which I decided needed to be investigated. I looked in his wallet again. There were two cards I didn't know anything about and three separate receipts of payments worth thousands together and also not matching our joint accounts. So, three unknown cards in total. The panic hit me, this had to be an affair of sorts. What was on these cards and who were they spent on? Then I noticed huge amounts of money had been taken from our accounts bit by bit over the last year or so, but I hadn't previously noticed the smaller amounts as there was such a large sum in there from our house sale. Still a very significant amount was missing. I was furious and called him into the room.

"Jim," I said. "Do you have any secret credit cards I don't know about?"

"No," he replied quickly.

"Right," I said sarcastically.

"It's true," he yelled.

"Oh, so I'm not going to find a MasterCard with the numbers… on it here in your wallet am I?"

"No," he said.

Was he for real I thought?

"Ok," I said, and out came the card.

"Oh," he sighed.

Right.

"So I wouldn't then find a Visa card in there too would I?"

"Nope, I don't have any more."

OMG, he had to have lost his mind. I had his wallet right there in front of him.

"Ok, Jim here it is."

"Oh," he sighed again.

Then I questioned him about Amex. "Would I be able to find three receipts in your wallet?" No was his preferred answer again. And almost just for laughs, I pulled it out.

"Oh well, you won't find the card," he said. "I hid it at work."

I had a little look in all the nooks and crannies and low and behold the last card almost like magic from universal entities flipped out and into my hand!

"Who are you?" I screamed. I was trembling in temper crossed with the realisation of what was clearly being shown to me.

He didn't know what to say at first, he hung his head in shame or maybe sadness he had been discovered. He tried to cover it by explaining each card away in some unrealistic ridiculous story. One was his old company card. The other was new and the other was to pay off the lounge from the renovation. I demanded the receipts but I never saw them. And after the yelling was over, he went back to his sister's place again. They were no real help to him and they sat him down and asked the serious question of why. They wanted to help me as they could see what he was doing but he didn't know why he was doing it. He told them he knew he had stuffed up big time. He rang me to apologise however I wasn't budging this time. I was so upset and the answer to the question of the affair was still not even confirmed. At the time all I knew was in my eyes he wasn't telling the truth. So really, I guess anything was possible.

He told me the following week he would do anything to make it up to us. He was so sorry. He wanted to come home and make things right. He would jump through hoops to do what it took. Wow. This was the most passionate I'd seen him in ages. I told him I'd think about it. He tried to make good with me by inviting me away for the weekend to the footy in the city. I just couldn't bring myself to go and play happy families. We texted during the night though, him telling me how much he loved me and including lots of xxx's. So, after a while, he came back and coincidentally just in time for a letter to arrive in the post. It was a brand-new account at another bank we didn't bank with. It had a cover letter. "Thank you Jim for opening this account. I hope you will be happy banking with us!"

This man needed help and fast. He agreed. The money was going quickly too but we still could work on ourselves. So, after another excuse as to the new account letter, off we went to a sex therapist/counsellor. He was questioned and so was I. He said everyone brings their issues into relationships so he wanted to investigate more. We sat for a few weeks with him but seemed to be getting nowhere. By this time, I felt if we didn't move from our expensive rental that tiny bit of money left would be gone. So, I found a very rundown house across the road for a third of the price and a six month lease. It would house us while we were looking and help us save. Unfortunately, Jim didn't want to help with the move and unpacking, besides his clothes were all still at his sister's and that's where he wanted them to stay. He never really, wholly and solely moved with us, just had sleepovers.

Jim continued to do his many work functions. Two particular times stand out. Melbourne Cup and another in early December. On the day of the Melbourne Cup his work had put on a huge function, entertaining many clients in his industry. He had been out all day which I expected. I thought he would be home around nine or ten, he was still a dad after all and he always had a fair run with so many outings. I had been waiting at home for him, I knew he hated restrictions on his times out so I didn't call or text. I just had to trust he would get home at a respectful time. Midnight came, and he didn't. I waited until 1.30am. That's it I thought. It was a Tuesday night. Where would he even be at that time? The venue had already closed so I texted him.

"Are you ok?"

"Yes" was the response, then nothing, no explanation. Not good enough I thought and I rang with a calm tone.

"Where are you?"

"Out," he said. "I'll be home soon."

"But where have you been the last few hours? The venue closed ages ago."

"Oh, asleep in my car," he said. It wasn't right. He hadn't done that before. I was suspecting another woman and this behaviour was pointing directly at that. He arrived home very happy. He gave me a big kiss and cuddle and went to sleep, leaving me unsettled, to say the least. A couple of weeks later he rang me on a Friday. He had been out most of the week at work dinners, but everyone was going to a work colleague's farewell that day and he wanted to attend. Apart from the fact he had been saying how much he hated this guy; it was also our family time. The kids nor I hadn't seen him so I bucked up. He reacted very strongly about this get-together. Unusually so, considering his dislike of the man. I decided to tell him that it was ok, I would get a sitter and meet him. If it was just a group of workpeople meeting at a bar after work in the city then I could come. I mean he shouldn't be trying to avoid me. He had told me he felt obliged so I thought it was perfect timing to tag along and see what I could see. When I suggested that I come and meet him, he went ballistic.

"If you turn up, I won't stay at our home, I'll leave you again," he yelled. I told him I was coming so get prepared. He was stressed out of his head and I stupidly let him convince me that if I didn't turn up he would make sure we had lots of romantic times and family fun over the rest of the weekend. I reluctantly, more like stupidly, agreed. I let it all go that night. In hindsight I should have secretly gone to spy on him and never let him know my plans, I may have found my answer! I believed all his bullshit almost all the time. I think some of it was because I loved him, some because I must have had an addiction of sorts to him, and some because I wanted my family to stay together. I just didn't want the answer to be another woman.

It's amazing what you put up with when you want to see what you want to see. One week later I visited another clairvoyant. I was getting obsessed as I had to uncover the truth. I was desperate to look for answers. I'm aware not to tell them too much as to give them clues, often turning up not wearing a wedding ring. This particular one was to prove very accurate.

"There is another woman," she said sadly.

"She is brunette, she comes from another place in Australia, not Victoria, but Tasmania. She works with him at the same company but not in the same office, in another one close by and they have been together a long time, maybe five years. He loves her, she loves him, I think she fell pregnant to him, but not sure they will have it."

My body twitched. My heart felt like it was about to compete in the biggest race of my life, pounding hard but with an almost funny feeling that I knew what the race was all about and how I felt it would end. In my heart, I somehow knew it all.

I didn't socialise with all the people in his workplace anymore. Who could this female be? Of course, after this clairvoyant's bombshell, I wanted to scratch her eyes out, push her off her crystal ball chair, and maybe even for good measure stomp on her like all evil witches bearing bad news! I wanted her to be wrong. Maybe I wouldn't say anything to him, put my head back in the sand.

On the same day, I caught up with a male friend for lunch. He was in the same industry, and he knew Jim, but not well. He worked with one of Jim's other offices in the city. He told me most of the men who worked in his industry were having affairs, and he pretty much guaranteed Jim was too. Big call! When I arrived home, I mentioned this friend's comment to Jim, who just rolled his eyes. I asked him to look me straight and tell me he wouldn't cheat on me. He glanced my way for a second then finished his sentence looking towards the window. Not very convincing! When I got into bed, I decided to bring up the reading I had had that day. It was dark, and now as I look back, I so wished I had been able to see the expression on his face as I told him the info that was so secretly locked up in a vault! Now too, of course, it was my subconscious trying to desperately save me from the heartbreak I was heading for. His answer was completely predictable. "Silly clairvoyant. Night Zoe, see you in the morning," was all he had to say. And as you can imagine I was not about to fall asleep very easily. Hope he had panic attacks all night too!

I arrived home the next day to an envelope in the letterbox that felt like photographs could be inside. My mind raced wildly, could these be from a secret supporter of mine with information that would solve the mystery, or divorce papers that were to be sprung onto me unbeknown? It was all too confronting right then and there, so I went inside and left them on the kitchen bench. Later that night I jumped up and raced to the kitchen, the curiosity was too great. I swiped it off the bench and raced back to my half-finished wine in the living room. Ok, I'm ready. When I opened the envelope, I was pleasantly surprised. Horse picture after horse picture. It was Reunion, my old mare and her foal. How gorgeous. Just what I needed to see. The owners attached a note next to one pic, showing the foal standing in Reunion's feed bin and Reunion ever so patiently waiting for it to move. "What a tolerant mare your girl is." I sat with my wine and pondered the photos. Reunion may have moved to another family, but somehow she was still part of my life. A mum and her baby, what a special bond and one that reminded me of what was important here. My kids.

CHAPTER 14

THE TRUTH REVEALED

As Christmas came, so did the discovery that would once and for all change my world. We were staying with Jim's parents down the South Coast. It was New Year's Eve. The family always took the kids for a fun night out to the local fair to see the attractions and watch the fireworks. This time Jim was trying hard to escape at any opportunity he could. He'd come up with all sorts of excuses, saying things like he was going to the bathroom, but I'd find him up in a nearby park nowhere near bathrooms, and on his phone. Deflated, and over it, I would ignore him and stay with my kids.

When we arrived home Jim sat up watching TV, and I went to bed around 1am. In the morning he was up again early, and I could see he was out in the yard. I noticed his phone was sitting all on its lonesome. I picked it up. Could I guess the code? It's got to be worth a go with numbers I should have tried long ago. His PIN for his credit card. Bingo! I opened it. Heart palpitations begin once again! There was an unread message so I quickly looked.

Sarah. Who was Sarah? I had never heard of her. This must be the affair the clairvoyant talked of, however part of me didn't want to look, I was paralysed with fear, adrenaline pumping, I scrolled down and read the message. My heart nearly stopped. It read: Happy New Year. I love you, my Wonder Twin. You're the best. Then another message: Call me, but I understand if you can't. I felt a mad woman step into my body. I was like a woman possessed.

I ran with his phone down the hall and into his sister's room.

"It's true," I said as I shook uncontrollably at her bedroom door.

"I thought it was," she said. It was all leading to this moment. She just had that feeling I remember her saying. It reminded her of her husband's infidelity, she explained. I told her to get him and meet me outside and thirty seconds later he came to the door yelling with steam coming from his ears.

"Where's my fu…ing phone." Not OMG Zoe I'm sorry or something more appropriate.

"Who is she?" I asked.

"It's William's PA from work."

"At your work?"

"Yes."

"How long have you been having sex with her?"

"We have had a relationship for seven years now," he quietly muttered.

The sky felt like it was falling on me, and my body felt weak like I'd aged one hundred years instantly. I was flipping between confusion, sadness, and anger. Did I have tears welling in my eyes, or were those tears coming from hate and therefore allowed me to picture myself with shards of glass ready to pierce his heart? I couldn't comprehend all this, and I couldn't distinguish my feelings. Then temper set in again harder. Those tears were real regardless. I threw the phone straight at his head, striking him on his forehead and producing a spot of blood as I did. Oh, shame about the blood as I thought of all the lies he had told, and my reality was syncing together and I could see again! I picked up the phone and he tried to grab it away from me. I threw it far away into a rock and it split in two. The other part of Jim, the extra limb he had grown, the evil Jim was destroyed, for the moment anyway, except I wanted and needed more information. This was the time for him to explain and I could see he was on the edge of blurting stuff left right and centre so I had to be smart, time was of the essence, so the questions flowed and he answered.

"She started at the company seven years ago, and we became extremely close five years ago."

The calculator was going off in my head. My math was poor on a good day but as I thought about it, I realised Jim wanted to leave me five years before. It fitted in perfectly.

"Was she married?" I asked.

"Yes," he replied.

"Any children?"

"No," he replied.

"What was the Wonder Twin comment?"

"Oh," said Jim, "It was our nickname for each other."

I almost vomited on the spot! How pathetic. Whose idea was that? Jim wasn't good on pet names, hence this ridiculous one, I guess. He was usually straight up and not into that sort of thing.

"But we never slept together," he blurted. "We are just really connected."

What the! Come on, no sex? Seven years! We were at the twelve-year mark, so that meant five years into my marriage this occurred. So connected, I thought, and no sex? They socialised at work sipping champagne and playing lawn bowls at a city club. Did he ever see her at her worst? In her old tracksuit, hair messed up, giving birth to your children maybe? Or being in a real relationship, budgeting finances, cleaning the house, or grocery shopping? No, I'm sure he didn't! Wake up to yourself Jim, I thought. This person got to present herself at her best at all times. Not so hard to seduce or be seduced by someone when it's uncomplicated, fun, and exciting? And by the look in his eye, he was smitten. It was my worst nightmare in full swing. I felt betrayed by him and by her too. The one thing I feared and resisted and turned a blind eye to but came at me hard. It almost felt like I had no real chance as I didn't ever know exactly what I was fighting as Jim deflected, lied, gaslighted, time wasted, stonewalled, appeared defensive, and ultimately cheated on me on some level.

This guy I thought I knew, seemingly was in love, and it wasn't with me. I felt like I was in another world, that it couldn't be real. Pinch me, I needed to wake up. He finished talking and got into his car to drive somewhere. He was good at running. All the counsellors told me he would run from everything. But that was no news to me, he had been doing that for the last few years. Instead of sitting to work stuff out, he ran away as far as he could get and frequently.

I got into my car and followed, leaving the kids with his family. We were out of control. I lost him within two minutes out the driveway but thought he might be heading to a nearby beach, and I was correct. He was at a park up on a cliff face. Half my luck he might have been going to jump, nasty yes, but I was irate, I couldn't have cared less at that point although I wanted to know more from him. I should stop him, he was no good splattered on the rocks and I guess deep down I wouldn't want that regardless of the result. Fury feeds crazy thoughts. So I ran so fast up the hill to where he was trying to escape and rethink his next story. I was fuelled by adrenaline. He saw me and started to come back down. I was yelling obscenities at him as I wanted him and the world to know what this man had done to me and the kids. He had let us down, let me down. He had taken all our dreams and plans for a fabulous future and dumped them carelessly in a deep dark black hole never to be seen again. He had hurt me, lied, and tricked me to believe in him, to believe in us as a couple but also as a family, it was unforgivable. He had tried to show me he didn't care anymore with his actions, but I didn't want to see it or trust that it could be real, that he didn't care anymore the way he used to, the way he promised he would. He broke our wedding vows. He did things I never thought he could. I trusted him, gave him the benefit of the doubt, and let him hold my beating heart for way too long. He never protected me as he should have. Jim, you let me down and tore my soul apart. We drove back separately to the house.

I asked his family to look after the kids. I had to go. Go somewhere away from him. Home to my mum and dad and to find out more about this girl and where she and her husband lived. Did her husband know? He was soon going to find out that's for sure.

The four hours home seemed like an eternity, sobbing and shaking the whole way. I asked mum to do some detective work and as I knew her last name, I had her find all of them in Tassie. I went to the electoral roll and because I knew he was constantly visiting certain Eastern suburbs, it was there I found them, I was right. In the meantime, Fran did a Google search and found her husband Robert, and the name of the company he worked for. When I got home, I rang Jim's work. It was only the second of January, and most people were on holiday, but I spoke to a holiday temp, asking her for Sarah's number. She was hesitant at first, but I quickly added I was a friend from overseas and was only here briefly and just had to see her. And that wasn't so far from the truth, I did just have to see her, but I was no friend!

The phone call was quick, as she didn't answer. But in a short time, she got back to me, sounding nervous, and so she should. The phone call was a blur as all the emotions shadowed my thoughts and left a foggy haze. I demanded to know what the hell was happening. She was a good actress, this girl. She toned it all down immediately which reminded me of Jim's similar behaviour, they were tarred with the same brush. I think people, well couples in particular, rub off on each other. They were Wonder Twins for a reason and that reason could have been because they thought so alike. One of my first questions to her was did her husband know. I hate myself sometimes as I'm so trusting and gullible but hey, it's who I am. She said she and her husband were separated so it didn't matter to him, I believed her, this devil. Who believes the devil? Stupid me. She was also a Scorpio star sign, and I knew they had a horrible sting! So, I dropped that point for the time being at least. Smart girl, she was, taking all the attention off her husband who may in fact just care what she had been doing after all. The questions flowed, luckily as with most women I got more from her than him. Although pretty much all of what they spat out was false anyway. Except for the obvious like saying I'm attracted to your husband, he is very good looking, we are just extremely connected, hence the Wonder Twins. I gagged.

"You know, the old cartoons," she almost gushed. Wonder Twins deactivate as they smash their fists in the air together.

"That's us," she sighed.

What world were they caught up in, I hissed in my head. Kiddy land?

Unfortunately, she forgot she was dealing with a family who was once a happy unit of husband and wife and children. She was taking a dad away from kids who adored him. I'm not sure people sit and think of the consequences. Just the nice feel-good emotions away from reality! I tried to confirm with her how long it had been going on. She differed from Jim. Five years in total she told me, not seven. When she started at his work, but not longer. We emailed every day and signed off with our signature WT. And like with Jim, she said there had been no sex yet. Yeah right. Five years of, I love you my wonder twin, and being so connected and attracted and all with no sex. Bull crap, he wasn't sleeping with me I thought, he must have been sleeping with her!

"I'm so sorry. It's all been blown way out of proportion, I've had this happen to me too, so I know what it's like," she said.

"Why?" I asked.

"Well, my husband cheated on me, it was awful," she said.

So, you think it's ok to do it to someone else? I shouted in my head! Shameless. The conversation softened slightly as she tried to calm me. I can't remember all the questions I asked her but there were many. Nearly two hours' worth. She even explained the New Year's Eve message as a silly message she had sent most of her friends as well, all varying slightly. She then started saying she called everyone Wonder Twin including William the CEO. What a load of rot I thought! The conversation ended with another apology and a comment on how well we might have gotten along in different circumstances. I doubt I could be friends with someone like that.

My emotions were still high, in fact, I would go as far as to say out of control. I had believed this man for so long, he lied to me for ages. The betrayal ran deep. It's the only way to describe it. The embarrassment was like being tossed aside and forgotten for another superior model. One who may have elevated his status again. Just like I had done for him in my magazine days. That is all gone now. Kids were my life, they were and still are the most important thing by far. Casual clothes, stress, and a more normal life with more restrictions were not what this man needed or wanted anymore. A life of meaningfulness and true love was being shadowed by what felt was a temporary, shallow champagne-injected lust. I was, though, a woman scorned.

The following day I spoke to Jim on the phone and the words that came out of his mouth were few but cut like a knife. Words like the Sarah message I found previously. Both, I will never forget.

"Do you love her Jim?"

"Yes, you could say that," he said softly. My body convulsed and my stomach churned. It's strange. It felt so bad to hear these words, this truth that he spoke I didn't want to know about, but then something drives you to ask more, to know more. Aware that it will hurt, the truth needs to be heard.

"In fact," he then added. "If I had met her fifteen years ago, before you, I would have married her instead."

Just kill me now! My mind went into a coma for a moment. I asked him to repeat it. I couldn't have heard it right. We had a wonderful marriage and now have two beautiful kids. How could he wish to just make our lives together vanish and replace us like this? The sorry that Sarah had said in turn came out his mouth too. He was sorry he hurt me so much. I know I never would have done this to her if the roles were reversed, I thought.

I was confused. Part of me wanted to smack his arse all over town. Embarrass him, as he embarrassed me, to tell the world what he had done, how much he did hurt us. Make the truth known! That was the strong yet angry side of me.

The sad, weak, abandoned me thought differently and unfortunately at that time fear and past feelings of love took over. I look back and I'm ashamed I was going to give in to him once again with what I thought was to be a possible reunion. Dog with a bone gone crazy or just plain stupid and weak, I thought I was done. The strong Zoe screamed as loud as she could, but the love-addicted Zoe locked her out holding her kids with her in the same compartment. It was the kids that mattered most to me, and it affected the decisions I was making. These kids deserve a dad to wake up to every morning. To have a male role model, at least in some way. I wanted to hold our family unit together. Judge me or not. I believed I was doing my best. But with all that was happening, I was flipping from sad to angry and back again. The kids were never that close to him, but I wanted to ensure they had their best chance of having a good relationship with him.

He arrived home two days later to talk. It wasn't an angry reunion. By this time, I had gone through the throws of real rage, and the anger was just simmering under the surface of the total despair, sadness, and hurt I felt. I expected he would once again agree to stay if I asked him to. We sat, talked, and cried, and talked and cried some more. He said he just didn't love me the same way he once did, and felt like we were more like best friends living together. He didn't think he could give me anything more, and certainly not the happy marriage I wanted. Didn't he understand that marriage, a relationship is constantly changing and growing? It's not always going to be rosy, and not always going to be perfect. It may have felt like we were just friends but that made sense as there was another woman who had taken my place to love. I cried again, and so did he. He added that he thought I was a fantastic mum and had been a wonderful wife to him. "Why do you have to leave, and why are you doing all this?" I asked him. I just couldn't get my head around the fact he didn't love me anymore, but still saw me as his best friend. There was no more of a real answer other than what I discovered and what I had heard directly from their mouths. We reminisced about old times, when we met, how I felt, and how he felt. The wonderful stories these love bubbles had provided and beyond the burst. Our love it seemed had somehow endured past the point of rupture. The conversations this time were only full of compliments, cuddles, tears, and love, but not a happy secure love, a past love from one party that seemed his affection was irretrievable.

I accepted his resignation from our marriage. But of course, you know me, not without a fight. He left the house and our marriage. I even had his sisters telling him not to go, as they truly believed he was making a huge mistake and would only want to come back within a year or two, as they all too often do. I agreed of course, so within days I asked if he wanted to give it another go at the counsellors. Yes, he said he did. You never know, he thought he would try again. So, our yo-yo continued. I know when I reread this book, and have it printed that you the reader must think I'm a pathetic girl who just can't let go. That's what I'll most likely be thinking. It was clear as day in front of me after all wasn't it? But we both had a part in it all. I didn't want it to end, but neither did he. One thing I do remember asking him at the time was "what would you do next if counselling didn't work?" He replied confidently that he would like to re-partner and have more children. He had it all planned out, and neither I nor the kids were part of his new dream. Why couldn't I just accept it and leave? Lock me up, honestly, I needed an emotional, and psychological detox from him.

In between, I decided to look a little further into the whole Sarah thing. I wanted to know more! So off I trotted into his head office to surprise this woman who had mercilessly and callously ruined a family, to do some interrogating. I rang from the lobby, giving her the chance to come down to me, when there was no answer, I popped upstairs and asked for her at the desk. I told them who it was. She was busy, they replied. I then had a text from her saying to wait ten minutes. She would be out soon. This girl was a slippery character. I wasn't used to such conniving people. I had worn my heart on my sleeve for my entire life. What you see is what you get. She knew the best way to overcome this was to befriend me, and that she managed to do for a mini-second. She smiled sweetly as she approached, although I detected a slight nervousness. Most women would be terrified of getting a visit from their lover's wife. But here she was in front of me, the woman who had been having some sort of a relationship with my husband for five years and she barely broke a sweat.

We walked to a nearby café, and like our phone conversation, we spoke for an hour and more. She didn't seem to have much loyalty to Jim at all. She made off statements such as she had been getting worried that Jim was stalking her. I'm assuming it was some kind of strange tactic in a bid to pull at my heartstrings so she could save her marriage, or maybe it was just a simple case of deflection.

"He has an obsession with me more than I thought," she frowned. I looked at her hiding my anger, I could have jumped the table and squeezed the life out of her with the rage that had built up inside of me. I quizzed her again. I wanted to know every detail I possibly could, even down the to Melbourne Cup Day, which of course she denied being with him that late in the night, insisting she left well before. Proves nothing I thought! Sex, or no sex it's an affair, of the emotional kind at least, and it didn't sit straight with me at all.

She said she and her husband were split but had decided to give it another go just like us. Their marriage had been on the rocks because she wanted to move home to Tasmania as her grandmother was sick. Rob… as she started to say, but changed the word to my husband, had said no. Little did she know I knew exactly who he was, and his name, but I was keeping that to myself. I could play this game too! It was beginning to make sense. From the information she freely began spewing out, I figured out that each time Jim wanted to leave, she had been separated from her husband. Each time she went back to him, Jim would come crawling back to me. I knew Jim had told me he hadn't sent Sarah any of the photos from our overseas trip, but it was another story I wanted to debunk. So, I asked Sarah up front,

"Which photos did Jim send you from our trip to America?" Hook line and sinker, she fell for it, telling me everything! "Oh, mostly from Central Park," she chirped. I knew it. Then she gave me more damning evidence. I didn't get many pics when we were there because our bike broke down at the start of the path, and we didn't manage to get all the way around. She then said she and hubby had a huge fight and ended up going home which was why Jim had sent them to her.

"Oh, really," I said. "So, when were you guys in New York?" I asked.

"Oh, around the time you were," she said. I felt sick again.

"I think we may have missed you by a day." All I could think of was the weird behaviour and the nights Jim spent out alone. Had she missed us by a day?

We ended there with her apologising again to me and saying that she was definitely going to keep away from Jim because she didn't want to encourage him to stalk her!

I left angry. Unsure of what I would hear and believe of her story before I had come to meet her, I was now certain of many things, but some of the pieces of the puzzle were still missing and incomplete. I went to Jim again and told him of my findings. He denied some, agreed with others, and I was no closer to finding the pieces I needed to understand. He didn't even query why I had gone and didn't seem surprised but denied some of the allegations, agreed with other things and some of the stories just didn't match at all. He kind of blew it off. He was nervous but played it down as best he could. They had tried to get their stories straight, but just couldn't quite manage it. Liars can't lie straight in bed. They weave so many lies they get tangled in their web of deceit, and Jim and Sarah were proving that to be true.

A woman scorned is never a good person to be around. I was keeping it together on the outside, but inside I was like a volcano waiting to erupt. Meanwhile back in payback land from my emergency plane ride I prepared to dish up Spaghetti Bolognese. The kids had already eaten, and Jim still hadn't sat down to eat his which was waiting on the dining table for him. I looked out the corner of my eye in time to see Crumpet jump up onto the table and start snacking away at Jim's dinner. I gave a silent chuckle thinking "karma's a bitch Jim, enjoy that tasty cat slobber" as I walked over to top it up with another spoonful of Bolognese before he walked in and sat down. Yum, Yum, Yum.

Unfortunately, Polo was getting older and all his allergies had caught up with him. He grew weak and I called Jim to tell him I thought it was time. He was quiet, but agreed to come and see him. He had had a bad turn and just wasn't picking up. We took him to the Vet and he agreed, it was time for him to go to sleep. We were both devastated and stood by his side to give him one last hug and kiss. Jim was a mess and looked totally broken. I knew it was from his mate passing, but as we stood at the surgery door, I wondered if the tears were also about our relationship as it seemed to coincide with our ending too. Goodbye Polo. What a great dog you were.

Jim had begun to hang out more and more at a local gym that was connected to the pool complex where he swam. It was very small, and not so glamorous, hardly the kind of place anyone who was seriously into fitness would hang out at. There was never anyone there. But Jim seemed to attract them, and in no time, he set his attention to a new woman—Amanda. If he hadn't briefly mentioned her in a passing comment, I wouldn't have even picked up on it. In the weeks to come, he dropped her name a couple more times, and I remember seeing a text or two from her as well. When I asked about her after yet another slip of her name, he casually responded saying "Oh it's just the young PT that ran the gym, she was wishing me luck in races." Yeah, right I thought. Surely, he didn't think I was that stupid. One day he brazenly announced he had been invited to jump on a flight to Las Vegas to join her for her birthday. You're kidding, right? In what world was that ok? There was a twenty-three-year-old PT asking a supposedly married man with kids, who was trying to get his marriage back on track to have a little fun time away. It was shocking to me that he found nothing wrong with this. Not on! Back to the counsellor we went.

The next counsellor we attended was short-lived, only two sessions in fact. The first was to hear the story and leave Jim with a question he was to answer in the next session the following week. Turning up for our second session, she asked him to answer the question she had posed to him to think about. "Could he move home again and make this marriage work?" she asked. While he thought for a moment before answering, it gave him some more food for thought. "It has a chance of being saved," she stated. Many marriages had come out the other side in better shape than before she had told us, even after affairs. Jim pondered for another moment before looking downwards and sadly answering, "no, I'm not ready." He said he didn't want to close the door, but made it clear he didn't know if he would come back again or not. It was too much for me, I stormed out the doors, and anger overwhelmed me again. He met me outside, and I asked him to look at his phone to check if he had been in contact with Sarah again. He said no, so I snatched it from his hand and ran to my car in hope of reading another message I could nail him on. I'm not sure why I wanted to, it was clear he had decided to leave us again, at least temporarily. It made no sense, even to me, what point there was in finding out who he was in contact with. I already knew I didn't have his heart but was hellbent on finding out who did. Was it Sarah, or was it, Amanda? Maybe it was someone else? Who knew? My anger clouded my judgment and when he reached the car, we struggled over the phone. I pushed him away, so I could get in alone and give myself time to check his phone, but he pushed his way in before me, and I had no choice but to drive home with him inside constantly trying to grab back his phone. My head was pounding with stress. I was yelling at him, and he was yelling at me trying to retrieve his phone. It was exhausting.

When we arrived home, it continued. The anger and betrayal I had built up over the years of being treated so badly had now exploded. I wouldn't let him get away with what he did. He had to feel the pain I was in. I had given him the benefit of the doubt for so many years, good years, and the better part of my life. The least he could do after all that deceit and fooling around was to come home to his family and make it up to us by being a good husband, and father. We were owed that. I can't believe I'm saying this, but I was willing to work through the affair. God knows why. But for the sake of the tears from my children, I was. They were young, and at an age separation, divorce, and fighting could damage the way they looked at relationships. The kids were good, strong kids, who were told that dad was visiting his sister, and I had hidden all of it from them as best I could and continued to shield them from the ugly truth by spending time with them, loving them, taking them on outings and of course riding our ponies. In my opinion he should have seen all of this and at least met me halfway to putting in some kind of effort. But instead, we cried again, and fought again, mostly over the finer details of the secret affair. After all the time that had passed with me not knowing, I still felt stuck on the whole Sarah thing. I had to feel satisfied somehow, I couldn't explain why. I knew all I could extract, but the stories continued. I'm not sure how much truth I ever discovered honestly. But hey I had to give him hell even if I never found the truth he deserved it, and so did she. I felt like she was getting off scot-free. She played a big role in this too, and she knew what she was doing.

At the end of our battle that day, Jim asked if I wanted to get help from a counsellor alone. It may help with all the issues that have been going on. Yes, I thought, I was feeling like I was losing my mind. He said to give him until March to sort himself out then he would be able to come back fully repaired and into the marriage. And we agreed that we would stay faithful during that time. Why couldn't I just let go? Please Zoe, for the love of God! Let go!

This all occurred around late October. By November I had decided to try and cheer up a little and went out for a night with friends. Jen and her friend, another single mum, whose husband also had had an affair, came out with us. Her husband had openly left the marriage after she found out, and he was still with the other woman. She needed a night out to help her cheer up too!

So many affairs around me! I remember Jim's sister once telling us that she worked with a girl who was married to a guy who travelled a lot. He had married this lady, had two kids, and what seemed to be a happy normal life, alas not so. The sneaky man had a double life happening. He had a girlfriend on the other side of Australia with two kids as well! He used to spend half the month with one, and half the month with the other. He would buy both ladies the same car, birthday presents, clothes, etc. as to not muck up his story. He had played this charade so well that it was decades when he was finally found out. He had become too complacent, and probably too cocky, leaving one to go to the other, he left some info and a photo of the girlfriend behind that aroused suspicion and ultimately uncovered his deception. Unbelievable the lengths a cheating person will go to!

Anyway, I was out at a bar with my girls sharing a bottle of champagne when this guy comes over to dance with us. We all had a groove on the dance floor, Jen taking happy snaps as the night proceeded. Then this guy wandered over, he seemed a little crazy though as he started coming up to girls including us again, to try and take off our shoes and attempt to suck their toes. He was drunk as a skunk and had a weird foot fetish that was over the top. Jen's friend had her foot taken, then there was an attempt to get mine. He accidentally pushed me off the back of the seat while he was trying to get hold of my foot. Jen was very amused and took more shots of us all until we managed to push this guy away to other more accommodating victims. He was out of luck and became such a nuisance, the security guys ended up escorting him out. We met lots of people that night. I sat with a guy visiting from Tarragal and we got on well. He told me he loved my company, and that made me feel nice. It had been a long time between compliments, and a long time of being rejected too. I left him with his friends and the girls and went home. The next day Jen emailed the pics through. I didn't look at them all, just a few, but giggled seeing them on my computer, not thinking much of it. I hadn't done anything wrong, but I still felt compelled to tell Jim regardless, who never even flinched.

Over the following months, Jim and I had a few nights out. One night we caught up for a party. I was all dressed up and feeling good about myself for a change. The night was going great. We were having a ball, laughing, drinking, and catching up with friends. He dropped me home, without a kiss or hug, and said he'd see me the next day. I told him a week later how I thought he would make a little move on me that night. But all he said was he still didn't feel the desire to be sexually involved with me yet. The blow hurt.

As March approached, I became nervous but also happy that Jim would be coming back. I asked him what day in March he was thinking of joining us, as the first week had already hit. Would he be back before the end of March? "Yes," he had said, he would be coming back then. Bang on the 31st of March he calls.

"It's me," he said angrily.

"What's wrong?" I asked.

"I better come home, I need to show you something."

"Ok," I said wondering what he was angry about. He arrived five minutes later with a yellow envelope in his hand. He said nothing as he handed it to me to open. I pulled out a typed letter that said, "To the husband, this is what your wife has been up to while you're not around. She is cheating on you." In the envelope were Jen's photos, but of course I was the only one in the shots dancing and sitting next to my girlfriends with this crazy guy, attempting to suck our toes. I was speechless.

My initial reaction was to defend myself. I had already told him about the night, and regardless I had done nothing wrong! There was nothing with this guy, he had danced with everyone, and had been running around to all the girls. He said to me that thankfully someone was looking out for him. I thought for a second, who would have sent these?

"The letter came from Tarragal," he said. What, I thought?

"I don't know who sent it," he said. Maybe Jen is trying to catch you out and tell me of your bad behaviour or it's that guy you mentioned who lived in Tarragal, but in my mind, I was thinking, I hadn't done anything wrong, and Jen knew that, absolutely no way would all this be correct. Jim then stated loudly "That's it! I couldn't possibly come home now! See you later." And he stormed away.

How ridiculous, as if I'd be cheating, although I had every reason to I reckon. This was just another attempt of Jim's to discredit me and find a reason to blame me for the whole unhappy marriage thing. He needed a scapegoat, and he needed ammunition. But he was grasping at straws and desperate to try to set me up. How disgraceful. Who could do that to his wife and the mother of his children? Hadn't he made enough mess and created enough sadness? No, he was mental and the lies were just getting worse. I rang Jen, she was appalled. We sat for a minute, and that's all it took to figure it out. The photos were not sent by Jen to anyone, just me. Not even the other girl who was with us. The Tarragal thing must have been because of the guy I had mentioned to Jim in my night out story. Maybe he thought the pics were of him. The envelope was definitely stamped from Tarragal, but he had an office there and would often get mail from them, so that would have been easy enough to set up. The date on the back of them was marked February of that year, not November when we were out. They were stamped with the photoshop located in his building! Upon closer inspection, he had changed the date on the printed stamp on the envelope from February, that's when he got hold of the envelope and pics, to March, all in black pen.

I was flabbergasted at how seriously screwed up and mean and nasty he was. All to provide a reason why he didn't want to move back in. Insane! Jen rang him to throw some abuse his way, lashing out, she said to him "Don't blame me for something you have done! And do not use me! How could you treat her this way? Be a man. Don't keep lying and dragging something on when you have no intention of honouring it. What a joke to make this photo thing up, you are a sick, sick man!"

And he was. He continued to deny that it was a setup. I told him the only way he could have got these pics was to take a copy on disc or email them to himself. He was always over at the house, with or without me and he had plenty of opportunities to do it. I asked him why, but he denied it like everything else he had ever done. Was he not embarrassed? Did he not have any conscience? Or maybe he just didn't want to be the bad one and it makes it easier to leave if it's not his fault.

This was pretty much the straw that broke the camel's back for me. I know… it took me a while, I see that myself, trust me. I went into full swing and decided to call Robert, Sarah's husband. My marriage was wrecked and was not salvageable. I had nothing more to lose. My time for forgiveness and patience had run its course and there was nothing left. I had lost it all, and if Jim was going down, so was Sarah. I know it's not the most loving thing to do, but hell neither was five years of an affair. Let's just see if Robert knows about all this!

On the day I called Robert, Jim had been away on a business trip to Singapore and was going to pop in and visit Izzy and Harry while he was there. He was due back to see the kids on Sunday night but no, Jim wasn't to be seen until Tuesday. I wondered if he was on a business trip at all. It was probably another of his outlandish stories and he was probably shacked up with Sarah or Amanda or any one of his girls that I would no doubt find out about one day. He was going down and I intended to make it anything but easy for him. I rang a friend's wife that Jim worked with asking if she had seen him or heard from him. She said no, but I think he is due back from his holiday in Bali any day now.

"What?" I said. "He said he was away on business," I squealed.

"No, he took holiday leave, and went with someone to Bali," she informed me. Bloody liars, it never stopped. I shouldn't have been surprised. Straight after that, I made the call to Sarah's husband Robert. "Hi Robert," I began. "You don't know me, but my husband works with Sarah."

"Oh, you mean Jim?"

"Oh, dear yes, how do you know?"

"I've known about your husband for some time", he said. "They have been texting and sending picture messages to each other for years." I guess Robert found out before me. But didn't track me down. I think he should have at least given me the heads up so I knew once and for all. He started recalling what he knew, but he sounded like he had worked through his emotions about this outcome, whereas I was just beginning to.

Robert remembered seeing a text from Jim two years ago at six in the morning on a Sunday. He said Sarah said Jim was just checking how she was and wished her a great day. He asked her why he was texting, but she had no answers. He said he asked her many times what the texts were that kept coming from Jim's number. Robert received and paid the bills, so it was easy for him to notice these things. She told him she was sending pictures of Robert's niece to him. Why would you be sending pictures of my niece to some man at work I don't even know? From there on in, it was a slippery slope into divorce for them he said.

"I'm not with Sarah now, I just left her a few weeks ago, he said. I then proceeded to tell my whole story to him. He was very interested but seemed not as shocked as I was, having already found out about the bulk of it. One of the first things he told me is that they had had a fight on New Year's Eve, and he left the venue before midnight, hence the lovey-dovey vomitus texts to Jim. Although he didn't know of the Wonder Twin text. Robert and Sarah had never split up, this was the first time. The occasion that Sarah talked about being cheated on was actually by Robert a few years back, but Robert told me it was just texting cheeky messages, no meetings, and he thought Sarah was just trying to pay him back by using Jim.

I mentioned the trip to New York and the apparent fight at Central Park etc.

"Nope, he said, never happened, any of it." We were in New York but not riding through Central Park, and certainly not fighting!

"You were there too?" he asked.

"Yes, I believe at the same time."

"Interesting," he sighed.

Then I told him all the other stuff. Credit cards, accounts, secret meetings, phone calls, Eastern suburbs outings, Melbourne Cup, and much more.

"We would have to have our heads in the sand if we didn't believe they were sleeping together," he said. I was speechless. Strangely I was hoping the sex wasn't happening, but hey what was I thinking? Then I told him all about Thailand and the strange behaviour. He quickly butted in.

"Did you say you were in Thailand then? So were we!"

My heart stopped. This was all a setup. It had to be. He was a bit shocked too. There may have been a crossover of a few days either way, but it seemed we were there together. These two were so sneaky. Jim deserved an Oscar for all this acting. So did she. A fine performance had been taking place for years. Now I know why the decisions to go away were so sudden. I felt happy to know all of this but even more betrayed and very angry.

Jim stormed into the room at our home, after obviously knowing something was up with so many missed calls from me. I hung up from Robert as he said he thought we should nut it out together without being on the phone. I flew toward him screaming, "How could you do this?" The fight went on for an hour or so… It was truly awful. "I hate you!" I screamed, and he yelled, "I hate you too!" Don't ask me why he was hating me, I hadn't had the affair, or lied, but he had. I think he was probably upset that I had found him out and ruined his fun. I was not some wilting lily about to let it all go so easily. I wanted him to pay, although now I see what I should have done was save my energy and just release it all and let him go. There was screaming and tears for the whole fight. Emotions were high.

"I'm walking away from all this," I said.

"Fine," he said.

I sobbed. It's amazing how many tears you can produce. They must have been close to drying out, surely!

For the next few months, he lived with his sisters and popped in to see the kids once a week, if they were lucky. I think this was the life he wanted. A free one. To see other girls, work, and go to the gym. He didn't want the family anymore. The kids were devastated. They had seen him come and go so often now that they had finally stopped believing he was ever coming home. It was so hard to see their little faces and hear the sad words "When was Daddy coming home?" When they ever got into trouble for anything they would often burst into tears, the only words to come out were, "I hate Dad, why has he left us?" Or they would be extra hypo and aggressive in their behaviour acting out, purging their pain. They had been seeing Jane, our counsellor for a year or two which they enjoyed, but ultimately no amount of help can bring back your dad. This was hard to deal with, and as time went on it became even harder. Kids get so affected, and in some ways, you can help them with little stuff, but deep down they are changed forever and often never forget. I had a deep sense of guilt around them carrying all of this. It wasn't their fault, and they shouldn't have had to endure our fights or see it all unfold. It broke their hearts.

CHAPTER 15

PICKING UP THE PIECES

So there I was. I didn't have a husband anymore. Or a real father to my kids. I was stuck living in a dumpy house. Actually, things were shit! I felt like I'd been dragged through the washing machine, spat out, and dragged back in on a never-ending cycle.

I was constantly teary, which often spilled into sobs or gut-wrenching shouts and screams to the universe with demanding answers to my simple question—"Why?!" I remember some days as clear as a bell, and some others not at all. I found it nearly impossible to get excited about anything, and I couldn't concentrate on my kids as well as I liked. I was distracted and down a lot. I visited Mum and Dad for a good while on my nights off. I was lost and reverted to playing a child again to give me some kind of peace and comfort. A warm loving feeling that was desperately needed. I hung out with them like in old times. It was nice. I felt too weak to get myself together and socialise the way I knew I loved. Well not right then, I didn't.

Apart from working in the jewellery trade, my life was pretty simple for a short time, but I soon needed to recreate myself, and become one with the big wide world. So, I got myself together and started looking for another place. I made that my mission and it kept me happily busy. I'd try and focus on my beautiful children, and maybe eventually date some guys. I was beginning to crave some attention it had been years since I had been paid any, and I knew I deserved it, soon.

I had met Phil, Natalie and Owen's best friend, a few years back. I didn't know Phil very well, but he seemed charming, cheeky, and a whole lot of fun. And he was single! Perfect and just what the doctor ordered. He was a few years younger than me, but that was fine. He had been interested in me a year back he had said, but knew I wasn't ready, as I was still chasing blindly after Jim. He said he thought he'd wait. He asked me out. We chatted and flirted and after a couple of dates we ended up together in the bedroom. It was weird being with someone else after so long with one person, in a silly kind of the way it was like I was cheating on Jim which was completely unfair. He'd taken everything else from me, now, here his memory was taking my future too? Not a hope I thought, I liked Phil, he was fabulous.

He adored me and told me how amazing I was, and how much he wanted to have me. Wow, different from Not Tonight Jim. And when it came to a sexual connection it was there. I didn't think I'd be able to want to have sex with any other men after Jim, but something casual was just what I needed. And it was good, really good! Of course, in the back of my mind I wondered why he was so good, but hey who cares if he had lots of practice before me? The only thing I was interested in was the here and now. I had spent years living in the past, I didn't want to waste a second more doing it now. Phil made me feel better about myself. Natalie was happy too. She thought for a sec we could have made it work, but Phil and I were both in agreement it was a casual thing.

I continued to work with the pearl company with Natalie as I was enjoying it. This confident peacock was constantly surrounded by admirers and was often invited to amazing places and lots of functions and fairs. Let me tell you, it was sometimes hard to keep up with her. At least I wasn't a wallflower. I could usually hold my own. Confidant by nature and also loved being the centre of attention.

My life had begun to change, and I finally felt alive again. Maybe sometimes too alive for my own good. I think I was partying more than I had in my twenties! From being shoved in the back corner, to being centre stage again, the bubbly, carefree, confident Zoe slowly began to emerge again. Unfortunately, without Jim, but hey, his loss. I wasn't going to let a man bring me down a day longer. I was certain my life would soon be so full of wonders and new experiences that I wouldn't look back. I could feel it in my bones, my new life had started.

It's never easy though. To think of moving forward away from someone you loved and adored and into the unknown single world again is terrifying. Leaving security, money, a companion, and your kids without one of the other parts of them, their dad in the way they used to have him. I believe the key to it is discarding that fear. I had to work hard on that topic, as we all know from this experience with Jim, I struggled. I knew there were techniques to help me, and I was determined to find them and learn.

Surround yourself with strong powerful and loving people, and think forwards, not backward of what you can achieve alone not relying on a partner. To find yourself once again. I started my journey to do just that. I found a great way of finding the calm in my life once again and not getting too carried away in anxiety by keeping track of my thoughts and not letting them run away with me.

Imagine yourself in his arms again, which is so easy to do, then stop, change the picture, step away from him, turn him into a black-and-white picture and shrink him down until he fades away. I found this helped to self-regulate and to lose the nervousness and start to feel complete again, alone without him but happy knowing you're never really alone unless you live in fear. I had all the crazy feelings of a breakup resurface regularly. That fear of being alone and just wanting him back, settling again and not standing strong like I should be, on my own two feet, but the visuals would rein those thoughts in and I could re-focus. There can be great value in being alone, recalibrating, and sitting in discomfort long enough to be able to say to yourself that I'm ok again, I can be alone or with other people and still, be ok, and still be me.

Sometimes an old friend can do the trick in shifting your mood and place in life and that's just what Gabriella did for me in an unexpected meeting. It was so nice to see her again, my ex-partner in crime from our PR company, Show Pony. With her beautiful blonde almost unforgettable curly locks, she looked at me with her big brown eyes and smiled. Now, this girl was one of those powerful, strong people you need to keep close to you. She is the epitome of "sisters are doing it for themselves", "girl power" and "god created man first, but then you always start with a rough copy". Don't get me wrong, she loved men but had a very strong belief of how she was going to be treated with respect. She was ambitious and very independent. She loved the good things in life, and expected nice pressies from her guy, but still wanted a name for herself. She was a bit of an extrovert like most of my friends, so she was good to be around and when we chatted about my current status, she was sad.

"You helped make him who he is today."

"How could he walk away from such a gorgeous girl?"

"You were so successful before he stepped into your life."

"You had everything."

"You're not going to let a man destroy you like this, are you?"

Well, I don't care if that info was correct or not, keep talking girl!

We had deep discussions one night for hours. I walked away on top of the world, stronger than before. She was a part of my old life, a person who loved and supported me, and believed in me. Yep, you can join my gang again, with pleasure. During our outings, she introduced me to many a friend. This was key for me at the time. Friends can be saviours and keep you busy and happy if you are struggling to keep things together.

In between times, Natalie suggested I start my Jewellery range too. Of course, she would always want me to sell her range, but instead of taking on three or four others to sell, she thought it was better to start my own and build up a successful range than be an agent for others. I took her generous advice and experience, planning my own, and putting together ideas and designs.

I was also lucky to have Kelly, and a friend of Natalie's—Dave, who was also a jeweller. Dave was fabulous. A boy version of Natalie. He lived in Tasmania. Natalie had met him on her travels years back and they were the best of friends.

They urged me to head to Hong Kong with them on what was to become my first buying trip! It was amazing. I was lucky to have these great people to help and guide me, and I loved spending time with them too. At this point, there was not one negative person in my life. What better way to move on? It was so exciting.

We all stayed together in a hotel. We shopped, got prices, and looked at designs. I learned so much. I was surprised that it was pretty hard to learn how to buy right. You need to know your stuff. I couldn't have done it without them. They taught me everything there was to know, and their passion for the industry quickly rubbed off on me. At night we'd have dinner, then head to a bar to meet other new acquaintances, before partying late into the night. We had a day or two off, having massages, going to the hairdressers, having high tea, shopping at markets, and tasting the local food. Not always a great idea to eat from the markets as we found out a few times. Maybe it's only the locals who can stomach chili crab and prawns from the night markets?

I even managed to get up to my old tricks, cracking my coccyx bone and getting just a little too tipsy at a bar. I had met a pilot who had asked if I wanted a drink. Ironically, he looked a bit like Jim (only cuter!). Natalie ran over to me to ask if Jim had flown in to meet us. It wasn't deliberate by me in any way, but obviously, I was drawn to a certain-looking guy, and it seemed they were drawn to me too! He bought me a few drinks before a walk to the crowded dance floor proved tricky. I was caught behind a few patrons, one pushed into me, and I fell to my demise. Very, very painful! Thankfully the rest of our trip was event free, and we landed back home safely. It was an amazing trip, and I was chomping at the bit to create my empire. My new adventures had started, and my heart raced with excitement.

On my arrival, I discovered my grandad had also grown sicker from his cancer which had returned. It was heartbreaking to see him so unwell. It would have been hard for him to have seen all the grief I was going through over the final couple of years he was with us. He loved me so much, and I love him too. As most grandparents will tell you, it tears them up inside when their babies suffer. Everything that upset me upset him, he was such a beautiful man, and after a long time of sickness and suffering, he passed away to join my beautiful grandma on the other side. They were finally free of suffering and knowing they were together once more made it easier to let him go.

After grandad's passing, we were feeling very sad. I noticed the kids in particular were all missing Polo a lot too. I thought it might be time to add another canine to the new group of three. We would appreciate the company. The kids were so excited to search for our perfect match. We were lucky enough to find the most beautiful doggy. She was a pretty, little English Staffy. And was she ever a girl! You would never mistake her for anything else. She was so dainty. We called her Kimba. We lived right opposite a dog park, and the kids loved walking over each day to take her for a play. They'd laugh hysterically watching Kimba's antics as she socialised with the other dogs. She was a naughty one though, always escaping during the afternoon when I was at work. She would hear the puppies arrive with their owners, ready for a game, and didn't want to miss out. So over, under, and through the fences she climbed to join in.

Luckily there were many nice animal lovers there, including a lovely girl who only lived a couple of houses round from me. Louise and her hubby Warren. They were fantastic, and any time they saw Kimba out, they would either call me or just returned my little nuisance home, plonking her back over my fence.

Louise and I became very close. And like Katy and Richard, I had a similar situation with her. She would come over during the week, and we'd cook for each other and share a glass of wine. It's so nice to have a friend as a neighbour.

In between time my loss of funds from my separation meant we had to plan to sell India's pony as with no money coming from Jim other than the minimum child support payment, we had to fend for ourselves, and sometimes sacrifices had to be made. Jim had cut us out financially and spent what money we had left. Tough times, but we were tougher.

I was lucky enough to find a wonderful lady to lease my horse paint to as well, which enabled me to keep him. Before we finally moved Bug, India's most recent pony, on, we went to a huge annual Welsh show in Sydney with both our ponies. Kelly by this time had purchased a new one for herself, so it came too. The kids had been quiet for a while, so it was about time they caused a little drama. Well, that's how it normally rolled in our neck of the woods. It was very hot at this event, and out in the arenas, there was no shade. India had lots of classes to do, and we are made to wear heavy jackets with shirt ties and vests. Not great for the heat. Poor India had been in and out for hours and although she had water, she finally collapsed from heat exhaustion. We put her in the shade and made her drink. She recuperated and took Bug for a walk over a bridge. A lady and two young girls commented on how calm and well-behaved India's pony was. She was chuffed. She had one class left. It was a lead class, so she wasn't on his back. As she was practicing running the pony up and down the grass section, she stopped to pass another pony. She was the right distance away from it, but unfortunately it was out to get Bug as naughty ponies sometimes do, and made a beeline for him. Narrowly missing Bug, it slammed into India's hip, with its hooves flying everywhere. She collapsed to the ground in tears. That had to hurt. I ran to her, and we sat her in a chair as the officials were brought over and the ambos came by to check her out and make sure she was ok. Her hip was badly bruised, they thought, and she had copped another big hoof mark to her body. At least not her head this time, I thanked our lucky stars. Two little girls ran over. The ones that had admired how quiet and well-behaved Bug was earlier.

"Are you alright?" they asked.

"Yes," India sniffed.

I thanked the mum and suggested we catch up that night at dinner.

There was a team of these nice people. The Stanhope Stables team. The best little riders you can imagine, ranging from six upwards. Maggie was the mum's name. And the owner of the Stables and trainer was Victoria. We all had a fabulous night. Talking and laughing and drinking a little too much considering we had to get up early with the horses. I'd found out Victoria was also a regular at Level Six, a fab bar in the city. Perfect. We should catch up. And so we did. I had more new friends. Victoria had a boyfriend, John. The most generous, lively guy around. He was very sweet and very flamboyant.

After my Hong Kong trip, I met a totally vivacious and even dare I say, a little arrogant, real estate agent. He was only very young. Twenty-three! But seemed very mature for his age. Yeah, I know what you may be thinking—there was a big age gap. He had all the moves, and I kinda fell for him at that moment. He made me laugh, and he was really interesting, and sexy, not to mention very forward as well. I was standing at the bar when I accidentally bumped him.

"Oh!" he said loudly. "Are you trying to get into my hoody?" (He was wearing a sweater with a hood attached.) It was all tongue in cheek, and a little corny too, but I loved it and laughed.

"Yes, well yes I was!" I replied.

"I thought so," he smiled.

"Girls these days are always trying to do that when I'm not looking."

"Hi, I'm Sydney."

"Hi, I'm Zoe." I know the pickup line sounded naff, but he had this confidence that enabled him to carry off any geeky silly line. After a couple of hours at the bar sharing cocktails he ended up being a fun and naughty distraction for me for a while.

One night out at a restaurant with my other blonde friend Fran, we sat next to a group of guys. Four of them. We thought they were on a bit of a boy's night, but it turned out their wives were sitting next to them. The boys were chatting amongst themselves and not with the girls. I ended up talking to the guy next to me while the other boys struck up a conversation with Fran. They were lovely although a bit tipsy as they had been there since lunch but fun and full of interesting stories. It took them a while to tell us they were there for one of the wives' birthdays. In fact, the guy next to me was a very well-known photographer. We hit it off straight away and started chatting about the world and all its ways. We got onto talking about family. His mum was a famous astrologer. I brightened up more as I got to tell him about all my out of this world kinda stuff. He loved it. We had a lot in common and just really connected. But… he was married and his wife who didn't even glance her hubby's way once, which is nice as she trusted him, was sitting across the table. It was weird. For a moment I thought it was a setup to try and lure a third-party home for some sexual fun, as I had been offered that invitation a few times before at many bars. Anyhow they ended up leaving but not before my business card was asked for by one of the other guys next to him regarding work prospects. Fran leaned over to me and asked if I thought I would hear from him as he was a little too friendly to me.

"No, no, he was married, nothing will come of that and it shouldn't." But it was a shame in a way as I felt something special. Maybe I had just been deprived too long of attention and felt connections more strongly around that time.

Fran and I by this stage were having fun so we decided to kick on to the next venue. Fran was ready to party, insisting on buying me this flaming cocktail at the next bar. It was busy and we were being pushed from pillar to post. Fran handed me this huge blazing thing and we walked away from the bar into the crowds. All of a sudden I felt a warmth creep around my ear, and then I spotted something out the corner of my eye, and before I knew it my hair went up in flames, engulfing my face. Fran dropped to the floor in hysterics leaving me and my fiery hair to figure things out. Good work Franny! Fortunately, a nice guy nearby saw and patted my hair down leaving a lovely aroma of burnt feathers and a shocked look on my face. After dragging my very supportive friend from the floor we agreed, no more cocktails that contained fire!

The next day I woke to see an email. It was him, the photographer from the night before! Oh my gosh, that made me sort of nervous. It read that it was amazing meeting me and that he felt something between us. He added it wasn't often you come across someone like that who you could get along with so quickly. He wrote that he got into huge trouble with his wife when he got home (I could understand that), but it was worth it just to spend that moment with me. Hmmm. After a couple more emails explaining how he felt it stopped. And that was the way it had to be. I certainly wasn't going to do a Sarah!

Fun without hurting others I was certainly having. And apart from the normal girl/ guy fun, there was more! I'm not sure if all of this stuff was happening back in my twenties but I certainly can't remember being offered such invitations. If it wasn't random pretty girls approaching me in the bathrooms suggesting to join them for the night then it was a girl or guy approaching you at bars suggesting the same but with their partner as well. I had one gorgeous Eurasian woman stop me in the bathroom while visiting Adelaide to tell me how beautiful and sexy I was and then try and plant one on me! Then at two separate bars, I was approached by a guy and girl combined who I chatted to for a while innocently. Eventually, I was asked if I would join them for the night detailing exactly what wild things they wanted to get up to. I declined but was flattered. Then the last one was a very attractive girl who after talking a while at the bar introduced me to her husband, he then proceeded to invite me back to theirs as they had an open relationship and his wife had met a guy to take back as well but was approving the girl (me), he had secretly chosen first! OMG, these people were for real. Now I don't mind new experiences, but this was getting ridiculous! To be honest, the excitement was a breath of fresh air, but I just wanted a safe, monogamous, loving relationship, a family-oriented one.

Back to more sensible normal experiences, I think. Work! I was enjoying my time with Natalie and the jewellery industry, I was going out a couple of times a week, meeting new people, getting the male attention I desired, and getting to know myself again. Who I was without Jim. Don't get me wrong. I would have rather been at home with my husband and kids playing happy family, but I tried all that to the enth degree as you have read and at the end of the day you can't make someone stay.

"Let it go" as they say. And if you can't rediscover yourself in a marriage, then I guess you have to as a single person. Jim had told me over again about how the Sarah thing was all a big mistake, and they weren't together and would never be, but there was that uneasy gut feeling that that wasn't the case. You've heard the well-known saying. "If you love something, set it free, if it comes back, it's yours, if it doesn't it never was." Great saying but unfortunately, I wasn't in the mood for letting him go with any sort of love involved. Nope, this man had wrecked me and the kids in so many ways.

Not very Buddhist like I know but I had to let him go because he was hurting me too much. If he felt as though he needed to be free, then bugger him. I wasn't about to let him back to be mine again! Be free my wretched bird, and don't come back! We started to share time with the children, I had five days a week, and Jim twice a week. It was hard to say goodbye, but on the plus side, I had time to myself which was nice. Time to be me again and catch up with friends. The money issue or lack thereof was still causing strife, but the solicitors were dealing with that. Jim wasn't budging which made it hard, and from what I had gathered was not completely honest with his salary. So, a court date was locked in, and I knew this would wrap everything up and finish some of the stresses I still had. Well, it should do.

CHAPTER 16

BACK ON TRACK

It's funny the feelings you get when you start to live a single life again. On one hand, you feel alive, young, naughty and wild, and free. On the other you feel sad and lonely for that deeper connection you know exists out there with someone. It had been sad living through that pain, and even sadder seeing the kids still battle with it. I'm sure there are people out there who would be happy knowing they were no longer tied down (just like Jim had). They could date people forever, live the life they want in the way they wanted it, and not be inhibited by anyone else. But I'm a bit of a fan of relationships and marriage so that wasn't me.

In saying that, I was in no rush to do it all again so soon, as I needed to focus on myself and the kids. I believe there are not too many so-called soul mates out there for us anyhow, like that photographer said. So having found one person I wanted to spend my life with had been hard enough. Could I find another? Yes, maybe I could, but I think you need to heal first and that takes time, and it should. We can't expect another Mr. Right to fall in love with us while we're crumpled up in a ball shedding bags of psychological crap, can we?

In between times, my pony was also helping to lift my energy sky-high. Have you heard about Equine Therapy? It's a very real thing.

Horses can help on so many levels with anxiety, ADD, autism, cerebral palsy, dementia, depression, illness of the mind and body, and spiritual empowerment. I discovered it firsthand. I wondered why I'd been able to cope so well in past stressful situations, and that was when it dawned on me that all my horse encounters were supporting me on so many different levels. The therapist said horses teach you to relax and be in the moment, develop boundaries, focus, create internal balance, resilience, and non-verbal communication. Horses are our four-legged, albeit expensive yet heaven-sent angels from the universe. So, as I was healing through these beauties and getting back out in nature, being with my kids, and my friends, reading my books and of course focusing on my will to pick myself up and get over this, I kept on moving forward in the ways that were needed.

I also believe that confidence in yourself attracts others and in turn breeds success. When you walk down the street with a happy yet secure look on your face it draws people in and they want to know you. People are attracted to that and they want a slice of what you have. You make others feel great about themselves when you are happy, free, and positive. Maybe that's the aura I needed to show before I met Mr Right again. Lots of work was still needed and I knew that. I took quiet moments to reflect and set myself new goals. I slowed my life down in certain ways to regroup, think, and plan and I kept those friends close by just in case I had a down time. I knew they would always remind me and smack me around a bit and help put me back on track. I am lucky I'm generally a positive person and don't usually get depressed, which helps. I remember Jen telling me once that she sometimes felt like it was hard to cope but she used to just put one foot in front of the other and smile. Taking care of yourself without a doubt is the top priority as without great mental health we can't tend to others very well or more importantly our kids. They rely on you being there and being present. I think if there was going to be any time I might have suffered from depression it was at this difficult time, and there were times I did feel rather down. There were days I'd cry to Mum on the phone in tears with how I was going to do this on my own.

Of course, I was blessed as Mum always said Dad and her will be there for me and help in different ways. Parents. Thank goodness for them.

I changed the way I thought, filling my mind with wonderful pleasant things. As you change your thoughts, the world seems to change before you just like that. I've heard the saying before that you are what you think. I do believe that sad and negative does what sad and negative thinks! Changing your behaviour can change your mood. There are so many habits and mannerisms that are built into us through genetics and some are learned through our time on this planet. Some may help us and be a positive influence and some definitely hinder and often prevent us from truly being the most fabulous people we can be. Grieving is paramount to moving forward into a better place and maybe looking at what habits we have accumulated and which ones we need to shed and which ones enhance our life and will help us on our way.

I used to write down my thoughts and look for a pattern or belief that could be causing the negativity. I found when it was clearly in front of me it was easy to pinpoint the problem and therefore try to eliminate it. I always had resentment, blame and bitterness pop up along the way, although I've learned over time that people and events don't make you feel sad or happy, it's our beliefs that do, maybe our expectations in some ways, although I do believe expecting the finest and the most amazing outcome for yourself is important. Aligning your vibration with the best possible outcome. We often think we should feel a certain way when certain things happen but, once we change that set way of thinking, things start to move in a very different direction. When I let go of Jim and all our plans and stopped fighting so hard for our marriage to work I realised that I was going with the flow of what was presented to me and I wasn't blocking the new way forward that was all leading to better things. No one can make you feel a particular way, you are the controller! I had to stop and think about this one. You are the controller of your life. What matters is how you react and what you choose to believe about yourself. I've found challenging those unconstructive thoughts helped the most. Is it going to be of assistance to me to feel better if I react in that way? Will it change the outcome? I tried to let go as much as possible, to follow the current not swim against it. You feel so much freedom within when you don't let things bother you, you relax and breathe it all out. I always found it hard to let go of anything and lived my life in a full dog with a bone way. Sure sometimes it worked but sometimes like in my marriage, it didn't. I wasn't planning on dropping my passion, drive, and determination traits but when it came to holding on too long to something that didn't serve me that's what I would try to curb. I did well for a while and as life usually throws curve balls I was able to practice what I was preaching and used the exercises all over again. It was often like a weight had been lifted from my shoulders the moment I let whatever was bothering me about Jim go and the negative patterns that were limiting me. It was the greatest feeling and I realised I'd held on for way too long.

I had found meditation in my early twenties, so this was where I looked for comfort as well. My years of studying the spiritual side of life and the supernatural occurrences helped me to tap into my soul and trained me to go within and connect with the part of me that knows how to heal itself. I tried to harness the strength to remain calm in the face of change and remembered my mum saying, worrying won't change tomorrow. The meditation I practised was mostly done alone at home or with my pony, sitting on a rock in the bush watching the sun set in the peace and quiet or sitting on the grass amongst the trees in my pony's paddock, letting the soft breeze against my skin, blow my troubles away.

Because of all the counselling and the self-awareness literature I had studied, I noticed it didn't take too long before my self-esteem and zest for life returned to normal. It felt like a new lease on life for me. I started to look to challenge myself more. What could I accomplish on my own? How capable and successful could I become? How proud would I feel about myself moving forward with strength and confidence?

Certain aspects of my life started falling into position. Any issues and roadblocks I had faced before, I now looked at it as opportunities to grow. I was inundated with fabulous opportunities and the more amazing I felt the better it got. Whatever I needed usually came to me and often just when I needed it the most. Admittedly it was mostly just in the nick of time, but it was always there just the same. My life was becoming great again. It was different, but not in a bad way at all. The new Zoe was beginning to bloom into a more mature conscious one, a grown-up one.

I was doing well with my wholesaling for Natalie and others, and I was close to finishing my very own jewellery range. It was so exciting putting it all together. I had bought a few bits and pieces, along with some diamond jewellery from Hong Kong while I was on my travels. I sold mine in-between times to test the waters. Our customers were so good to me. They were only too pleased to help, and to top it off they loved my choices, and so did the customers because they sold nearly straight away.

There was no better feeling to me, and the ease of how it happened only confirmed to me I was on track. I had gained enough knowledge to be part of the jewellery world for real. Building my name all by little myself. I was doing it alone! It kind of felt like when you stood up by yourself on a surfboard for the first time or rode a bike as a kid unassisted. I didn't need you anymore Jim.

After most of my stock sold, I had researched enough to notice that flower designs were coming into style so I thought about how I could focus my range around a flower theme. By the time the next fair was on in Hong Kong, I was ready to buy my next jewellery collection. I still needed Kelly, Nat, and Tom to check in with me, but I knew what I was after. It wasn't too long before I found a manufacturer that suited my purpose. The basic design was there, it just needed my final touches. I sat with them in absolute excitement. This was going to be the range that people would know me for—I just knew it. It was beautiful. I changed a few things around like colours, designs, and sizes, and tailored it to me. And the name… I would call it "Wildflower by Zoe". It took six weeks for delivery. That time was never going to come around fast enough! I was excited as I waited and counted down the days. I thought of what I could offer my clients to help sell this lovely range. I decided to do a photo shoot and I would supply point-of-sale cards to put into their windows.

My clients were excited to see what I was going to produce. The support I was getting gave me more positive feelings and drove me harder. My business cards were also printed, and once my precious Wildflower cargo arrived, I was ready to go! Everyone I saw wanted it. I was chuffed. And within a month or two it was sold out, and then the calls started rolling in. "Zoe, we need more of the same." "Zoe, how quickly can you send the stock?" "Zoe, we love it and so do our customers!" It was on fire, and a reorder was in need. My range was in demand and my efforts were being appreciated. This was my time to shine.

As I was busy doing all this, I made amends with Mia and Chris. Mia was lovely enough to send me a card asking if we could forgive each other and let it all go. It was unexpected, but it was perfect timing to release all those preconceived ideas and harboured feelings toward them. Let it go! Let it go! Although not as close as we were back in the day, we maintained a friendship afar as they moved away to a different state. We were all young and sometimes things can get blown out of proportion. I even forgave Sarah and Jim, refusing to let it burden me any longer. Maybe they were truly in love, and to be honest what could I do. Best of luck to them. Love can be powerful.

Hopefully I'm only halfway through my life, and up till now, it's been a rollercoaster of new, scary and wonderful experiences. I have many years ahead and now that I have worked out how to be me once again, I can continue my way on this planet, feeling more capable of overcoming most situations life can throw at you. And I'm fairly confident I will find a solution to those bumps in the road.

Oh yes, that's right, the little bumps in life, I was trying hard to ignore the big ones remember? So let me finish my opening story and follow me to the next chapter my friends, there's still a little more to come.

CHAPTER 17

LOCKED UP

So, back to my birthday. This happy day was not looking like it was going to be very happy after all. I can assure you there were plenty of memorable moments, but they were not of the beautiful, cheerful kind. As I mentioned leading up to my birthday I was sick. I should have taken it as a sign and never even thought of trying to push myself that day. On reflection, I should have stayed in bed. But Jim and I had an arrangement with each other to mind the kids on our respective birthdays to give the other a child-free day and night out with our friends to celebrate and I didn't want to let any of the girls down. I'm sure they would have understood, and now knowing the outcome, I wished I'd not let Jim take the kids and instead stayed home with them.

I awoke that day and swallowed a tablet that was hopefully going to get rid of the headache I'd developed and enable me to attend a hair appointment at lunch and then meet my friends a little later. On the way to the hair salon, India threw up in the car and Max soon followed. After an agonising drive home covered in vomit, I cleaned the kids up, and Jim soon arrived to take them to his apartment. I was supposed to get them the next morning but as fate would have it, it would be much earlier.

I dragged myself out to the restaurant in the late afternoon feeling ok, but soon after I sat and took my first sip of champagne, I began to feel sick and was starting to burn up. I knew I couldn't stay any longer. So, after an hour I told the remaining few friends who were on their way not to come as I was going to bed. After a few hours, I was woken by a missed call and message. It was Max. He was crying explaining India and him had been left alone. Dad was nowhere to be seen, and Max needed me to come now.

I called the number back and an Asian man spoke in broken English.

"We have your children, it's ok we keep them until you get here." I was given his unit number, and I tore across town to Jim's place. I panicked. He had never allowed me in his unit, not once, even to see the place my kids stayed in two days a week, and I was soon to find out why! After I buzzed frantically on the unit door I was let in by the Asian gentleman. When I arrived upstairs the kids were waiting in the doorway of Jim's apartment with the man who had spoken to me on the phone. I thanked him again, as really if it wasn't for adult help who knows what would have happened. The kids looked grey, as I'm sure I did, we were all so sick, and it was crazy that any of this drama was even happening at all.

I led the kids inside the unit and with a slightly flustered voice, I asked them some questions.

"Where was Dad?" When was the last time you saw him?" The kids were so upset, but very relieved to see me, so they both tried to talk at once, Max led the way.

"We put ourselves to bed after we arrived because we had been vomiting and had such bad diarrhoea. Dad gave us Panadol to take away the temperature and we fell asleep. When India woke about nine o'clock vomiting, she called for Dad but he didn't answer."

"I went looking for him as I was scared," India added, dishearteningly, "He promised us he would only ever be in the next room, but I couldn't find him, so I woke Max."

"Yes," Max confirmed.

"I wanted to get help straight away, but India said to wait as she hoped he was not too far. India although the younger child used to be the braver one. Max often fell to pieces over things fairly easily, so it didn't surprise me that she took charge and tried to calm the horrible situation. She added, "After what felt like an hour he didn't return, and we needed medicine and help as we couldn't stop being sick."

Max continued, "India held the door open so we didn't lock ourselves out and I went for help, but it took a while to find someone who was home and the Asian man was the only one who opened his door for us."

All the feelings I had with Jim previously came flooding back to me engulfing my sick body. Why would he do this? I know he had become a very different person, but who in their right mind would leave kids under ten alone at night and to top it off, while they were so sick? I called his mobile but there was no answer. I left a message to his arrogant recorded voice.

"Call me, it's an emergency." It's amazing how even after all the things that had gone down between us, I still thought for a second that he might have been hurt. I always gave him the benefit of the doubt. Note to self… Stop doing this!

I began to look for something that might help me get an answer. I thought I could find his phone (as he hadn't answered) or keys as that would mean he hadn't gone far, however after looking in his bedroom I discovered more.

I knew the kids were never allowed in his room. I guess he had private things in there now, Sarah's lingerie for one. Looking through his room I found Lovey Dovey Wonder Twin photos together, arms locked firmly in place, laying on top of the underwear in the drawer of the other side of his bedside tables. His side had boxers and matching pics. I winced and felt stupid again thinking of what he had said to me about her only the other week.

"Oh, I haven't seen Sarah in over a year," he would say, and "I won't ever be seeing her, you have always been wrong about us, and we will never be together." Oh my goodness, note to self: stop believing him, Zoe! Well after a look around there were no keys, no phone, and no wallet to be seen. He wasn't there and by the looks of things was nowhere close. The kids then added, "We were scared someone had broken in again."

"What do you mean?" I asked. They explained that Jim had a robbery a few weeks before. This man had left his kids alone after a robbery had taken place at the apartments as well. Who was he becoming? A soulless being? I texted him, "Call me." Again, no answer. I looked around further and on the kitchen bench I discovered an insurance note, under their joint names. He had bought her a car! After having our family VW repossessed leaving me carless, he went and bought her one. How could he? I am the mother of his children and gave him the best years of my life. Well, a life he cared nothing for anymore. I was standing in his unit on my birthday, two scared sick kids in tow and wondering what had become of him. I tried to regroup and think about my next move and went into the car park with India to see if his car was there. I assumed it wasn't going to be, as he had his keys, but I had to check just the same. As India and I stood in the oily stained spot that was his, I considered my options. Do I take them home now?

Wait to give him a huge serve, or go looking for him?

My decision was soon made, and in came the man of the moment bolting down the adjoining road like the cool, collected fancy pants metrosexual athlete that was now my estranged husband.

"What have you done with the fucking kids?" he yelled.

"What have I done with them?" I moved closer glaring at him and poked my finger at his chest.

"How dare you leave them alone, sick, and frightened. And I know all about you and Sarah." By now I was close to his face. The gut-wrenching feelings that used to stick with me on a day-to-day basis all came flooding back! Focus Zoe. See him in black and white, shrink him down in size, manifest what you want, love is the answer, like attracts like, let it go, God, use those techniques you memorised I panted to myself. Self-help books don't fail me now! Yep, I needed an injection of good advice immediately. Probably the advise I should have given to myself would have been "run get out of there ASAP!" but my memory recall was frozen. Frozen from a man who had meant so much in my life, a man I was getting, in fact nearly gotten over, but he had such a hold. I got closer to him against his body, and up to his face with a need to get answers straight away. He pushed me away, falling back, I felt my nail scratch his neck.

At this point I should have gone, his lies were getting too much to handle, and he hated me now knowing anything about his life, especially his secret life with Sarah. He couldn't stand that I still had some sort of a hold over him, I was linked to his children and would always be around. He asked me to go back upstairs from the carpark to inside his apartment to talk about this calmly, which I agreed to. He took India and me upstairs, and India waited with Max in the loungeroom while he took me into his hidden den of a bedroom and tried to make out he was only missing as he was putting out the garbage. What, for over an hour? With sick kids in tow, with your keys, car and phone? And then I muttered…

"Nice holiday snaps and lingerie!" Yeah of course Jim, I was so wrong about Sarah.

"We went to the Greek islands together," he softly spoke. "Sorry, please don't take the kids tonight." No, I refuse to leave them with you. Goodbye. I left his apartment with the kids, all of us sick, exhausted, and to be honest trying to understand what had just happened.

As I drove out of his street, I noticed two streets away, his car was parked facing the wrong way and parked crooked, sticking out into traffic. A frantic stop the car anywhere anyhow moment and run to the apartment to deal with the mess he had created. Easy to see Jim that the lies were true. I arrived home, hugged and supported the kids as best as I could, and with a big sigh fell into bed again. In the morning, I spoke to Mum. We talked through the whole story. She asked me with a worried tone if I thought Jim would set me up and lie and make out a different turn of events. I laughed and blew it off saying to Mum how could he? It was all him. I had been sick in bed. He had managed to do all this himself. It was him, not me in any way. How do you think he would even manage that?

Mum wasn't so sure. She was a lot more sceptical than me. More switched on to what people, namely Jim, were capable of. Goodness Mum, please don't be right. But as I sat handcuffed in the back of the police car, I finally realised my mum's truth. Luckily my parents were quick, arriving swiftly at my house, Mum stayed with the kids and Dad followed to the station to join my nightmare. I was put into a cell, photographed, fingerprinted, and interviewed. They explained Jim said I had assaulted him. I was dumbfounded, and I of course denied all of this, but I was in shock. How could this man I once knew turn this all around on me? I was able to speak to a lawyer and was told not to say any more. I found out Jim had driven straight to Sarah's place and went to the local police to try and get an AVO. Was he mad? I wasn't trying to see him, I was rescuing my sick kids from a horribly dangerous situation. Someone phoned me to come and get them, Jim. And assaulting him? What world did he live in? It was a pending criminal charge and something I didn't deserve.

Until the court date the AVO stayed in place, but it had a clause for Jim to see his kids every week. We would exchange them in a pre-arranged spot but I'm sure you can guess it right. He never saw them. Four months went by, and nothing. I can't tell you why he made that decision, it baffles me to this day. I would look after my babies. It was tough, as for many, many years, my daughter in particular had anxiety when it came to being left alone. The once brave girl had vanished and even her primary school teachers had issues with her anxiety of being left at school without me or the fact she found it near impossible to go on school camps. While waiting for the case to be heard, we were able to subpoena phone records. I found out while I was phoning and messaging him on the way to his place that night, he had called Sarah over a dozen times instead of answering me and my emergency calls.

I also found out how he had convinced the police that night to place an AVO on me. That was mind-blowing. Jim and I had visited a counsellor who was the mother of one of the kids' schools friends maybe two years prior. She probably shouldn't have offered as it was unprofessional seeing people you knew as friends first. In any case, we did. In that session, she knew how I'd been going, and how sad yet frustrated I was. She asked me how I was feeling. In an exasperated, humorous way, I stated, "Oh Margo if I could kill the guy I would", and smirked. She laughed empathetically.

I remember that day she called me back after I left the session, and said, "Be careful, I think he is trying to set you up." What? I thought at the time. Set me up? Like how and for what? All I was focused on was getting our marriage back on track. She then informed me he had called her straight after the session saying that's a death threat she made, you need to report it immediately. I was gobsmacked! She explained to him I was joking but he insisted she report it and she did. I told her that I was disgusted she had done that as she knew it was said as a joke. She agreed but said it was her job to follow his demand in a legal obligation sense. She wanted me to know about the future, to give me a heads up on his plans. I decided to wipe her from my friend' list but to be honest, I thought what she said was ridiculous and how could he ever do this especially when it was so far from the truth, so I didn't take heed of this information. Hmmm, probably should have.

The court case arrived, and we had to have representation, which cost a fortune. As we turned up to court there was no Jim to be seen. He was a no-show. My lawyer presented our case, the story, the facts, and the truth. The judge shook her head, outraged and after muttering a few sentences announced how sorry she was to the kids and me and the stress he had caused, and that the evidence spoke for itself. The AVO and accusations of assault were dropped immediately, as was the case itself. I was happy but it did leave a fresh scar. I had worked through so much. I shouldn't, couldn't let this tarnish my healing. I was contacted immediately afterwards and was introduced to the Victims Support Scheme. The NSW Government provide services to victims of crime, supplying counselling, financial support and a recognition one off payment. I also really appreciated the acknowledgment that something did actually occur against myself and my children. After the years of being gaslit I finally felt seen and relieved. The immense support especially from my assigned councellor really added to how I was healing and growing and finding myself once again.

Soon after, my divorce papers showed up. Yep, hand me the nearest pen. I would not object! We ended up going to the family court about six months later to sort out financials and custody arrangements.

I ended up getting three-quarters of the time with the kids. As I turned up to the final day to sign the orders, Jim and Sarah were standing with a newborn child. His new life and new family. Would he repeat the same pattern with her? Time would tell on that one. I had my babies to look after and show love to, and that's certainly what I planned to do.

"Back to normal life again and stay away from toxicity and Jim!" I said to myself. I knew there is always cause and effect, so I would make sure there was limited contact with Jim. I would not let him ruin my recovery from this addiction to him and sabotage the progress I had made.

My take thus far on events to date is certainly interesting, to say the least. I would try to never be naive when it came to certain people in my life, but I would always try to remember the good out there too and hoped it outweighed the bad—the eternal optimist I am.

I immersed myself in my life with my kids, family, friends, and my four-legged friends once again. Take two it seemed. When you don't succeed, try, try again.

Getting back into work was the next step, it always kept me happily occupied. One afternoon while driving back from an appointment I received a phone call from my horsey neighbour. She sounded slightly flustered as I answered and started her first sentence with "Don't worry it's all ok now but…" I know it's a perfect way to try to stop someone from getting too concerned as I've done it myself. Just not sure it works as she had barely finished her sentence when I started asking the what's, where's, and why's. She quickly told the story of how as she was pulling into her driveway, and she spotted a dark-haired man in a flannelette cream and black shirt lassoing one of my horses as the other was tied to the fence. The street I lived in was half residential, half acreage. I lived at one end and my friendly neighbour lived at the other and in between was where I kept my horses. We always kept an eye on each other's horses, so she stopped the car and ran down to see what was happening with them and who this man was.

She said he was almost relieved-looking as she approached him.

I told him I was a friend of yours and asked what happened. He told her he was glad she arrived as the two horses were a bit of a handful. All I could think of while she was telling me this is I can't cope with much more.

He just moved in last week to the cottage behind your paddock and if I may say so he is kind of cute! He told me he hadn't met you yet but as he was moving his things in he saw your two cheeky monkeys about to play dodgem cars with the traffic.

I told him you will be thrilled he was there to rescue them.

He said to tell you it's no problem at all as he loves horses and it was added excitement for the day.

I thanked my neighbour and rushed home making sure to stop at the florist for a big bunch of flowers and then straight to his cottage. I turned up a little flustered and knocked on the door. A tall, dark-haired man opened it and stepped forward with a surprised look on his face. I almost threw the flowers at him in appreciation but also nervousness as he was gorgeous. My neighbour had played this one down.

"Thank you so much," I blurted. "I'm Zoe the owner of the two crazy horses you rescued."

"Oh they are just beautiful and I love horses a lot so it was seriously my pleasure."

"I'm happy to help you with them any time if you need assistance, maybe we could have a beer one afternoon in the paddock?"

"Yes, I quickly responded, that would be great." We swapped phone numbers and said goodbye.

With that, I walked back to the car and jumped in wondering if once again my horses had led me to what I needed and wanted. A warm fuzzy feeling engulfed me, maybe this was going to be a really good thing.

THE END

ACKNOWLEDGMENTS

This book is dedicated to women. Women of all shapes and sizes, all nationalities, and all personalities. We rock. And let's not forget horses — they rock too!

Writing my first book was weirdly enough laborious and uncomplicated all in the one. Setting down on paper my deepest, darkest and sometimes funniest moments was an extremely cathartic experience and pleasingly satisfying. Unravelling those memories to have it make more sense on paper took a long time, years in fact. I'm thrilled to say it's here! It's hot to trot and I'm ready to let people into Zoe's world.

— I WOULD LIKE TO THANK THE — FOLLOWING PEOPLE

My parents, for embracing parenthood with love, guidance and kindness, and of course getting me to adulthood in one piece, all considering. My dad is a tower of force with a soft centre. My mum is an old, wise soul and my ever patient sounding board, listening to all my crazy stories and providing solid advice. I wouldn't trade either of them for the world.

My sisters. Who could ask for better siblings to share a haunted house and childhood antics with. They are both beautiful people and I'd be lost without them.

My grandparents. They, like my parents, helped shaped my life. My grandma showed me resilience and adaptability, and my grandad was a rock and taught me to always look for fairies in the garden, that magic is real.

My two children. Life without these angels would be unimaginable.

My Son, you have a kind and warm nature. Quietly determined and always wanting the very best for everyone.

My daughter, you are sassy, beautiful inside and out, and wise beyond your years.

To my partner, for encouraging me on this journey, to read, consider, write, to rewrite and write again, and never stop learning. When I felt frozen in the writing process you have kept me inspired. You have been an undeniable support with an abundance of fabulous ideas.

To my girlfriend, my horse sister. Your technical prowess and emotional support has been a huge part of being able to finish this book. If it wasn't for you, I may have had this book saved in a wrong file, irretrievable or accidentally erased forever.

My Publisher, Clark & Mackay. Thank you for taking my manuscript and turning it into a book. You go above and beyond. You are a talent and the best!

And of course my girlfriends, you know who you are. Love you all.

ABOUT THE AUTHOR

There would have been no better star sign for Zoe Fanning to be born under than that of the vibrant Leo the lion. She is fierce, vivacious, brave, and definitely not afraid to roar!

Zoe entered the world in the 1970s in a picturesque seaside suburb in Australia.

She was raised by a loving family in a round house on a hillside that was also inhabited by some friendly ghosts, alongside neighbouring horse paddocks that became her constant source of entertainment.

Her obsession with horses led her to compete in horsemanship studies and events where she excelled.

Along with her equine skills, she is a gifted singer who performed songs in many bars and clubs across the country.

Zoe worked in media, sales and marketing and dabbled in journalism, including food and wine reviews, before eventually having her own weekly column.

She is a mother of two beautiful children she adores, and a firm believer in the law of attraction, coupled with a philosophy to appreciate and value each and every day.

When she is not with her beloved horses or family, Zoe can be found travelling the world sourcing diamonds and gemstones.